CEDAR MILL COMM LIBRARY
12505 NW CORNELL RD
PORTLAND, OR 97229

WITHDRAWN
CEDAR MILL & BETHANY LIBRARIES

Buried in Books

Titles by Kate Carlisle

Bibliophile Mysteries

Homicide in Hardcover

If Books Could Kill

The Lies That Bind

Murder Under Cover

Pages of Sin
(enovella)

One Book in the Grave

Peril in Paperback

A Cookbook Conspiracy

The Book Stops Here

Ripped from the Pages

Books of a Feather

Once upon a Spine

Buried in Books

Fixer-Upper Mysteries

A High-End Finish

This Old Homicide

Crowned and Moldering

Deck the Hallways

Eaves of Destruction

KATE CARLISLE

Buried in Books

A Bibliophile Mystery

BERKLEY PRIME CRIME
New York

BERKLEY PRIME CRIME
Published by Berkley
An imprint of Penguin Random House LLC
375 Hudson Street, New York, New York 10014

Copyright © 2018 by Kathleen Beaver
Penguin Random House supports copyright. Copyright fuels creativity, encourages diverse voices, promotes free speech, and creates a vibrant culture. Thank you for buying an authorized edition of this book and for complying with copyright laws by not reproducing, scanning, or distributing any part of it in any form without permission. You are supporting writers and allowing Penguin Random House to continue to publish books for every reader.

BERKLEY is a registered trademark and BERKLEY PRIME CRIME and the B colophon are trademarks of Penguin Random House LLC.

Library of Congress Cataloging-in-Publication Data

Names: Carlisle, Kate, 1951- author.
Title: Buried in books / Kate Carlisle.
Description: First edition. | New York : Berkley Prime Crime, 2018. | Series: Bibliophile mystery ; 12
Identifiers: LCCN 2017061357| ISBN 9780451477743 (hardcover) | ISBN 9780698411128 (ebook)
Subjects: LCSH: Women bookbinders—Fiction. | Women detectives—Fiction. | Murder—Investigation—Fiction. | Books—Conservation and restoration—Fiction. | Rare books—Fiction. | BISAC: FICTION / Mystery & Detective / Women Sleuths. | GSAFD: Mystery fiction.
Classification: LCC PS3603.A7527 B87 2018 | DDC 813/.6—dc23
LC record available at https://lccn.loc.gov/2017061357

First Edition: June 2018

Printed in the United States of America
1 3 5 7 9 10 8 6 4 2

Cover art by Dan Craig

This is a work of fiction. Names, characters, places, and incidents either are the product of the author's imagination or are used fictitiously, and any resemblance to actual persons, living or dead, business establishments, events, or locales is entirely coincidental.

PUBLISHER'S NOTE: The recipes contained in this book are to be followed exactly as written. The publisher is not responsible for your specific health or allergy needs that may require medical supervision. The publisher is not responsible for any adverse reactions to the recipes contained in this book.

This book is dedicated with gratitude and joy
to Librarians everywhere.

ACKNOWLEDGMENTS

Many thanks to Anna Links and the American Bookbinders Museum in San Francisco for providing so much insight and historical perspective to the art and craft of bookbinding. I appreciate your patience and assistance—and your delightful museum store.

To senior editor Michelle Vega: much like Obi-Wan Kenobi, you came into my life when I needed you most. Your intelligence, warm encouragement, and wonderful good humor have helped me in so many ways. Thank you!

I am grateful every day that I get to work with the smart, savvy, insightful, and deliciously witty literary agent Christina Hogrebe. Thank you for everything you do for me.

This book would surely not exist without the incredible support of my husband, Don. Thank you for your constant love and support through so many years and so many books. And thank you for helping to concoct the most awesome signature cocktail ever. Let's have another round, shall we?

Chapter One

"The name is Wainwright," I said to the conference volunteer seated at the registration table before me. "Brooklyn Wainwright."

The young woman gave an absent nod and began to skim the thick stack of envelopes standing upright in the box in front of her. Not exactly the friendliest greeting, but the crowd was huge and the woman was probably feeling overwhelmed. Halfway through the stack, she stopped suddenly and gaped up at me. "Wait. You're Brooklyn Wainwright? Wow. I signed up for your workshop."

"Oh." I smiled. "I hope you'll enjoy it."

"I know it'll be fantastic," she said brightly. "I'm, like, your biggest fan."

"That's so nice." I peered at her badge to catch her name. "Thanks, Lucy."

For the fifth year in a row, I had been asked to present the bookbinding workshop for the annual National Librarians Association conference. It was a real honor to be asked because there had to be hundreds of talented bookbinders among the librarians who attended every year. I was doubly thrilled that the conference was being held in San Francisco this year so I wouldn't have to lug all of my supplies and equipment halfway across the country.

Sighing inwardly, I admitted that I would've been looking forward to the workshop a lot more if I hadn't botched up my schedule so badly. But nobody here needed to know that.

Lucy flipped her pink-streaked hair away from her face and continued to stare at me as though I were a rock star. Her former boredom had turned into wide-eyed excitement. It was fun, but also a little intimidating. She knew me and my work. What if she hated the workshop?

"I saw your *Alice in Wonderland* pop-up display at the Covington Library," she said. "It was amazing."

"Thank you." I sensed the people in line behind me getting antsy to move things along. I turned and flashed an apologetic smile.

But my new biggest fan didn't seem to notice the impatient crowd. Instead, she leaned forward and whispered loudly, "Everyone says you're going to dish about the murders during the workshop. I'm so psyched!"

"Uh . . . what?"

She nodded eagerly. "Is it true you found a body inside the Covington? What a rush!"

"Umm, no, I . . ." I had no words. The fact was, I *had* found a body inside the Covington. More than once, to be honest. But I wasn't about to discuss the details with a stranger.

She frowned at me, clearly confused by my reticence. Then

she began to nod slowly as if she and I were in on a secret together. "Ah, I get it. You're saving the gory details for the workshop. I understand. Don't worry. I can wait."

Snapping back into work mode, she pulled a manila envelope from the stack and handed it to me. "Here you go. This envelope contains your badge and your program book. It's got all the events listed, as well as the speakers' bios. And there's a map of the convention center inside the back cover. This place is huge, so we don't want anyone to get lost." She pointed toward the opposite side of the massive hall. "You can pick up a book bag at the south end of the auditorium."

"Okay. Thanks, Lucy."

"Enjoy the conference, Brooklyn." She gave me a conspiratorial wink. "See you at the workshop."

"You bet." A little dazed and a touch breathless, I stepped away from the registration table feeling like I'd just run a sprint. Pulling my rolling briefcase behind me, I began the long trek across the crowded room.

An enormous woman in pink bumped into me and kept walking, obviously in a hurry to get her conference bag. My head was so filled with questions, I hardly noticed.

Was someone spreading the word that I would be talking about murder? Seriously? I didn't even like *thinking* about the bodies I'd stumbled across, let alone using them as filler in my workshop program. It wasn't going to happen. Which meant that there were going to be some disappointed people—like Lucy, for instance. I sighed and shook my head. The conference had just gotten more complicated.

I'm a bookbinder specializing in rare book restoration, which means I make my living refurbishing old books. I also enjoy creating handmade books when I'm feeling particularly artistic. Unfortunately, in connection with my work, I happened to have stumbled across more than a few dead bodies over the past several years. And yes, the victims were all connected to the various books I had been working on at the time.

But that didn't mean I was an expert on the subject of murder! I absolutely refused to draw attention to myself or to these crimes simply because of my weird proclivity for finding dead people. Why would anyone think I would take time out of a bookbinding class to talk about murder?

When it came to any connection between rare books and murder, the only bit of information I was willing to offer was this: If you thought that books weren't worth killing for, you were dead wrong.

I scanned the enormous hall, noting that in the time it had taken me to register, hundreds more people had arrived for the conference. Dozens were waiting in line to register. Some peered around anxiously, trying to get their bearings. Others were gathered in small groups chatting and laughing and, in the case of the cluster of five women closest to me, shrieking.

I did a quick mental calculation as I studied the diverse crowd. There had to be at least eight hundred people milling around this cavernous space. Probably closer to a thousand. No wonder the noise level was deafening.

The racket didn't bother me. These were my people. Librarians. Book nerds. "And apparently a few murder fans," I muttered to myself.

I headed toward the south end of the convention center, asking myself all the way: Did I really need a book bag?

More importantly, did I really need to be here at all?

The organizers had called me months ago to ask if I would give a bookbinding workshop during the conference. I had said yes because I loved giving that workshop and it was a real thrill to be asked. Then somewhere along the way they had also roped me into giving a speech on book conservation. And if that wasn't enough, I had also agreed to donate a raffle prize. I was all for fundraising for librarians, but I had to ask myself why I couldn't have simply given a basket of books or a gift card. No, I had offered to take twenty lucky librarians on a three-hour "Book Lovers' Tour" of San Francisco. We were renting a bus and everything. Good grief. What had I been thinking?

Of course, all those months ago, I had never dreamed that I would be getting married to Derek Stone this weekend.

My gaze softened and I sighed happily at the thought of marriage to Derek—and almost crashed into a gray-haired man minding his own business reading the program booklet.

"Sorry," I stammered, and kept walking. It wasn't the first time I'd spaced out and almost injured someone lately. Whenever I thought of Derek and our upcoming wedding, I sort of lost consciousness for a few seconds.

I had considered cancelling my conference events this week, but after talking it over with Derek, we decided that it would be a good idea for me to keep to my original conference schedule. Because amazingly, every last detail of the wedding was taken care of. And Derek had pointed out that attending the conference would—hopefully—distract me from any pre-wedding jitters I might be susceptible to. He had a good argument there, seeing as how I was more than a little overwhelmed by the fact that his entire family—including his parents, four brothers and their spouses and children, and various aunts and uncles—had arrived from England several days ago. They had gone directly to Sonoma to visit my family so I wouldn't see most of them until the day of the rehearsal dinner. But still.

Derek had insisted that his family would be fine in the wine country without us and that my family would provide them with plenty of fun and friendship. It all sounded good in theory. But now that I was here, staring at this massive convention space and all of these people, I began to wonder if there wasn't something I should've been doing to welcome his family more personally. And what about the rest of the wedding preparations? Had I really completed everything on my list of bridal duties? I checked my watch. Would it be wrong to leave the conference after I'd just arrived?

Not just wrong, but stupid, I silently lectured myself as I made my way through the crowd toward the book bag counter. Attending this conference would be great for my business, my career, I reminded myself. I would make new contacts, possibly acquire some new clients, and reacquaint myself with old friends.

So I was here to stay. At least for a few hours. As I wound my way through the crowd, I realized that despite my neurotic compulsion to check all of my wedding lists on an hourly basis, I was happy to be here. I had always enjoyed this conference and I was grateful to the organization for all the good things I'd received by being a part of it. Besides, being among all these librarians made me feel nostalgic for my post-graduate years. Those were good times.

Even though I had never planned to work as a librarian, I knew that starting out with a degree in library science was one of the best routes to a career as a bookbinder. Consequently, everyone I knew in school had been working feverishly toward their master of library science degree back then. I had to admit it had been daunting to be surrounded by all of those highly intelligent, compulsively organized, overwhelmingly detail-oriented people. I used to cope by wearing T-shirts that said things like: *How many times have you washed your hands today?* and *Do you spell anal retentive with a hyphen?*

Instead of the quick laugh I always expected when I showed up wearing one of my dumb T-shirts, my gifted friends would actually spend an hour or two seriously discussing whatever statement I was displaying.

"It's simple really. You spell it with a hyphen when it's used as a descriptive. For instance, if you said, 'I hate my anal-retentive professor,' that would require a hyphen. But if you said 'I'm feeling rather anal retentive today,' no hyphen is necessary."

I chuckled at the memory. God, I missed them!

I finally snagged my book bag, a sporty navy blue backpack that everyone around me agreed was highly impressive. Especially compared to last year's offering, a cheap beige fiber tote that barely held up for the length of the event. Free conference bags—and free books—were an important part of the conference experience and clearly a contentious issue.

I tested the weight of the book-laden backpack and then slipped my arms through the straps. I decided to head for the coffee kiosk, when I heard someone call my name.

"Brooklyn? Is that you?"

I whirled around and frowned at the red-haired woman standing a few feet away. "Yes?"

She laughed and ruffled her short red hair self-consciously. "I know it's been years and I've changed a few things, but I don't look that different, do I?"

I blinked. "Oh my God. Heather? Heather Babcock?"

"Yes!" She squealed and grabbed me in a crushing hug. "I was so afraid I wouldn't find you!"

"I was just thinking about you," I said. It was the absolute truth. She had been one of my favorite people back in the day. "I didn't realize you were coming. Why didn't you call me?"

"I didn't know I was coming until two days ago and then it was like a whirlwind trying to get ready for the trip."

"Wow. I'm stunned. But it's a good feeling," I added quickly, grinning to hide the fact that I was in complete shock. Heather had been one of my roommates in graduate school and a best pal from the good old days. She was so beautiful and petite, with a delicate bone structure and short-short hair. She always looked like an adorable pixie to me, but today she looked almost . . . haggard. Like maybe she hadn't slept in a week. "Gosh, it's been . . . how many years?"

"Ten, maybe? You look fantastic."

"So do you." It had been twelve years, but who was counting?

"Yeah, right." She chuckled ruefully. "I do own mirrors, let's not get carried away."

"Don't be silly, you're beautiful," I insisted, but quickly changed the subject. "Do you have time for a cup of coffee?"

"Of course."

I bought two café lattes and two biscotti and we found a small table in the far corner. Within seconds we were talking and laughing like the old friends we had been, as if twelve long years hadn't passed since we'd last seen each other.

Heather and I, along with our best friend, Sara Martin, had been roommates back in library school. We had clicked from the get-go and became so inseparable that our classmates took to calling us the Three Musketeers. Sadly, though, a few weeks before graduation, Sara and Heather had a major falling-out when Heather found out that her boyfriend, Roderick, had been cheating on her—with *Sara*.

Heather had been inconsolable, especially when news filtered back that Sara and Rod had run off to get married. About a year later, I heard through the grapevine that Sara had caught Rod cheating on her. This was not a big surprise to anyone since Rod was adorable, but very shallow and prone to believing his own hyped-up PR. But in the end, Sara forgave him and they were still together, as far as I knew.

Heather and I avoided the dreaded subject of Sara and Roderick. Instead, Heather talked about her fulfilling job at the local library in her small town, and I told her all about my adventures in bookbinding and my relationship with Derek. I didn't mention the wedding, worried that my happiness would make her feel even worse. After thirty minutes of chatting and catching up, we both sat back and smiled.

"It's really good to see you," I said wistfully.

"You, too." Heather's smile turned enigmatic. "So, are we ever going to mention the big fat bitchy elephant in the room?"

I reached across the table and grabbed her hand. "I didn't want to ask."

She raised an eyebrow. "But you're dying to know."

"Sorry," I said, wincing. "But yeah, I would love to know if you've had any news or run-ins with . . ."

"No." Heather inhaled quickly, as if she were about to take some horrible-tasting medicine. "I haven't seen Sara in twelve years. But I have a friend who has a friend who knows her, so I hear things."

"I hope you intend to share what you've heard."

She chuckled. "Absolutely."

I frowned. "Do you think she'll be coming to the conference?"

"I sure hope not," Heather said. Her jaw tightened and her eyes narrowed in unrepressed fury. "Because I swear, if I ever see Sara Martin again, I'll kill her."

Chapter Two

I'll kill her.

Heather's words still rang in my ears two hours later as I left the convention center and headed for home. I only lived four short blocks away so I was lucky to be able to walk and take advantage of the late spring sunshine. But even the radiant warmth couldn't keep the intermittent shivers from skittering down my spine each time I pictured Heather glowering as she uttered that phrase.

Had she meant what she said? It was hard to tell. As soon as she said the words, she quickly waved them away and laughed at her "little joke."

Whether she'd meant it or not, it saddened me to see how bitter she remained over something that had happened twelve long years ago. Yes, she had been betrayed by two of her closest friends. Yes, it had been devastating. I could verify that. I had been there to cry with her and feel her pain. She had lost her boyfriend, Rod, but we had both lost Sara's friendship that day. It was rough for a while, for both of us, but as the years flew by, I managed to completely forget the incident—until today. Of course, Rod hadn't been my boyfriend, so I didn't have the same emotional investment. Still, I had figured Heather would've been over it by now. Wasn't twelve years a long enough time to mourn the loss of a jerky boyfriend?

Apparently not, because here she was, still playing the victim. That was probably a little harsh, but wow, I'd had no idea how deeply Sara and Rod had wounded her. I tried to relate, thought of Derek and myself in the same situation, and wondered if . . . Nope. That would've never happened with us. Though it did give me pause to reconsider how Heather could still feel so hurt.

Heather had managed to graduate with the rest of us, obtaining her masters in library science and then moving back home to Wisconsin. I emailed her at least a dozen times but she never responded. I tried not to take it personally and instead chalked it up to her need to distance herself from anyone connected to the unhappy incident. But I had definitely lost her as a friend. I had never considered myself a victim of Rod and Sara's treachery, but now I realized that I had lost *two* good friends in the upheaval.

At Fourth and Folsom I waited for the light to turn green. Trying to change the subject in my head, I thought about the Book Lovers' Tour I was giving tomorrow afternoon.

After finishing our lattes and promising to get together again, Heather and I had separated and I ran off to track down the raffle coordinator. I wanted to see if enough people had entered the raffle contest to fill the small tour bus the association had hired.

"Oh my God!" Patty, the coordinator, had squealed. "We've

got over a thousand raffle entries! Everybody wants to take your tour."

I frowned, not sure I'd heard correctly. "Are you serious?"

"Yes! Isn't it fabulous?"

I was still skeptical. "Do they all know the tour is tomorrow afternoon?"

"Oh yes, it says so right on the ticket and all of our volunteers have been reminding people about the time."

"Okay. Good."

She squeezed my arm. "We are so excited, Brooklyn. At five dollars a ticket, that's over five thousand dollars for the scholarship fund!"

"Holy moly." *Pressure's on, Brooklyn*, I thought. "I sure hope everyone enjoys the tour."

"You're kidding, right?" she scoffed. "They'll have a blast."

"Yeah. Well, thanks." Still in shock, I had walked away, feeling a little numb as I left the raffle center. I had thought that the tour would be interesting and informative, but now I realized I would have to make sure it was fun and fabulous for the winners.

The light turned green and I crossed Folsom Street.

I smiled, remembering how the coordinator grabbed my arm in excitement. "Nothing like a happy raffle coordinator," I muttered to myself. "So that's good news."

But then there was the bad news, I thought, as my mind wandered back to Heather and her disgruntled state. I refused to believe that Rod had been the great love of her life. Sure, he had been cute and fun, but he certainly had not been worth her spending the rest of her life wallowing in a state of abject misery.

But that was just me.

I'll kill her.

I came to a dead stop—no pun intended. Once again I was struck by the cold certainty of her words. I could still see the expression she wore and it gave me another chill. And now I wondered why she had only blamed Sara. Rod was just as much to blame, if not more.

If it were me, I would have killed Rod instead, I thought.

"Wait, no." I said it out loud and glanced around, hoping no one had heard me say any of the above.

"Don't even *think* it," I hissed under my breath. It was like tempting fate or something. Honestly, though, if given the choice of getting rid of either Sara or Rod, it was a no-brainer.

And by *getting rid of either Sara or Rod*, I meant, like, banishing one of them to a campus in the frozen tundra. Nothing violent. No killing. I did a quick mental back step, hoping to appease the karma gods before they got together and smote me.

And there went another cold chill. I rubbed my arms and vowed to stop thinking about this stuff.

I couldn't help it, though. Seeing Heather again had reminded me of all those angst-ridden days back in graduate school. Rod had spoiled everything when he transferred to our campus during our last year together. First of all, he was ridiculously good-looking, with dark, scruffy hair, piercing blue eyes, and a sly, sexy smile. For Heather it was love at first sight. She was head over heels and everyone knew it, including Rod, and that spelled trouble as far as I was concerned. He used to tease her all the time and play little games with her, taunting her with the fact that there were plenty of other women around campus who found him appealing.

He was funny and fun, but he wasn't very nice, I thought, remembering. Even at the time I'd thought he wasn't worth Heather being so gaga over him. She deserved better. But Heather never seemed to notice. She was simply blown away by his smile and his charm. He liked to shake things up, he always insisted. And he did. Everything in our little world changed when he arrived, and not in a good way.

Before Rod showed up, Heather and Sara and I had been inseparable. The Three Musketeers nickname had suited us; we were fiercely loyal to each other. We went everywhere together and always had a good time. We knew every last detail of each other's lives and could finish each other's sentences. And since we were tagged with the Three Musketeers label anyway, we made it our credo to be *one for all and all for one.* I would have done anything for those two girls and I knew they both felt the same way about me.

Rod changed all that. He was like a bright star and my two roommates weren't the only students who were blinded by the light. After testing the waters with Heather and Sara and several other girls, Rod eventually chose Heather as his girlfriend. I always thought it could've gone either way between her and Sara. And Sara, in her defense, seemed to take his decision in stride. But apparently she was determined to win him back. And eventually she did.

Heather did not take it well.

A truck honked its horn, snapping me back to reality. The

sidewalk was crowded and I needed to pay attention to where I was going.

At the next corner, I pressed the walk button and tried to relax my shoulders as I waited. Obviously, I was still unnerved by the conversation with Heather, but I shook it off and quickly walked the last half block home.

I keyed in my security code and stepped inside the lobby of my apartment building. Once the front door was closed tightly, I hurried over to the old freight elevator and jumped inside just in time, hitting the up button. The ancient thing shuddered and moaned, then began to move. But instead of ascending to the sixth floor, the elevator headed down.

"Rats," I groused. Someone in the garage downstairs must've pushed the button just before me. With a shrug, I leaned against the rough wood wall to enjoy the ride.

This beautifully rustic elevator had been one of the selling points when I bought my apartment five years ago. I had also loved the exposed brick walls, the polished wood floors, spacious rooms, and awesome view from my front window. Not to mention a great location south of Market Street—otherwise known as SOMA—within walking distance of the Giants' baseball stadium.

I chose to overlook the fact that the old elevator trembled so much that it often felt as if the entire building was shaking. I preferred to consider it an integral part of our state-of-the-art security system. After all, an unwelcome stranger couldn't exactly sneak up on you if they were taking the elevator.

Unfortunately, in the past there had been a few unsavory characters who had figured out that they could get to me by taking the stairs. We had worked that out with cameras and video screens at the front door and video screens in everyone's homes to make sure nobody got into the building uninvited.

I brushed off that unpleasant topic and turned my thoughts to Derek Stone, my gorgeous fiancé and the man I intended to spend the rest of my life with. He had taken the week off to finish up a few of the wedding chores he'd volunteered for, such as choosing a "signature cocktail" for the wedding reception and picking up family members at the airport.

I smiled at the thought of finally meeting the rest of his large family. So far I'd met his parents and his younger brother Dalton. He had three more brothers coming to town, along with their wives and children, plus three aunts and uncles and various cousins and more children. It seemed that this had become the wedding of the century for the Stone family since every last one of them was showing up for the ceremony this weekend. Or maybe they just wanted to experience the thrill of traveling on a luxurious private jet from England to San Francisco. Derek was pulling out all the stops to make sure his entire family was here for the most special day of our lives.

The elevator reached the garage floor and shimmied to a stop. The doors opened and I saw Derek standing there. His eyes lit up. "Darling."

"This is such a nice surprise," I said, as he joined me.

He leaned in and kissed me. "What are you doing home so early? I thought you'd be at the conference for hours."

"I just went to register and then wound up talking to a few people. What about you? Where have you been?"

"I finished my errands," he said. "Then I stopped off at the office to make sure there were no shenanigans going on while the boss is away. And now I'm home. And here you are."

"Isn't that fun?"

He kissed me again. I sighed and laid my head on his shoulder. Sometimes it startled me to realize how much I loved this man. Almost equally as startling was the fact that he loved me back, just as much.

I gazed up at him. "When you say *errands*, what exactly do you mean?"

His grin was lopsided. "You'll be happy to hear that I've managed to narrow down our signature cocktail choices to two. I'll make them both for you this week and you'll be the final judge."

"I'm up to the challenge," I said.

"Of course you are." He chuckled, then shook his head. "Just be grateful you didn't have to work your way through the twelve other contenders."

"Twelve." I stared at him, finally comprehending. "You're inebriated."

"Not in the slightest." He shrugged. "I took the smallest sips of each."

"Didn't Dalton go with you?"

He scowled. "And therein lies the problem."

"Oh no. Did you get him drunk?"

"Certainly not. He did that all by himself."

"Will he be all right?"

"Of course," he said gently, knowing I had a soft spot for his baby brother. "I poured him into a cab and sent him back to Dharma."

"I hope Savannah doesn't blame me," I muttered. Not that it was my fault, but then, we were sisters. It rarely mattered whether something was actually my fault or not.

Derek's brother Dalton had recently moved from England to Dharma to live with my sister. The two of them had fallen madly in love last year while Savannah was under suspicion for murder. Dalton had come to town to help us solve a tricky cryptology question. His top secret job at MI6, England's mysterious intelligence agency, had something to do with breaking codes.

"She might not blame you," Derek grumbled, "but I do."

I smiled. "Why?"

He wrapped me in his arms and buried his head in the crook of my neck. "Because you weren't with me."

I rubbed his back, laughing. "You're right. It's all my fault."

He chuckled. "I'm glad we agree."

After a moment, I asked, "You didn't drive home, did you?"

"No. The taxicab dropped me off and I jogged down to the garage to grab some client notes I left in my car."

"Good."

I knew Derek was barely inebriated, but I still would've been worried to know he'd driven home. In most situations, he was in complete control, the master of his universe. But right now he seemed a little more stressed out than usual. Maybe he was worried about the wedding.

I thought about it for a half second and shook my head. Derek, stressed? About the wedding? No way. He had been looking forward to the big day from the very moment he had proposed.

Straightening, he gazed at me and touched my cheek. "What's troubling you, love?"

"What? Me?" I leaned back and gazed up at him. "Nothing. I thought something might be wrong with you. You seem a little stressed."

"Not a bit." He regarded me for a long moment, then frowned. "But something happened to you, I can tell. Was it at the conference?"

I blinked and shook my hair back. How did he do that? Not that I minded him being able to gauge my every emotion and thought by osmosis, but it was disconcerting nonetheless.

"I ran into an old friend," I admitted.

He stroked my cheek with the back of his hand. "Tell me about it."

The elevator quivered to a stop on the sixth floor and the heavy door slid open.

"Let's get out of here before the door shuts," I said, shifting my rolling briefcase around. "I'll tell you all about it inside."

He slipped his arm through mine. "I'll hold you to that."

We walked down the wide interior hall to our front door. As always, once inside the house we headed for the kitchen to regroup and chat. I left my rolling briefcase and purse by the dining room table and sat down on the barstool facing the kitchen. Derek found some crackers, put them in a small bowl, and set it on the bar. Then he removed a bottle of wine from the cooler and poured one glass. After handing it to me, he grabbed a bottle of water for himself and took a seat on the kitchen stool across from me.

As soon as we were settled, Charlie, our sweet cat, came out from hiding and wound herself around my ankles.

"Hello, my darling one," I said, and reached down to scratch her soft neck. As I sat back up, Derek raised his bottle.

"Cheers, love," he said, and we clinked our drinks together.

"Cheers." I took a sip of the cabernet sauvignon, savoring the richness and flavor. Setting the glass down, I reached for a cracker. "So how are your parents doing?"

"They're having a delightful time at your parents' home in Dharma. They planned to tour the new wine cave this afternoon."

"Without us," I groused. "Maybe I should have backed out of the conference after all."

"You can still back out if you want," he said gently, reaching out to squeeze my hand. "But then where would you go? What would you do? You'd be here, underfoot. In my way."

I laughed, as he knew I would. "That's such a lovely thing to say."

"Seriously, love. I remember hearing you say how eager you were to attend this conference."

"Oh, nice," I said, scowling. "Throwing my words back in my face."

He laughed. "That's my style."

"Vicious." But I chuckled, because it wasn't his style at all. Derek had always been unfailingly kind—except for those times when we had faced down cold-blooded killers. Then he could be more cutthroat and diabolical than anyone on the planet. I appreciated both sides of his personality and they gave me two more reasons to love him.

"Admit it," he said. "If you stayed home, you'd be bored out of your mind. There's nothing left to do for the wedding. You've planned every last detail down to the minute."

"I know. Robin told me I'm a disgrace to bridezillas everywhere." I grabbed another cracker and chomped down. "I'm just feeling grumpy because everyone's in Dharma having fun and I'm not there. Ordinarily I love this conference, but since you're home and our families are having a blast together, I sort of feel like I'm forced to go off to work every day."

"I'll be going into the office a few times this week as well. Aren't we a sad pair?"

I flashed him an accusing look. "Don't pretend you're not perfectly happy staying in town while our families frolic in the wine country."

He chuckled. "I admit I'm rather relieved to be away from it all."

I considered that for a moment. "Guess I need to adopt your attitude."

"Everyone should," he said, biting back a grin.

Rolling my eyes, I held out my wineglass. "I'm going to need more of this."

Chuckling, he poured more wine into my glass. I took a sip and ate another cracker. Finally Derek leaned forward and rested his elbows on the counter. "Are you going to tell me what happened today?"

With a shrug, I said, "It's not a big deal, really. I ran into an old college friend. Graduate school friend, actually. We had an interesting conversation. I'm still mulling it over."

"Graduate school. From your time in Austin?"

"Yes." I had received my masters in library science at the University of Texas at Austin, which was also one of the best schools for bookbinding and archival studies in the country.

"And this was a good friend?" Derek said. "Was it one of your Musketeers?"

I was taken aback. "You remember me telling you about that?"

"Of course." His gaze was solemn. "I remember everything you've ever said to me."

I laughed, but then tried to think back over our time together. What else had I told him that might come back to bite me? "Now you're scaring me."

He chuckled. "Tell me about this friend, darling."

With a sigh, I gave him the basic details of my hour-long chat with Heather.

"She said it out loud?" He shook his head in disbelief. "That she would kill this other woman?"

"Yes."

"Did you believe her?"

"Good question." Did I? I had to ask myself. "No, of course not. I mean, she was angry, but you know, it's one of those things that people say. There's no way she could've meant it. But . . ."

"But you never know," he said, finishing my thought.

"Right." We exchanged wary glances. The two of us had

seen enough dead bodies to know that almost anything could motivate someone to kill another person.

Deep in thought, I swirled the dark red wine in my glass and stared at the way it coated the inner surface. "I should've just asked her if she meant it. That would've been smart."

"It might've been awkward," he said. "What if she told you she was just kidding? Would you have believed her?"

With a groan, I said, "I don't know. There was so much rage in her tone." I blew out a frustrated breath. "After twelve years, she's still so angry. Isn't that a little sad?"

"Some people hold grudges for a lifetime," he murmured.

Gazing at him, I had to wonder if maybe Derek had known someone like that.

I sighed. "I guess it's a good thing Sara isn't coming to the conference."

"Are you sure she's not coming?"

I smiled wistfully. "To be honest, I wouldn't mind seeing her again because we used to be such good friends. But I'd hate to be around when she and Heather see each other for the first time."

"That could be unpleasant."

"You can say that again." I took a quick sip of wine. "Now that I think about it, I'm not sure I'd like to see Sara after all. Both she and Heather really changed after Rod showed up. They weren't much fun anymore. Always competing for his attention and spending way too much time fluffing their hair and putting on makeup and worrying about what to wear. And then once Sara snagged him away from Heather, she became insufferable. Their final confrontation was awful."

"It still bothers you."

"We were so close and . . ." I shook my head. "It was sad. Needless to say, the Three Musketeers totally fizzled."

"No longer *one for all*?"

I chuckled. "Hardly. We all went our separate ways and never spoke to each other again. Until today."

He leaned forward and reached for my hand. "I'm sorry, love."

I squeezed his hand. "Don't get me wrong. It was wonderful to see Heather. I've got a lot of great memories of the three of us. She was always so smart and she had a wicked sense of humor. God, we had a good time."

"Darling, it sounds like you used to have a wonderful friendship. If you'd like to invite her to the wedding, it wouldn't be a problem."

I stared at him. "I didn't tell her about our wedding."

His eyebrows shot up. "You didn't?"

I shook my head, mentally replaying the conversation with Heather. "I couldn't be sure of her reaction. She seemed to be so angry still, I didn't want to make her more miserable than she already was. So I never mentioned it. We just kept talking about her. Her problems, her anger, her pain. Her life since college."

"Then on second thought"—he paused—"perhaps it would be better not to invite her."

"I agree. She might not appreciate all the joy and happiness in the air."

"True," he said, then added sagely, "Too much joy and happiness can be a real downer."

Chapter Three

Early the next morning, I rushed over to the convention center to give my speech on book conservation. It was a dry subject, but I always tried to infuse a little bit of lightness into the talk.

"That was absolutely the most inspiring speech I've ever heard," a young woman gushed. "It's like you looked straight into my soul and spoke directly to me."

I almost laughed at her overwrought words, but her expression was so sincere, I didn't dare. Besides, I loved talking about book conservation and the need to preserve our oldest books and treasures. It was an important topic and I was strangely exhilarated after speaking for the last hour to an auditorium filled with librarians. "I'm so glad you enjoyed it. It's important to take good care of books."

"I believe in books," her friend whispered. "We have to save them all."

"Those are words to live by," I said with a firm yet positive nod.

"Can I take a picture with you?" the first girl asked.

"Sure, as long as you send me a copy." I handed her my card with my email address on it. "I'll post it on my social media pages."

"Oh, awesome!" She quickly sidled up to me and held her phone out as far as she could. "Smile!"

After pressing the button twice, she whirled around and beamed at me. "Thanks again. You're my idol."

"Uh, thank you. Thanks for coming." As she walked away, I found myself wondering what she would think if she could see me working alone in my studio with no makeup, tossing back chocolates, wearing sweats and Birkenstocks. Ah, the glamour.

"Wow, you made her day."

I turned and found Heather standing behind me. "Hi. I thought we were meeting at the restaurant."

"I had a little extra time so I popped in to listen to your speech. You're good." She nodded for emphasis and smiled at me. "Really good. I was impressed."

I grinned as I gathered up my notes and tucked them into my briefcase. "Thanks. I get a little zealous with the message sometimes."

"Zealous is good. Especially when you're preaching to the choir. I should think everyone here would want to save the books. For librarians, it's our mission in life."

I winced a little at the way she phrased it. "Was it too preachy?"

"No, don't worry." She chuckled as we headed for the door. "And I'm glad to see that some things haven't changed."

"What do you mean?"

"You were always so conciliatory back in school."

She made it sound like a bad thing. "I was?"

"You don't remember?" She smiled and shook her head. "You were always the one who looked at both sides of an issue or tried to play devil's advocate when someone got carried away. A teacher would give you a compliment and you would immediately search out all the reasons why everyone else in class was just as good. You were always so annoyingly *fair*."

"Wow, that's harsh." I gave a weak chuckle, but I wasn't feeling happy. She made me sound completely boring.

"That was a compliment." She laughed and elbowed me lightly. "Seriously, I'm amazed that you're still as self-deprecating as you always were."

"No I'm not," I argued. "I can be a selfish pig when I want to be."

Heather laughed again. "If you say so."

We walked out into the sunshine and headed over to Third Street to my favorite Thai restaurant in the area. Heather's words were still rattling around in my brain and I had to force myself to let it all go.

Lunch was delicious and the conversation was fun, lightening my mood. I asked a ton of questions and Heather did a lot of the talking, but eventually she got around to asking me what was happening in my life. That was when I finally mentioned the wedding to her.

She blinked and dropped her chopsticks. "What?"

"We're getting married this Sunday."

Her eyes went wide. "But . . . but . . . what are you doing here?"

I smiled. "I know it's weird. At first I was going to cancel my conference events, but then Derek and I realized I didn't need to. We planned it all really well and now everything is basically ready. Our families are up in the wine country all week, getting to know one another, enjoying each other's company, and eating good food. And Derek and I are both home, taking it easy. Sort of."

"But that's . . . that's crazy!" Heather sat back and stared at me as if I had two heads. "You should be freaking out and terrorizing caterers and making unreasonable demands. Or at the very least, packing for your honeymoon."

I hung my head in shame. "I'm already packed."

Her eyes widened in horror. "You. Are. Sick."

"I know," I said, laughing. "But I can live with it. And better yet, Derek can, too."

"Wow." She had to pause and breathe. "Well, congratulations on your wedding. If he's as wonderful as you say, I know you'll have a beautiful life."

"Thanks, Heather." I wanted to wish the same to her, but I couldn't. My friend was still stuck in the past and it was breaking my heart.

Heather insisted on paying for lunch—"Consider it a wedding gift," she said—and after a minute of half-hearted arguing, I gave in and let her pay. We walked back to Fourth Street and then split up. Heather continued on to the conference center while I headed for home to change into more casual, comfortable clothes for the Book Lovers' Tour that afternoon.

Once home, I took my tour file from my desk drawer and read through my notes for the hundredth time. I knew my city intimately and I'd given this tour before, but never with strangers. I wanted to be clear and concise and entertaining during every moment of the trip. Okay, I knew that was a pipe dream; I just hoped it would be interesting and fun for everyone. Including me.

I found my itinerary and easy directions for the bus driver and set them on top of my notes. I planned to go over each stop on the tour with the driver before any of the raffle winners got on the bus.

Also in the drawer were my handouts for the winners. I had hand-drawn a quirky map of the city with funny icons for each stop, and added a short history of each point of interest. I had also made individual mini-accordion booklets for each of the participants. These would be a fun, colorful giveaway. Derek had suggested that I might offer to autograph the booklet if anyone wanted me to do so.

This was going to be a piece of cake, I thought, then laughed out loud. Because the truth was, I was so nervous, my hands were shaking.

"Never mind," I muttered. Dashing down the hall to my bedroom, I checked my outfit and hair and makeup one last time, then strolled back to my studio, where I packed everything into my rolling briefcase.

Charlie bumped up against my ankle and purred loudly.

"I'm sorry I can't stay and play with you," I said, giving her a quick scratch and a few strokes down her back. "But Derek will be home soon."

She swatted my shoe lightly and then sauntered off. To wait for Derek, I assumed. That was certainly what I would do if I were a cat. Or a human, for that matter.

I cleaned and freshened her food and water bowls, then wheeled my briefcase out to the hall and locked the door.

Ten minutes later, I was standing in front of the wide sidewalk outside the main entrance to the conference hall. I checked my watch and saw that I still had a few minutes before the bus arrived. Just enough time for my nerves to escalate into a full-blown panic attack.

"Ridiculous." I paced a few yards back and forth, taking comfort in the fact that I'd never had a panic attack in my life. Then again, it was never too late to start. In my defense, I was about to get married, so even though I knew it was all taken care of, there was still a tiny voice in the back of my mind screaming incoherently. Then there was this tour, with a bunch of strangers. Those two things started me off on a downward spiral, and after that, my busy brain took the bait and ran with it.

Pacing helped quell my nerves, so I continued to walk back and forth around the wide sidewalk by the entrance. I also took a few deep breaths, sucking in air while hoping no one would notice.

It helped to watch all the people coming and going. I was amazed that each of them carried what appeared to be at least a dozen books and I remembered one year when I brought back forty-six books from a conference in Chicago. I had to buy an extra suitcase to transport my treasures back home. Once again, I was grateful that the conference was in San Francisco this year so I wouldn't have to deal with that issue.

Okay, good. Books had taken my mind out of panic mode and into a zone of comfort, at least for a few minutes. I continued to concentrate on mundane thoughts as I strolled back and forth along the forecourt until a horn honked, pulling me out of my daydreams. I looked up in time to see a shiny white mini-coach pull into the passenger loading area.

"Saved by the bus," I said, then waved to make sure the driver had seen me. He pulled to a stop right next to me and I had a moment to admire our transportation for the afternoon. The charter service had called it a "luxury mini-coach bus" and promised it would seat twenty-five people.

The door opened, and to my complete shock, my mom and Meg Stone, my soon-to-be mother-in-law, stood there waving madly.

"Yoohoo, Brooklyn!" my mother cried, as she climbed two steps down to the sidewalk.

"I'm right here, Mom."

"Ach!" She wrapped me in her arms and gave me a little squeeze. "Blimey, aren't you a sight for sore eyes, then?"

"What are you doing here?" Was it my imagination or was my mother speaking Cockney? "Not that I'm not thrilled to see you."

As soon as I was free from my mother's arms, Meg grabbed me in her warm, viselike grip. "It's wonderful to see you, Brooklyn. You look beautiful."

"Thank you, Meg. It's great to see you, too." I leaned closer and whispered in her ear, "When did my mother start speaking with a British accent?"

Meg's face lit up. "Isn't she adorable?"

"Huh." We held each other at arm's length for a moment and she gazed warmly at me. Her bright blue eyes twinkled with charm, reminding me of Derek.

Mom pulled me back for another hug and I held her tightly for a quick moment. "I'm still in shock. How did you get here?"

"We haven't seen you all week," Meg said. "So we decided to come into town."

"That's wonderful," I said, glancing from Mom to Meg and back. "And here you are. On my bus."

"Wouldn't miss it for all the tea in China, now, would we?" Mom stepped back and opened her purse. "Where's me kettle 'n' hob?"

I flinched at her mangled attempt at British slang and stared at Meg. "What did she just say?"

Meg laughed. "She's looking for her phone. She wants to know what time it is."

"How did she get . . . Never mind." I gave an inner sigh. At least with my mom around, I'd be too busy to have another panic attack. "You'll tell me later."

"Of course, dear," Meg said, patting my shoulder.

We all stood in a circle and gazed at each other, grinning like loons.

"So really, what are you doing here?" I asked, once my initial shock had started to fade.

Meg squeezed my hand. "Derek told us you were giving a tour today and we decided to come along. Do you mind?"

"Cor, she won't mind," Mom said, winking at me. "She's not a bloody wanker, now, is she?"

I gaped at my mother, who had apparently gone full Cockney after spending three days with Derek's English parents. Who weren't Cockney at all, by the way, but that didn't matter to my mother.

Meg didn't seem at all fazed by my mother's oddball behavior. She had happy tears in her eyes as she hugged me again. "I'm positively thrilled to be back in San Francisco. I can't wait to watch you make Derek the happiest man on the planet."

"He makes me happy, too," I whispered.

She sniffled as she stepped back, and ran her fingers through her chic, short cap of gray hair to distract herself. "Dalton is happy here, too. And Savannah is wonderful. I couldn't be more delighted. It's all just . . . perfect."

Mom wrapped her arm around Meg's waist. "We've been laughing and crying all week."

"I hope that means you've been having fun," I said.

"Oh, so much fun," Meg said. "John may never leave Dharma."

Mom beamed at her. "I'd be perfectly happy if you both stayed forever."

"Don't think we're not considering it," Meg said with a laugh, as she fondly tucked Mom's arm through hers.

"That would be fantastic," Mom cried. "You know, there are a couple of houses for sale near us in Dharma."

I was so relieved that my mother's real voice had suddenly returned, I didn't really pay attention to their conversation.

Where had she picked up the Cockney inflection? And how did she know all that British slang? Hmm. I eyed Meg reflectively.

Just then the bus door opened again and a tall, muscular man with skin the color of rich, dark coffee stood there looking at us. He wore a red golf shirt and khakis, and looked formidable, to say the least. I supposed if any rabble-rousing librarians wanted to cause trouble, I could count on him to crack some skulls.

"Who's in charge here?" he asked.

"I am," I said, raising my hand.

He consulted his clipboard. "You're Brooklyn?"

"Yes."

"I'm Lawrence. Come on aboard and I'll show you what's what."

"Sounds like a plan." I checked my watch.

"We'll wait out here," Mom said.

"Okay. The rest of the group should be arriving in a few minutes."

"We'll have them queue up," Meg said.

"Thanks." I checked my watch again. I would have just enough time to go over the itinerary with Lawrence and figure out how to operate the PA system before the winning librarians arrived for the tour.

I climbed the steps and handed the man my itinerary. He studied it for a long minute and made a notation on the side of the map. "Okay, give me the rundown."

"See the five smaller circles?"

"Yeah."

"Those are the places I plan to talk about in a general way.

You don't have to stop because we won't be getting out of the bus. But if you're able to slow down for a minute, that would be great."

"So if there's no place to stop and park, I should just keep on driving?"

"Right. If there happens to be a big parking space right in front, feel free to pull over. But I don't want you to go to a lot of trouble. I know we're about to hit rush hour traffic, so if you can't find a parking place right in front of any of them, don't worry about it. I'll just blather on for a few minutes about its significance as we drive to the next site."

He gave me a cockeyed grin. "Blather. I like it."

"It's what I do best." I looked at my own map. "Okay, so the two points marked with the bright red stars are the places we'll be featuring on the tour. That's where we'll be parking and getting off the bus."

I pointed to the list along the side of his map. "I explain each of them in this column."

He took a minute to study the map and read my explanation along the side, then nodded. "Okay, looks easy enough. Those two places all have big parking lots, so it shouldn't be a problem."

"I hope not."

He stuck the map onto his clipboard and set it on the dashboard. Then he grabbed a small box from the passenger seat and pulled out a lavalier microphone. "Let's test this." He clipped it to my jacket lapel. "Just speak naturally."

Easy for you to say, I thought, but went ahead and followed directions. "Testing one, two, three, four."

My voice echoed through the bus.

"You're a natural," he said. "Now, why don't you test out your seat? It's adjustable."

"Oh, nice." I would be sitting up front next to Lawrence. The seat swiveled, which meant I'd be able to look out the front windshield to see where we were going and also swivel around to talk to my tour group. "This is perfect."

He gave a quick nod. "Then I think we're good to go."

"Right." I smiled. "We just have to wait for our passengers."

"There's a good idea." He sat in the driver's seat. "Give me the word as soon as everyone's here and I'll take off."

"Okay." As I gazed back at the rows of comfortable seats, I took in a deep breath and let it out slowly. I was nervous again and I didn't know why. It had been only a few hours ago that I had given a speech in front of two hundred people. Why would a little bus ride freak me out?

Maybe because these were contest winners with high expectations? Or maybe it was simply because I'd never done something quite like this before.

But it would be fun, I told myself. I knew my town intimately and I loved all of the places we were going to visit. Besides, I was hardly the first person who'd ever come up with the idea of a book lovers' tour of San Francisco. There were whole companies devoted to the subject. Of course, most of those groups tended to stick with the tried-and-true hotspots around town as well as the great old bookshops like City Lights in North Beach and Green Apple Books on Clement Street. There were other tour companies that specialized in one particular author or another, giving readers a glimpse, for instance, into Amy Tan's Chinatown or

Dashiell Hammett's haunts. I'd actually taken the Hammett tour a few years ago and our small group had ended the evening with dinner at John's Grill off Union Square, where the Maltese Falcon held court. It was both fascinating and yummy.

Of course, if I'd had all day for this tour, I would have driven everyone out to Sonoma and up to the top of Glen Ellen to explore Jack London's wonderful cabin in the woods. Maybe someday I would take my own tour group up there.

But for today, since this tour would last for only three hours, my plan was to focus on *books.* What better way to entertain twenty librarians? We would pass by two of the city's most historic bookshops and drive through at least one well-known literary neighborhood. Then it would be off to visit some of my all-time-favorite book-centered places around the city.

The librarians began to arrive just as Patty the raffle coordinator came running up to hand me a list of the names of the winners. "We don't want any party crashers," she said with a semi-frantic grin.

"No, we don't," I agreed, giving the list a quick scan. "Especially since there's no more room on the bus." With my mother and Meg joining the tour, we would have just enough seats for everyone on the mini-coach.

"Have fun!" she cried, and ran off to take care of her next task. A raffle coordinator's job was never done.

As each librarian climbed aboard the vehicle, I introduced myself, checked their name off the list, and then gave them a small sparkly mesh bag that contained the goodies I'd assembled for the tour. The little handmade accordion books were in there, plus a copy of the map and itinerary and my business card. And just in case, I had tossed in a generous handful of wrapped chocolates. I didn't want anyone to go hungry.

Once everyone was on board, I gave them a brief rundown of the tour. "I'll show you plenty of fun, book-related spots, but we'll only leave the bus at the two locations indicated on the map."

There was a bit of commotion while everyone pulled the maps out of the goodie bags.

"Our driver's name is Lawrence," I said.

"Hey, gang," he said, giving a friendly wave as the librarians called out greetings.

"And in case you're wondering, we have two suspicious stowaways on the tour." I smiled. "My mother and my future mother-in-law paid me a surprise visit, so I've got them sitting right up front where I can keep an eye on them."

Mom and Meg were thrilled with the laughs and enthusiastic applause and stood and waved at everyone.

"Finally," I continued, "please take lots of photographs. My email is on my business card inside your goodie bag, so be sure to send them to me. I'll post them on my website and my Facebook page."

I assured everyone that the tour would take only three hours and that they would be back in plenty of time to enjoy the conference dinner and tonight's keynote speaker, a famous author who wrote books about books.

Five minutes later, with everyone in high spirits, Lawrence pulled away from the curb and we took off on our adventure.

"A three-hour tour," I sang under my breath, then tried desperately to banish the tune from my head.

After only a few blocks, the driver turned onto a narrow one-way street and slowed down as we reached a small modern, glass-fronted building. There was an empty space directly in front, so he pulled to the curb and came to a stop.

"This is the American Bookbinders Museum," I said, pointing out the window.

"There's an actual museum for bookbinding?" the blond woman behind me said, awestruck. "That's amazing."

"What do they have on display?" her friend asked.

"So many cool things," I said. "Unfortunately we won't be able to take the tour today, but if any of you have an extra hour this week, I would highly recommend a visit."

A hum of excitement spread among the librarians as they imagined the possibilities. Yes, we were a nerdy bunch, but it still gave me a thrill to know that they all loved this stuff as much as I did.

"As you might have noticed," I continued, "the museum is only two blocks away from our conference center. It's a virtual celebration of books and bookbinding. Not only do they have a fabulous museum store, but they've also got two really interesting exhibits going on right now. One is on papermaking, which I always find fascinating, and the other is an exhibit of antique letterpress printing presses. It's the largest collection I've seen anywhere and they're all in functioning order. And once a day the curator and his staff get all of the machines operating at the same time. I can't tell you how much fun it is to watch them all operating at once." I grinned. "Well, fun for me, anyway."

Everyone on the bus smiled and nodded in complete understanding. These were my people, I thought again as that warm and fuzzy tingly feeling spread across my chest.

"I love museum stores," a woman in the last row said with a sigh, and her seatmate laughed. Some others joined in the conversation and I turned around to face the front, assured for the moment that everyone was having a good time.

Lawrence pulled away from the Bookbinders Museum and continued down the one-way street until he reached Fifth Street, where he turned left. A few blocks later, he turned right, easing slowly onto Market Street, and then inching his way a few blocks before turning left on Kearny. Skirting Union Square, we headed toward Chinatown. I turned and faced the group in order to mention a few of the landmarks that Amy Tan had featured in her books.

"Also," I continued, "if you do get a chance to visit Chinatown, be sure to stop in Portsmouth Square, where you'll find a lovely marker commemorating Robert Louis Stevenson, who spent some quality time in our city."

That started a discussion of other literary landmarks around town, so I gave them directions to a street near Russian Hill that was said to be the fictional home of Armistead Maupin's characters in his *Tales of the City*.

Finally we turned left on Pacific and headed west toward our next stop.

"In just a few minutes we'll arrive at the Covington Library," I explained, "where we'll leave the bus and take a short tour." I gave a brief history of the Covington and listed a few of the most important pieces in their massive collection. "Sadly, we'll only have a half hour, so we're going to concentrate on the displays in the main hall. But I promise you won't be disappointed, especially when you meet our tour guide."

I had wrangled my dear old friend Ian McCullough into talking to the group for a few minutes. Ian had been the Covington's head curator for years and had recently been promoted to president. I knew the librarians would find Ian both entertaining and brilliant.

I texted him to say that we were ten minutes away and he responded immediately, so I gave myself permission to relax for a moment. Everything seemed to be working out just fine.

As we crept toward Pacific Heights, I happened to glance over at Mom and Meg, who were seated in the first row behind the driver. They were practically shaking with excitement.

What was that all about? I wondered.

The friendly blond librarian across the aisle noticed as well. "You two look like the cat that swallowed the canary. What's the scoop?"

Meg glanced over her shoulder at Mom, who gave her an enthusiastic nod. "Go ahead. You can tell her."

"Tell me what?" the blonde said.

My shoulders grew stiff as Meg flashed me a coquettish smile. "Brooklyn is too reserved to mention it, but she has developed quite a reputation as a crime buster over the years."

My eyes widened as the blond woman shot a quick glance at me, then turned back at Meg. "How's that?"

Mom and Meg exchanged another glance, then Meg said, "Our Brooklyn is famous for finding dead bodies."

"That's right," Mom said, aiming a warm smile at me. "She's my little murder magnet."

"Mom, Meg, stop that," I said, hissing, but they ignored me.

Mom was on a mission. "And she's very close friends with the homicide detectives around town."

Meg nodded with enthusiasm. "I believe she's got that nice policewoman on speed dial. Don't you, dear?"

My mouth fell open. "Wait, what?"

"You mean Inspector Lee," my mother said, ignoring my sputtering. "Such a nice gal. Tough as nails, but she has the prettiest hair."

"Does she call you whenever somebody dies?" an older woman in a purple sweater asked. "Is that how you see so many dead bodies?"

"No," I insisted. "That's not—"

"Hey, is this about those murders?" a skinny bald-headed man asked from one of the middle seats.

"Yes," Meg said loudly.

A woman in the back row spoke up. "I heard she just has to show up and bodies start to drop."

"True dat," Mom said, winking at me. So now instead of Cockney she was speaking *gangsta*?

Someone else chimed in, "I'm surprised the Covington Library still allows her to work there."

Horrified, I tried to catch that person's gaze. "No, that's not even—"

But my words were drowned out by a buzz of comments. And three rows back, a woman sitting next to the lady in purple wore a puzzled look. "Did somebody die?"

"Not yet," Mom said gleefully. Turning in her seat to face the crowd, she added, "But hold on to your hats, folks. We're about to tour the scene of a real-life murder!"

Chapter Four

"You two are in deep trouble," I whispered sharply, sounding like a parent disciplining her wayward children. I didn't like the feeling.

"Now, sweetie, don't blame Meg," Mom pleaded. "We both thought it would be fun to inject a little sparkle into the tour. You've got to admit, you could liven it up a touch."

While that might have been true, I wasn't willing to go there with her. I love my mother, but really, I felt as if I'd been ambushed. And now, my mom apparently had a willing ally. Suddenly I was outnumbered.

Meg scooted forward in her seat and reached out to pat my knee. "She's absolutely right, Brooklyn dear. To be perfectly honest, we heard several of the ladies talking about it in the queue. So the subject of your, er, proclivity for murder was bound to come up eventually."

"Are you kidding?"

Meg shook her head. "Oh, no. They're very interested. You're quite a celebrity in that regard. I think that's why everyone is so enthusiastic about the tour."

I winced. "You think they actually expect me to talk about the murders?"

"Of course," Mom said. She took a quick glance at the librarians, then looked back at me. "Wouldn't you?"

I hung my head. I should've known something like this would happen at some point, especially after Lucy, the very first person I spoke to yesterday at the registration desk, had gushed about my involvement in murder investigations.

It was bad enough that I actually *was* prone to stumbling over dead bodies. But now to find out that everyone on the bus was hoping to hear some tidbits of gossip about my unfortunate habit? That was just plain weird. And a little disturbing.

Was that why there were so many raffle entries?

"I can see you're distressed," Meg said kindly, "but you have a gift, Brooklyn. You save lives, for goodness' sake! Believe me, these ladies and gentlemen would dearly love to hear how you faced down a cold-blooded killer—in a bookshop of all places!—and survived to tell the tale."

"And that makes it book-related, too," Mom said brightly, seeing the glass half full as always.

I almost laughed at her reasoning, but I managed to restrain myself.

"Don't be angry, sweetie," Mom whispered. "You'll get wrinkles."

It wasn't easy, but I chose to ignore that comment. "I'm not angry, Mom. I just don't need you to encourage them."

"We won't say another word," Meg insisted, and pantomimed locking her lips together and throwing away the key.

"But if we do happen to say anything," Mom said, pushing her luck, "I really think you should do the talking, Meg. Your voice lends an air of *Masterpiece Theatre* to everything. Don't you think so, Brooklyn?"

"Oh, Becky, that's a lovely thing to say," Meg said.

Mom smiled at Meg. "We Americans think everything sounds better with a British accent."

I mentally rolled my eyes. Was that the reason why my mother had tried on the Cockney accent?

I couldn't think about that right now, so instead I brushed the entire conversation off to concentrate on my tour duties. Coughing to clear my throat, I raised my voice to be heard over the many conversations going on throughout the bus. "As we reach the crest of the hill, you'll want to look to your right for a breathtaking view of the San Francisco Bay. The fog is starting to roll in, but you can still see the Golden Gate Bridge in the distance."

"Ooh, I see it!"

"It's beautiful."

The Golden Gate was always a crowd pleaser.

Staring at the view, I let my mind drift back a few years to the day I visited a charming little house in the Sea Cliff neighborhood, tucked away in the shadow of the Golden Gate Bridge near China Beach.

Without warning, the shocking image of a dead body flashed into my head. He was the second victim I had ever encountered. I had been looking for a book in one of the back bedrooms of the house and found a body instead. A bullet hole had been etched neatly into his forehead. I was told that he died instantly.

Someone laughed sharply and I flinched.

"Whew." I blew out a shaky breath and wondered where in the world that memory had come from. Was it caused by seeing the bridge in the fog? No way. I saw that view all the time, especially when I was traveling up to Dharma to visit my family. No, it had to be all this talk of murder that had brought that ugly image back to the forefront of my mind.

I glanced over at Meg and Mom, who were deep in conversation together, no doubt plotting their next subversive move.

I swiveled around to face the front and saw that we had only a few more blocks before we arrived at our destination. I made an effort to concentrate on my breathing and felt my shoulders begin to relax again. Five short minutes later, Lawrence parked the bus in the Covington parking lot.

Pasting a cheery smile onto my face, I turned my chair around to face my librarians. "Remember, we've only got thirty minutes to see several exhibits, so please stay with the group. You can always come back for a longer visit later in the week. For now, let's go see some amazing books."

There were cheers from the librarians as they jumped up and filed out of the bus. I stayed in my chair, taking a minute to organize my notes while everyone else was leaving.

Once the librarians were outside, Lawrence spoke up. "You

know, your mom is going to sneak into wherever it was that you found that body."

I cringed a little. "You heard that?"

He grinned. "Well, y'all are sitting right next to me so I could hardly help it. But I'll let you in on a little secret. I hear every conversation going on anywhere inside this bus." He pointed to the high, curved headliner above his seat. "Sitting here, with these acoustics, I catch all the chitchat."

I stared up at the coach's ceiling. "Ah, the sounds are amplified by the arch. I'll bet that comes in handy sometimes."

"You bet it does." He studied me for a moment. "So. You find dead bodies."

"Not on purpose."

"But you found one in there." He jerked his head in the direction of the massive library.

I grimaced. "Actually, I found two bodies in there."

"At the same time?"

"No. There was a year or two in between."

"So it's really true."

"It doesn't mean anything," I insisted. "It's just my weird luck."

"That's something bigger than luck, my dear."

"Maybe." I shrugged. "I'd better catch up with the group. Lord knows what trouble my mother will get into if I don't."

He chuckled. "She's cool. So's her friend."

"That's my future mother-in-law."

"Looks like they might be ganging up on you."

I laughed as I started down the steps. "Yes, and I'll tell them you noticed."

I caught up with everyone near the front entry of the Covington. Mom was playing shepherd, leading the way.

Once inside, their voices automatically dropped to a respectful hush, as proper librarians everywhere would understand. They practically tiptoed across the polished checkerboard marble floor of the grand foyer, stopping to gaze up at the sweeping staircases on either side of the large anteroom.

Ian came running up and gave me a big hug, then introduced himself to the group. He took over the tour guide duties, instantly charming the group with his easy warmth and his fascinating stories.

With Ian in charge, I was able to enjoy the tour as much as my charges did. I fell in love all over again with the four-foot-tall Audubon book of beautifully painted birds, the display of early Shakespeare folios, and the fascinating collection of nineteenth century poets' works, the highlight of which, for me, was the handwritten letters of Walt Whitman.

Ian made the librarians laugh and cheer with the story of how he beat out the Metropolitan Museum in New York to obtain the illustrated fifteenth century Ellesmere manuscript of Chaucer's *Canterbury Tales*. It involved a stolen masterpiece, a treacherous train ride into the Scottish Highlands, and a high-stakes poker game straight out of a James Bond novel.

After that, Ian led everyone down the wide hall toward the west wing. On the way, he told us how the grand Italianate mansion became a world-renowned museum and library known for its advanced techniques of book conservation, preservation, and restoration. He pointed to the antique Tiffany chandeliers that had been updated with state-of-the-art LED lighting to preserve the integrity of the books and ephemera on display. Behind the scenes, technicians studied every aspect of book conservation, including environmental controls, pest management, chemical and water damage, and the newest methods of fire- and earthquake-proofing areas where the rarest books were kept. Parts of his presentation were similar to what I had spoken of in my speech on book conservation earlier that day. It made sense, since I had done some of my most important conservation work right here at the Covington.

We wound up in the West Gallery, a space almost as large as the Main Hall. There were six smaller galleries branching off from the central room, and in the past, Ian explained, these smaller spaces had featured everything from an American cookbook exhibit to a fabulous baseball card collection.

"What I want to show you is right through here," Ian said, and walked over to the second doorway on the left. I walked in and was instantly surrounded by more Beatles memorabilia and ephemera than I had ever seen in one place. There were concert posters, album covers, clothing, and magazines. There was a left-handed bass guitar, apparently once played by Paul McCartney. There was even a Beatles candy bar wrapper behind the protective glass wall of a display case.

"Oh, Ian," Mom whispered, pressing her fingers to her lips as she gazed at the delightful presentation.

He flashed her a broad smile, then explained to the others. "Mrs. Wainwright was generous enough to loan the Covington a number of pieces from her extensive private collection."

I recognized Mom's vintage fan magazines from the sixties,

now individually framed and spread out across one wall of the room. And in the main glass case, holding a place of honor, was Mom's cherished ticket to the Hollywood Bowl to see the Fab Four on their first visit to the United States in 1964.

I had been visiting Mom last year when Ian showed up to ask if she would be willing to loan her Beatlemania treasures to the Covington for this exhibit. At the time I thought she was going to faint, she was so pleased.

I stole a glance at her now and saw her eyes tearing up all over again.

Purple Sweater Woman and her friend stared with interest at the glass display. "Cindy, look at the price on this concert ticket."

Her friend gasped. "Oh my God, seven dollars."

"Isn't that amazing?" Purple said.

"The original ticket price was reasonable enough," Mom said to the two women. "But I actually had to buy mine from a scalper."

"Oh, dear."

Mom nodded. "He charged me twelve dollars. My father said it was highway robbery."

Purple laughed. "Those were the days, right?"

I wandered over to a monitor on the far wall that was showing *A Hard Day's Night*. Mom and Dad had played that Beatles movie at least a hundred times while we were growing up. I still loved it.

A few minutes later I turned away from the movie to discover that the small gallery was empty. I guess I had been so wrapped up in the Beatles' world that I had zoned out for a while. Checking my watch, I saw that it was just about time to head back to the bus. I walked into the West Gallery, but it was empty as well. I left the gallery and started toward the Main Hall. The Covington was a large space, but I couldn't have lost everyone so completely in so short a time, could I? Where had they all disappeared to?

"Some tour guide I turned out to be," I muttered as I hurried back to the Main Hall. I had lost my people!

I stopped abruptly as the realization hit me. I knew exactly where everyone had gone.

Heading back to the West Gallery, I stopped at the very last door and peeked inside. Mom was pointing to the slick marble floor where Meg was sprawled, trying to appear lifeless.

"Brooklyn found the body right there," Mom intoned. "The guy was dead as a doornail."

Oh my God.

There was no use berating her. I just walked away. The good news, I thought as I wandered back to the Main Hall, was that at least Mom hadn't dragged them all down into the cavernous basement. That was where I had actually stumbled across my very first murder victim. He was my teacher, my mentor, my friend, and I still missed him to this day. It gave me shivers to think of him lying there, so I tried not to do it very often. I was pretty sure the Covington janitors had never been able to fully erase the bloodstains from the cement floor.

The rest of the tour went off without a hitch and I began to hope that maybe my tenure as a tour guide wasn't quite as disastrous as I'd thought. We drove across town to Bay Area Book

Arts, our final stop for the day and an absolute must-see for the serious book lover. The gallery at BABA was a wonderful treat with beautifully handmade books, cards, wrapping paper, and artwork on display as well as for sale. One of the instructors showed the librarians around the workshop rooms and quickly demonstrated the guillotine and the letterpress. I took a few minutes to check in with Naomi and Marky May, two old friends who ran the center. And if Mom and Meg slipped off to give a few librarians a private tour of the back hall where I had once found another body, I pretended not to notice.

On the ride back to the conference, the bus was quieter than before. Conversations were hushed and some people were passing around the items they had bought at BABA and the Covington. I took the quiet as a good sign that my tour group members were wiped out from having so much fun.

When Lawrence finally pulled up and stopped in front of the convention center, everyone applauded. My heart didn't exactly soar with happiness, but I was relieved that they seemed to have had a great time. Most of the librarians were effusive with their compliments and thanks.

"Best part of the conference, hands down," the bald-headed man said as he passed me on the way out of the mini-coach.

"I'm so glad you enjoyed it," I said, beaming.

"Absolutely," his buddy agreed.

I thanked them all for supporting the association and coming on the tour, then stepped down from the coach to shake hands and say good-bye to everyone. "Thank you again for entering the raffle. I hope you enjoy the rest of the conference."

After all of the librarians had gone their separate ways, I climbed back into the bus to collect Mom and Meg, who were still talking to Lawrence.

"Are you ready to go?" I asked, gathering up my notes and stuffing them into my briefcase.

"We're staying on the bus, Brooklyn," Mom said. "Lawrence has one more stop to make."

I was grateful that he was willing to drive us to another location, but puzzled by my mother's insistence. "That's not necessary, Lawrence. We can walk home from here."

Mom smiled. "But we're not going home, sweetie. Lawrence is taking us somewhere else."

I sat down in the passenger chair and gave Mom and Meg my best eagle-eye stare. "What's going on with you two? You've been very secretive all day."

They smiled serenely, but said nothing.

I turned and looked at Lawrence. "Do you know what they're up to?"

"Sorry, ma'am, but I have my orders."

"What does that even mean?" I asked. "I thought I was in charge."

"Dream on," Mom said.

Meg giggled, but didn't give up any information.

"Okay, ladies," Lawrence said, revving the engine. "Buckle up."

He drove a few short blocks toward Union Square and stopped in front of a pretty little restaurant on a side street. "Here you go, ladies. Last stop."

The three of us thanked Lawrence profusely, and he and I

exchanged business cards. I knew a gratuity had been included in the rental, but I slipped him an extra bit of cash for putting up with all of us, and then we climbed off the bus.

"What are we doing here?" I asked, looking around as Lawrence drove away.

Mom wrapped her arm around my waist. "Oh, sweetie. We just wanted to have a cocktail and chitchat with you. Lawrence was nice enough to offer to drive us."

I glanced at my wristwatch. "I should give Derek a call."

"That's not necessary," Meg said. "He knows you're going to be a little late."

I sighed. They had obviously gone to some trouble to arrange this, so I wasn't about to rain on their parade.

"Okay, then," I said, coaxing a smile onto my face. "Let's go have a cocktail."

We walked inside and the maître d' immediately led us to the back of the restaurant and into a narrow hall. I actually got a chill across my shoulders as he walked with us down that long, dark passageway. Then suddenly he turned and ushered me into a pitch-black room.

"Here we are," he said helpfully, and walked away.

"What do you mean? Where are we?" I honestly couldn't see a thing. "Wait. Can you at least turn on a light?"

Before I could start to get my bearings, the room burst into bright light and there was a loud shout of "Surprise!"

"Surprise? Where?" I was completely disoriented and had to wonder if I had suffered heart damage. Standing in front of me were at least thirty people. Staring at the faces, I realized I knew who these people were. But what were they doing here?

To my left was a long table covered with a white cloth. Beautifully wrapped gifts were stacked from one end to the other. Over our heads, pink and white crepe-paper ribbons were strewn every which way across the room. There were big white paper bells hanging from all the corners and gorgeous bouquets of white and pink flowers graced every other surface.

I still wasn't certain what all these people were doing here. They were my friends and family, but I wasn't at all sure I wanted to be here. And yet, I knew it was important that I stay. It was the most surreal feeling, almost like an out-of-body experience. I turned to Mom. "Are you sure Derek knows I'll be late?"

"Oh, honey," she said, laughing as she patted my cheek. "You've never had a surprise party, have you? No wonder you're so spaced out."

I swallowed. She was right. I'd never experienced the terror of a surprise party. Still breathless, I pressed my hand to my chest. My heart was beating way too fast. "So this is really a surprise party?"

"Yes."

"For me?"

"Of course. You're the bride-to-be."

"And Derek knew about it?"

"Yes."

"Why didn't he stop you?"

She laughed. "He mentioned you might not take it well, but that made it all the more fun to plan."

I let out a breath and gazed around the festively decorated room. "Well, you did a good job."

"I sure did. I'll go get you a glass of champagne."

"Yes, please." Under my breath, I added, "Maybe you should bring the bottle." But I pulled her back and gave her a long hug. "Thank you, Mom. It means a lot that you would go to all this trouble for me."

"Oh, sweetie, you're going to make me cry."

"Then we're even."

She swatted my arm lightly. "I'll get your drink, smarty pants."

And suddenly I was enveloped in hugs from all three of my sisters; my friend Alex; my best friend, Robin; my neighbors Vinnie and Suzie; several of my bookbinder friends from BABA; and a dozen or more other friends from all over the Bay Area. Even my cop friend, Inspector Janice Lee, was there and came over to give me a hug. And . . .

"Heather?"

"It's me." We hugged. "You can't believe how hard it was to keep my mouth shut about this."

I gaped at her. "You knew all along?"

"Yup." She kept her arm wrapped in mine. "Your mother called me last month and asked if I was coming to the conference."

Now I was really shocked. "So you faked your reaction to me telling you I was getting married?"

"Yeah." She grinned and squeezed my arm. "Pretty good, huh?"

"I'll say," I said, still blown away by my own mother's ability to organize something this major, all for me.

She hugged me again. "I'm so happy for you, Brooklyn. I just hope we can . . ." But she had stopped talking.

"You hope what?" I asked. "Heather?" Behind me, someone else had arrived, shoving the door open so that it hit the wall with a bang.

Heather's mouth opened and closed and she started to blink as if to clear her vision.

"Hi, everyone," the tardy arrival said. "Sorry I'm late."

Heather's face had turned a deathly shade of pale. "I—I can't believe you invited her."

"Who?"

But she had already rushed off so I whipped around to see what she was talking about. And stared into the face of someone I hadn't seen in twelve long years.

I suddenly wondered where my mother was with my glass of champagne, because my throat was as dry as a desert sandstorm.

"Hey, Brooklyn," the woman said with a cheeky grin.

"Hello, Sara."

Chapter Five

"I can't believe you invited her," Sara Martin said, her pouty bottom lip sticking out far enough to trip over.

"I didn't," I pointed out after I downed several large gulps of champagne. "This is a surprise party. I didn't arrange it, so I'm not the one who sent out the invitations. I didn't even know about it until I walked in here."

Another well-meaning ambush, I thought. Now Heather was upset. Sara was upset. And me? I needed more champagne.

"Well, still." In lieu of a decent comeback, she tossed her lustrous mane of chestnut hair over her shoulder. Sara was tall, willowy, and reserved—although that quality was tempered with plenty of snark. She had always dressed like a fashion plate and today was no exception. She wore a chic black suit with knee-high boots made of a soft, buttery leather that I coveted unreservedly.

Sara's perfect wardrobe reminded me that Heather, although petite, outgoing, and funny, usually dressed like a truck driver in her signature blue jeans and clunky boots. We had always laughed about the two of them being total opposites with me in the middle, with my medium height and blond hair. They were both beautiful in completely different ways, so maybe it was no wonder Rod hadn't been able to decide between them. In the end, though, he had made his choice. And shattered a friendship.

"You had to have known Heather would be here," I said. "I mean, if my mother called you, she would've called her, too. Right? Once upon a time you were my two best friends."

Sara waved that logic away. "But I saw you talking to her, all cozy and stuff. Why? She's such a wet blanket. How have you managed to remain friends with her?"

I reminded myself to breathe. Moments ago when Sara arrived, Mom had rushed over with glasses of champagne for both of us. As soon as we had them in our hands, I had dragged Sara down the hall in search of an empty room. There was no way I was going to stay in the happy party room with both her and Heather looking to start World War III.

"Sara, I haven't seen Heather in twelve years. Just like I haven't seen you in twelve years. You both slithered out of my life after graduation and I never heard from either of you again. I tried to contact both of you, but you never called, you never wrote." I shrugged. "I moved on."

She had the good grace to look remorseful, whether it was really how she felt or not. "I guess I could've emailed you."

I patted my heart. "An email? Such a personal touch."

She ignored the mockery. "But I knew you were angry with me so I kept avoiding it. And then it was too late."

"It was never going to be too late," I insisted. "But you're right, I was angry. You were mean and heartless to Heather and you completely ignored me. I no longer recognized you as a friend."

She scowled. "Maybe that's true, but I figured you would've gotten over it by now. Guess not."

"Oh, don't get me wrong. I'm completely over it." I took another major gulp of champagne and wondered where the bottle was. "Heather, on the other hand, is still hurting."

"Oh, isn't that too bad?" she said, all feisty again. "Well, tell her to get over it. My life hasn't exactly been a bed of roses, you know."

I almost laughed, but it would've sent the wrong message. Here I was, straddling the middle road between two women who used to be very important to me. And suddenly, I'd had enough. There was no way I was going back to being the rope in their personal tug-of-war. "I would love to hear all about your rough, tough life sometime. But right now, you don't get to be the aggrieved party."

"Why not?" Sara looked genuinely puzzled. "Heather was awful to me when I tried to reach out to her."

I was surprised. "You reached out to her? When was that?"

She shrugged. "You know, back in school. When she was kicking me out of my room."

"Oh, gee. Where's my tiny violin when I need it? When was that again? Oh yes. Right after you waltzed off with her boyfriend."

"There's no need for sarcasm."

I gave a short laugh. "Trust me, sarcasm is just about the only thing keeping me here with you."

"You can leave anytime."

It was tempting. But, "No. I want to talk about this. Did you see her again after she kicked you out of our room?"

"No." She was pouting again. "She never called me or tried to get together or anything."

"Did you expect her to?"

"Well . . ."

I plowed ahead. "Did you expect that bygones would be bygones? Did you honestly think she would call you up and say, 'Hey, kid, let's get together and talk about old times'? Are you crazy? You're lucky she didn't kill you."

"All right, all right." She paced from side to side in front of me. "Look, things were a little weird back then. I admit it. But it's been twelve years, Brooklyn. Come on."

I studied her for a moment. "I'm really trying to see this from your point of view, but it's hard. Rod betrayed her. More importantly, *you* betrayed her. That kind of pain doesn't go away easily. If ever."

"Oh, give me a break," she said sharply, firing a hot look at me. "We were in college, for Pete's sake. Name one girl who *didn't* steal someone else's boyfriend back then."

I could've named plenty of people, including myself, but that wasn't the point. "So you finally admit that you stole her boyfriend?"

She scowled, but I could read the guilt in her eyes. "It wasn't all my fault," she said, toughing it out. "Rod wanted to break up with her but she wasn't making it easy."

"Right, you're not to blame at all."

"Fine!" she shouted. Slugging down the rest of her champagne, she set the glass on a nearby table. "I'll take the blame. Does that make you happy?"

"Doesn't matter how I feel. You need to tell Heather."

"Oh sure," she said, rolling her eyes. "Like she'll listen to me."

"You could give it a try."

She was back to pacing again. After a moment, she turned and glared at me. "Tell me the truth. Don't you think it's time she got over it?"

"Maybe I do," I said, frowning. "But you and I don't get to put a time limit on her feelings."

Her eyes narrowed in on me and she leaned closer. "That's something at least. Seriously, don't you think she's just wallowing at this point?"

I hated to say anything, because I *had* been thinking that very thing. But I wouldn't betray Heather by admitting it to Sara. My mom used to tell me that men would come and go, but the two things that were certain in life were family and good friends. Heather and Sara had not only been good friends, they had been family to me. And Sara had tossed it all away. "Look, Sara . . ."

"You don't have to answer," she said, wearing a superior smile. "I can see what you're thinking."

"It doesn't matter what I'm thinking because again, it's not our place to decide for her."

She took a deep breath and let it out. Her eyes softened and she touched my arm. "I didn't come here to fight with you. I miss you, Brooklyn. I can't tell you how thrilled I was when your mom called me out of the blue."

I had never told Mom about Heather and Sara's fight over

Rod. All she knew was that the two women had been my best friends way back when. So why not invite them to be a part of my special day? Mom must've figured that since I was going to be attending the librarians' conference the week before the wedding, she would try to get the two of them to show up as well.

Sara's eyes welled up. "I don't blame you for still being mad at me, but I hope we can find a way to be friends again someday."

"I'm sure we will," I conceded. "If you tell me where you got those boots, I'll probably find a way to forgive you."

She laughed and gazed down at her feet. "Aren't they awesome? They're two years old but I'm going to wear them until I'm dead."

I chuckled. "I don't blame you. Look, I hope you'll stay for the party, but I'll understand either way." Then I turned toward the door.

"Wait," she cried. "Can I get a hug at least?"

I sighed. "Of course."

She wrapped her arms around me for a short moment. I could feel her breath stuttering and wondered if she was crying. Was she really upset about the situation or just feeling sorry for herself?

"Well, this is cozy."

I jolted back from Sara and whirled around in time to see Heather standing in the doorway. Why did I feel guilty? Of all of us, I was the one who hadn't done a darn thing. And yet . . .

She started to close the door and I grabbed the knob. "Heather, wait. Come back."

"Why?"

"Because," I said lamely, taking her arm and pulling her inside the room. "Look, we were all best friends once and I miss you both."

"I miss you, too, Brooklyn." Heather stuck her thumb out toward Sara. "But I don't miss this snake in the grass. Not one bit."

"Oh God," Sara moaned. "Get over it! I can't believe you're still harping on something that happened more than ten years ago. You are pitiful."

Heather got right up close to Sara. "And you are horrible."

"Stop!" I cried, waving my arms for emphasis. "This is ridiculous. We're not in grad school anymore. We're grown-ups and we need to act like it. If I've learned anything in the last few years, it's that life is too short to carry a grudge like this forever." I shook my finger at both of them. "You two need to work this out right here and right now."

"Why should we?" Sara demanded.

"Because . . . because this is my party and I say so."

As exit lines went, it was pretty feeble. Nevertheless, I gave them each a stern look, then turned on my heel and walked out, slamming the door behind me and leaving them alone in the room together.

"Do you think they'll come back to the party?" Mom asked, obviously upset after five long minutes had passed.

"Heather left her purse here," I said. "She's got to come back. Right?"

She squeezed my arm. "I had no idea you three had parted on such bad terms."

"I should've told you, but I didn't want to worry you." I sighed. "But it did get ugly there for a while."

"I'm so sorry. If I had known they would bring their bad feelings with them to your wedding shower, I never would've invited them."

I gave her a quick hug because she seemed to need it. My mother had the best heart of anyone I knew and she would worry herself sick over this, even though she had tried to do a nice thing for me. "It's not your fault, Mom. Don't worry. Everything will work out for the best."

"I hope so. But you know me. I just want everyone to be happy."

"I know. And I am." A little white lie, but it made Mom smile, so that was good enough for me. We stood at the bar, where I had gone directly from the other room to quickly replenish my champagne. Honestly, those two women had gotten on my next-to-last nerve, and what made it worse was that their little squabble had distressed my mother, who didn't deserve to feel anything but jubilant tonight.

Thankfully, though, it looked as if everyone else was enjoying the party. The music was wonderful, mostly classic standards, and the champagne was flowing. Two waiters wandered through the crowd carrying trays of the bubbly and hors d'oeuvres. I glanced around and had to smile. "Mom, you've outdone yourself."

"Thank you, sweetie. I had a little help from Alex."

"I thought I recognized those cupcakes." My black-belt, high-powered-businesswoman neighbor Alex Monroe liked to relax by baking cupcakes, which automatically qualified her for the world's-best-neighbor prize as far as I was concerned.

Along one wall of the room was a beautifully laid table with trays and platters and bowls filled with the most delectable-looking goodies I'd seen in a long time. It was all hearty fare since the party would encompass the dinner hour, and my mouth was starting to water at the sight of Kobe beef sliders, pasta salads, and chicken sate served with a yummy-looking peanut sauce. A massive cheese and fruit platter held down one end of the table while a fruit and veggie platter had been placed at the other.

A smaller table held four trays filled with an assortment of beautiful bite-sized pastries. In the center were two multilevel cupcake stands filled with Alex's glistening treats. I could swear they were calling my name, but first I had to make sure that my two erstwhile friends hadn't ripped each other's hair out.

"Oh, here they come," Mom whispered, staring at the doorway.

"Both of them?" I asked.

"This would be a perfect time to open your gifts," she said quietly. Her tone was almost pleading and I knew she didn't want me to tangle with them again tonight.

"Let me just welcome them back to the party and give them some positive strokes for actually speaking to each other."

She sniffled. "Oh, sweetie, that's so thoughtful. You'll make a wonderful mother someday."

"Mom, please. Get it together."

She laughed. "You'd better get used to those sorts of comments. Once you're married you'll hear them all the time."

I walked away, mentally cringing at the thought. But I supposed . . . maybe . . . someday . . .

Good grief. Maybe I'd had too much champagne.

"Impossible," I muttered, and began scoping out the room. Sara had walked to the far end and had begun chatting with one of my bookbinder friends from BABA. Heather was over by the cheese platter, talking to my neighbors, Suzie and Vinnie. I decided to talk to Heather first because she was closest to the food and that cheese platter was beckoning me. I strolled over and joined that little group for a few minutes until Suzie and Vinnie went to sit down and eat.

Alone with Heather, I said, "I'm sorry about what happened. I had no idea she would be here."

"That's understandable, since you had no idea I would be here, either."

I smiled. "True. So how are you holding up?"

"I'm doing better," she admitted. "We actually had a conversation."

"That's great."

"Don't get me wrong," she said, as she spread a chunk of Brie onto a cracker. "It was short and to the point. We're not exactly back to being the Three Musketeers, but at least we spoke."

"That's something, right?"

"I guess so." She took a deep breath. "I even asked her how Rod was doing."

"What?" I beamed at her. "I'm so proud of you. That was really bold."

"Wasn't it?" She sighed. "And guess what? He's here. He came to the conference with her."

"He's here?" I grimaced. "Oh dear."

"It's fine. Really." But she began to flex her hands open and closed as though she were trying to relax her muscles. "I should've gotten past this years ago. I can't tell you how many countless hours I've spent replaying those horrible scenes with her and Rod over and over in my mind. I guess they sort of got etched into my character. They became a part of me, so how could I let them go?"

I stared at her in admiration. "That's really insightful, Heather. I'm impressed."

"It's not a big deal, Brooklyn, but thanks." Her cheeks had turned pink and she took a big bite of the cheese and cracker, probably to distract herself from my words of praise. "I've got to say, this whole trip has been an eye-opener."

I nodded, knowing how she felt. "I just hope you feel better."

"I do," she said firmly, then frowned. "Or at least I will, eventually, once I've been able to figure out exactly what happened and how I feel about it."

"Sometimes it takes a while to process stuff like that."

She rolled her eyes. "Well, I've had twelve years. It's about time I worked it out."

I laughed and gave her a hug. "I really have missed you."

"You, too." She fidgeted with her short hair for a moment, tucking a strand behind her ear. "I should probably go, but I wanted to give you something first."

"You don't need to do that."

"Well, I saw this and thought of you, so I had no choice." She pulled a brightly wrapped rectangle from her bag. "It's not exactly sexy bridal lingerie, but I hope you like it."

"I love it already."

She grinned. "Maybe you should open it first."

"Oh yeah, maybe." I put my champagne glass on the table and began to unwrap the present. I knew as soon as I touched it that it had to be a book, but until I got the paper off, I had no idea which one.

And then I saw it. It was a battered copy of *The Blue Fairy Book* by Andrew Lang. I noticed right away that the spine was creased, the boards were rubbed, and the joints were wobbly. Still, I had never seen anything so sweet in my life.

The dark blue cloth cover featured a gilded witch flying under the full moon. It reminded me of late nights together in our dorm room, reading and laughing and studying and, yes, occasionally drinking cheap wine.

The Blue Fairy Book had been the first of twelve popular collections of fairy tales compiled by Andrew Lang. Each of the subsequent book covers sported a different color and that was how Andrew Lang named them. *The Red Fairy Book, The Green Fairy Book*, and so on. I think we three girls made it through the fifth volume before we finally called it quits. Or graduated. I couldn't remember what came first.

"You're going to make me cry." I opened the book to the title page and stared in shock at the publication date: 1889. "Are you kidding? It's a first edition. How did you ever find it?"

"I'm a librarian," she said with a light shrug. "I can find anything."

I grinned and pulled her in tightly for a hug. "I love it."

"I wasn't sure you'd remember."

"Of course I remember." I laughed as I sniffled away tears. "The three of us used to take turns reading this to each other after we'd finished studying. And usually after we'd shared a bottle of wine or two."

Heather laughed. "Leave it to you to recall the drunken parts."

"Those are some of my favorite memories."

"We went through so many of those silly fairy-tale books." She shook her head. "God, we were such nerds."

"I know. I loved every minute of it." I gazed down at the faded blue book cover, then opened it to a random page with a black-and-white illustration of a lovely woman surrounded by several large parrots. "I actually remember this picture. This is amazing."

"I'm sorry the book is a bit grubby," she said, frowning. "The cover is bubbled in spots and there's foxing all the way through. But hey, it's a first edition so that should give it a bit of pizzazz."

"You're too funny." I hugged her again. "This was really sweet and thoughtful of you. I absolutely love it."

"I'm glad." She grabbed two crackers and slid them into her pocket, then gazed around the room. "I'm going to sneak out while everyone's busy eating. Please thank your mother for me. I'm so happy I was able to be here."

"I am, too. Let's try to get together for coffee again before the conference is over."

"Yes, let's do it. I'll text you."

I held up the book. "Thank you again for this, Heather. I'm really touched."

She blew me a kiss and it hit me like a strong gust of warm wind. Blowing kisses had been something we used to do with each other whenever one of us would leave the dorm room.

I blew her back a kiss and we both grinned. Then she left and I had the strangest hollowed-out feeling, like I was empty inside.

"You look like you could use this," Meg said, handing me another glass of champagne.

I smiled. "How did you know?"

"It's one of my superpowers," she said lightly. "Now what's this lovely book?"

"A gift from Heather."

She took the book from me and turned it over. "Fairy tales. Isn't that wonderful? She's a good friend?"

"Yes," I murmured. "One I haven't seen in years."

Meg patted my arm. "I'm glad she could be here for you."

"Me, too."

She kept her hand on my arm. "Would you like me to fix you a plate, dear?"

I realized I was still staring at the open doorway and shook myself out of my pensive mood. "Oh, no. I can do it. But thank you, Meg. I think you woke me up."

"Sometimes it's difficult to see people from our past."

I blew out a breath. "You can say that again."

"Have something to eat. You'll feel better."

"I already do." I gave her a reassuring smile. "Don't worry. I'll go eat something and mingle with my guests."

"A perfect plan," she said. "I'll leave you to it."

Almost two hours later, the party was still in full swing. I had laughed and chatted with all my friends and relatives, all the gifts had been opened, the fabulous cupcakes were long gone, and plenty of champagne had been consumed.

And that was when Sara finally approached me.

"I should be leaving," she said, "but I wanted to let you know how much fun I had. Your sisters are great."

"I'm so glad you were able to come."

"Me, too. Even though we started out a little shaky."

I grinned. "Hopefully we can get back on track. Do you have time to meet for coffee sometime during the conference?"

"I'd like that, if my boss will let me." She grimaced. "Cornelia's been gunning for me lately."

Seemed like Sara made friends wherever she went. "Do you know why?"

"Basically she's jealous. I'm younger and prettier, and she resents that. You know the type." Sara grinned. "But what's she going to do, fire me? She needs me and she knows it. So let's make coffee a definite yes. If she doesn't like it, too bad."

We exchanged phone numbers and then she reached into her tote bag and pulled out an object wrapped in a brown paper bag. "I wanted to give you something."

I realized that I hadn't opened a gift from her earlier. Not that it mattered.

"You know that's not necessary," I said quickly. "I'm just happy you could be here."

"I am, too, but I still want you to have this." She stared at the worn bag covering the item in her hand and took a deep breath. "It's not exactly wrapped, but here." She thrust the package at me. "I hope you like it."

"I know I'm going to love it, whatever it is." I opened the brown paper bag and reached inside.

Her lips twisted into a mischievous smile. "I noticed that Heather gave you a book so I couldn't be one-upped."

I chuckled. "You're too much." I pulled out the book and stared at the cover in shock. "Oh my God. Sara, this is . . . it's amazing."

"You like it?"

"Are you kidding? I love it." I glanced at the spine. "I mean, I really love it."

"I kind of thought it would be perfect for you. Because . . . you know."

"I—I'm stunned." I turned the book over in my hands and stared at the beautifully gilded fore edge. It was a near-pristine, finely bound copy of *The Three Musketeers* by Alexandre Dumas. The book artist had taken the original colorful cover art depicting the three dashing soldiers, Athos, Porthos, and Aramis, along with their friend d'Artagnan, and incorporated it into the exquisite leather cover, framing and beveling the edges for a beautiful finished effect.

I opened it to the title page and saw that it was published in 1846 in London. "This is a first edition? I—I can't accept this, Sara. It's too rare. It must've cost a fortune."

"It's yours," she countered. "Look, Rod buys and sells books all the time. He found this one, and when I saw it, I knew it would be perfect for you."

"Are you absolutely sure?"

She laughed. "Yes, I'm sure. Besides, Rod can always find another one if he needs to."

I stared at the heavily gilded spine, then looked at her. "I'm just blown away. I'll treasure this, Sara."

Pressing her lips together nervously, she said, "You've got a wonderful heart, Brooklyn. You've brought us all back together and that's deserving of a gift as beautiful as you are. I hope you enjoy it and I wish you many years of happiness in your marriage."

My eyes began to water and once again I had to fight to keep my composure. "You're making me cry."

"Excellent," she said, grinning.

"No, really, I'm overwhelmed. I can't thank you enough."

She gave me a hug. "Enjoy it in good health, please."

"I will, I promise."

"I'd better get going."

"Okay. I'll text you tomorrow and we'll set up a time to have coffee."

"I'm looking forward to it. Especially the part where I tell Cornelia to kiss my behind." When she got to the doorway, she stopped abruptly, turned, and blew me a kiss.

Delighted, I laughed and blew one back to her.

I arrived home in time to catch Derek watching the late news. He turned off the television and patted the sofa cushion next to him. "Come and tell me how you enjoyed your party."

I sat down and he wrapped his arm around my shoulder. As if on cue, Charlie hopped up and squeezed herself into the minuscule space between Derek and me. I stroked her soft, furry back as I played back the events of the evening. "It was a little rough at the beginning," I admitted. "I didn't quite catch the concept of a surprise party so I spent a few minutes staring dumbly at all the faces. But I ended up having a really great time."

Chuckling, he said, "Your mother led me to believe that you'd walk into the house with a truckload of gifts."

"Oh, you won't believe all the beautiful gifts I received. It was almost embarrassing." I rested my head on his shoulder and sighed. "Anyway, Mom thought it would be easier on me if she took them home with her. She'll bring them over when she comes back to town for the wedding."

"That was thoughtful of her."

"She thought of everything. Or Robin did. Or Alex." I shook my head. "It was probably a group effort."

"You've some good friends, darling."

"I know." I smiled as I recalled how smoothly the evening ran. "Thank goodness, because I never would've been able to pull it off."

"Don't sell yourself short, love. I've seen you organize some rather impressive events over the years."

I stretched up to kiss his cheek. "Thank you. But I can't tell you how grateful I am that someone else was in charge. I got to enjoy myself and visit with friends I hadn't seen in a while."

"I'm glad." He shifted on the couch to make eye contact. "Are you ready for bed?"

"Almost. I'd like to look up something online first. It'll only take a minute or two."

He stood and pulled me up off the couch. "What is it?"

"A book."

He smiled. "Of course. Care for some company?"

"I would love it." As we walked into my workshop, I told Derek how my mother had invited the two women who used to be my roommates.

"Your Musketeers," he said.

"Right."

"You told me about the one woman, Heather. The other one showed up as well?"

"Yes. Sara. My mother didn't know we'd had a falling-out back in school. She just thought it would be a nice surprise for me."

"Very sweet of her. But it must've been quite a shock."

"I was a little freaked out, to say the least. I thought I'd have to play referee all night to keep them from killing each other. But they wound up talking it out and managed to remain civil." I held up my hand. "Let me rephrase that. They didn't even speak to each other again. But that's better than yelling and screaming, right?"

"Absolutely."

As I powered up my computer, I explained about the two books the girls had given me and the sentimental meanings attached to both of them.

"The thing is," I said, "I don't think Sara intended to give me *The Three Musketeers*. But then she saw Heather give me a book and she had to go one better. She even admitted it."

"So she just happened to have this expensive book with her," Derek said, his tone speculative. "And she decided to give it to you on the spur of the moment?"

"Yes. That's exactly what happened." I typed in my favorite book auction website and waited until it appeared. Then I entered *The Blue Fairy Book* into the search box and stared at the prices of similar books to the one Heather gave me. Most of them ranged from two hundred to four hundred dollars. "It was too much for her to spend," I muttered.

"Perhaps she was able to find a better price than any of these," Derek said. "She is a librarian, after all. She may have an inside source."

"I hope so." I turned back to the screen and typed *The Three Musketeers,* then waited for the results. I gazed up at Derek. "The book was wrapped in a brown paper bag, Derek. I doubt she brought it as a present for me. I think she was holding on to it for her husband."

"And she gave it away." His eyes narrowed in thought. "I can't imagine he'll be pleased about that."

"She insisted he wouldn't mind. Said he found it and he could find another one."

He frowned at me. "What do you mean, he *found* it?"

"Oh. Forgot to mention that Sara's husband is a broker. He buys and sells high-end books and ephemera."

"Ah." He glanced at the computer screen. "Do you think it'll be easy for him to find another one like it?"

"I doubt it." I angled the computer screen so he could get a better look. "Check this out. Eight years ago a book matching the same description sold for almost ten thousand dollars." I tapped the screen for emphasis. "Two months ago a very similar book came back on the market. Sotheby's has it listed for seventy-four thousand."

He let out a soft whistle. "If the book she gave you is worth seventy-four thousand dollars, I'm guessing your friend Sara is facing a very unhappy husband tonight."

"Unhappy?" I gave a short laugh. "More like homicidal."

Chapter Six

I spent the night tossing and turning, thanks to Heather and Sara. And okay, maybe the champagne had a little something to do with it, too. My dreams kept recycling over and over, and I found myself back in our old dorm room, tearing apart the books they had given me, then putting them back together, then pulling them apart again. What was that all about?

"You didn't sleep well," Derek said as I stumbled into the kitchen.

I groaned. "Oh, great. I must look ravishing."

He chuckled. "You look beautiful as always, my love." His fingers grazed my cheek and he pressed a light kiss on my forehead. I leaned against him for a brief moment, then stepped back while he poured me a cup of coffee.

"Bless you," I whispered, pitifully grateful that he had risen an hour ahead of me to make some phone calls and prepare our breakfast.

I took a sip of the strong brew, then sat down on the barstool. Charlie scurried over to greet me and I picked her up to snuggle for a moment. When I put her down, she circled and brushed up against my ankles a few times, then settled at my feet. "I kept dreaming of those books the girls gave me."

"Is that what had you restless all night?"

"Yes."

"But you're happy with the books, aren't you?"

"Happy? Oh, I am. The books are wonderful. But it was such a weird situation with both of the girls suddenly showing up at my bridal shower after twelve years of silence. I think that's what triggered the dreams, not the books themselves."

"I understand." He pulled two pieces of toast from the toaster and buttered them, then scooped scrambled eggs onto both of our plates. "But you did have fun at the party, didn't you?"

"Oh, definitely." I smiled, remembering. All in all, it had been a fabulous night. "Mom was amazing. I'll admit I wasn't thrilled to be surprised like that, but it turned out to be a complete kick."

"I'm glad, darling. Now tell me more about the books. You must have some theories after going online and then dreaming about them all night."

I chuckled. "Yes. As you know, Heather gave me an old book of fairy tales. That particular book used to have a lot of meaning for the three of us and I really do love it. I was frankly shocked that she remembered. But it was a sweet, thoughtful gift."

"And the other one?" he asked.

I shook my head, still confused. "Don't get me wrong, it's a beautiful book and I'm thrilled to have it. But . . . well, you saw what it was worth. It doesn't make sense." I took another sip of coffee as Derek added a piece of turkey bacon to each of our plates. My mouth was starting to water watching him. And he had that effect on me even when he wasn't giving me food.

He picked up the plates and brought them over to the kitchen island, where I was sitting. He sat down across from me and we began to eat.

"I guess I'm a little skeptical that Sara actually meant to give it to me. I think she was carried away in the moment and also wanted to make a bigger splash than Heather. So as much as I love the book, I'm wondering if I should give it back."

"Did your online source indicate that the similar book was still on the market?"

"I took another quick look this morning. They show that it was just sold."

"Just sold? That was fast." He sipped his coffee.

"Here's the thing, Derek. I think it's the same book."

He glanced up at me, surprised. "What makes you think so?"

"They described it exactly." *Another reason to give it back*, I thought. "I guess it's possible there's another copy out there, but I doubt it."

He gazed at me for a long moment. "So a friend you haven't seen in twelve years shows up and gives you a seventy-four-thousand-dollar book. And that same book was just sold to someone else."

I sighed, took another gulp of blessed coffee, and gave myself a moment to settle before saying, "It doesn't make sense, does it?"

Derek was contemplative as he took another bite of toast.

I snapped off a piece of bacon, popped it into my mouth, and savored the rich flavor. "What are you thinking?"

Frowning, Derek shook his head. "Everything about this situation smells fishy."

That was just what I had been thinking, too, darn it.

That afternoon, I gave my bookbinding workshop. I arrived early to find the studio and was happy to see that it was perfect for my class. There were three long, wide lab tables with an ample number of stools for everyone who had signed up. I arranged supplies and equipment for each student with a cutting board, utility knife, bone folder, sewing needle, scissors, pencil, awl, a small glue brush, and a metal ruler.

I had collected all this equipment over the years and used it whenever I had a class. Occasionally a student would show up with their own tools, but I was always willing to lend my own—as long as I was able to collect it all back when the class was finished.

I also gave each of them three different thicknesses of linen thread for the various bindings I'd be teaching, a stack of high-quality, acid-free paper for the pages, and several pieces of heavy bookboard for the covers. The pages had already been scored for folding and the pieces of bookboard were cut to the correct size for each book.

Once the students' spaces were set up, I moved to the front of the room to set out my own supplies. On a side counter I placed piles of decorative papers for the endpapers and lots of interesting cloth remnants for covering the boards. I had brought a jar of polyvinyl acetate, otherwise known as PVA glue, that I had mixed at home yesterday. I planned to pour small amounts into disposable plastic cups for each student. Happily, the association had given me a stipend to cover the cost of these supplies since they couldn't be reused.

And then I waited.

I had been giving this same bookbinding workshop for years at conferences and book fairs all over the world. I loved teaching this stuff. Sometimes I added more history and technique and stretched it out over an entire weekend. And once a year I offered a three-week intensive course at BABA that attracted artists and teachers from all over the Bay Area. But these short, two-hour classes were the most fun and generally attracted hobbyists as well as librarians looking forward to picking up a new technique or two.

Even though this would be a relatively short class, my attendees would go home with four small handmade books representing four styles of bookbinding. It was fast-paced and enjoyable for anyone who loved books and crafting.

In the back of my mind, though, was the nagging thought that one of my students might beg me to relate some grisly tales of murder. I wouldn't do it, of course, but the fact that the subject had already come up during the bus tour concerned me. It didn't help that my mother and Meg had fanned those flames. Still, I knew that Lucy from the registration desk, who had been so rabid about the subject, would be attending the class today, and that made my worry all the more real.

The students trickled in, including Lucy, and finally I had my full class assembled and ready to go.

I handed out name tags so I would be able to call on them by name. I took a few minutes to explain several different methods of bookbinding, such as Coptic, one of the oldest binding methods, similar to a chain stitch; Japanese stab binding, a good place to start since the pages are not made up of folded signatures but a stack of single sheets; and limp binding, which usually refers to a binding in which paper signatures are sewn onto cords and a soft cover is folded around the textblock.

I dispensed some general cautionary advice along with a touch of history. And since my students were all librarians whose days were often filled with rescuing badly treated books, I also devoted a few minutes to some quick and practical tips and tricks of book repair and maintenance.

Finally, I gave my inspirational mini-lecture on paper fibers and grain direction, followed by a dazzling speech about glue. And then we got down to making books.

"We're going to start with the accordion-folded book." I held up a four-by-four-inch sample of a cute little book I had made a while back. It had a grosgrain tie that wrapped all the way around to hold the book together. I untied the ribbon and pulled the book apart and the accordion-folded pages expanded. To my surprise, the students applauded and I laughed. "I'm glad you like it, because this will be the easiest book we make today."

I re-tied the ribbon and handed the book to Priscilla, the student closest to me. "I'm going to pass this around. Please feel free to examine it, unwrap and wrap it up again. As you can see, the front and back boards are covered in beautiful, gold-tone fabric and the 'endpaper' is actually the first page of the accordion. When it's closed, it looks like a nicely bound book."

"It's like playing an accordion," Priscilla marveled, as she pulled the covers apart and pressed them back together a few times. "Now I get it."

I smiled. "Keep passing that one around while we start making our own."

I had set aside thirty minutes to work on the accordion book project and most of the class came close to finishing. After promising to leave time at the end of the class to complete any unfinished work, I moved on to our next topic, the Coptic stitch. The best part of this bookbinding method was that it could be accomplished without using any adhesive.

Essentially, the Coptic stitch was a series of chain-like stitches that held a set of folded signature pages together and bound them to the covered boards. Again, I passed around samples of Coptic bindings to illustrate exactly what we would be making.

I had the librarians pick out fabric and endpapers before we started on the Coptic project since the front and back boards would need to be completed before the stitching began. I explained that this style was more complicated than it looked, but most of the students picked it up pretty quickly.

"Have you guys done this one before?" I asked, teasing them. But they insisted they hadn't.

"You're just a brilliant teacher," one of them remarked slyly.

"And you get an A," I said, laughing.

Halfway through this portion of the class, a woman named Amy raised her hand. "Has anyone else noticed that some of these tools could be really dangerous?"

It was her tone that had my antennae perking up.

"Yes," I said lightly. "As I explained at the start, the utility knife, the needle, and the scissors are very sharp, so please be careful." I tried for a nonchalant tone, but I could already hear a low-level buzz coming from Amy's worktable. Was it just a coincidence that she was sitting next to Lucy from the registration desk? The one who had been so excited to hear about murder?

Prepared for the worst, I strolled over to their worktable. "How's it going over here?"

"Amy brings up an interesting point," Lucy said. "Don't you think so, Brooklyn?"

"Actually, I'm not sure what her point is." I smiled at Amy, who was a pretty blonde in her twenties. "Can you repeat it for me?"

The others at the table were looking anywhere else but at Amy. But Lucy seemed happy that her friend had brought up the subject. She was sweet and a little naive while Amy had more of an edge. She seemed ready for a confrontation, but I wasn't sure why.

"Here's the deal," Amy said breezily. "Not only do you find dead bodies everywhere you go, but some might say that you bring the vibe with you." She held up the utility knife. "I mean, look at these tools. What else can we think when you simply hand them over to us?"

I smiled, which wasn't easy while gritting my teeth. "You

could think that I'm teaching a class in bookbinding. These are the tools that a bookbinder uses to create a book."

She rolled her eyes. "Well, sure. But what if someone in here is really unhinged? You hand them a knife and it sends them spiraling and they end up hurting one of us. What happens then?"

I glanced at Lucy but she would no longer make eye contact with me. I could understand that. Lucy had wanted to talk about dead bodies and all that fun stuff, but Amy was off on a tangent about me and my "vibe." And I didn't know why. I was teaching a class on bookbinding and we were making little books. Pretty innocuous stuff if you asked me. But I supposed I had to address her point.

"It's a scary world," I said carefully. "I try to make my classroom a safe environment, but these days there's always a slight possibility that something dangerous could happen. But do you really want to have a philosophical discussion about that right now? Because I'm sorry to say it, but you're disrupting the entire class and that's really not fair."

"I thought it was a perfectly straightforward question."

"Actually, it was confrontational and mean-spirited." I managed to smile as I said it. "As you'll recall, at the beginning of the class I asked everyone to be very careful with the tools because I didn't want anyone to hurt themselves. I offered to help anyone who needed assistance."

"Okay, fine," she groused. "Sorry I even said anything."

So now she was being a martyr. I sighed. "Amy, if you'd rather not continue with the class, I'll be happy to refund your payment." I glanced around. "That goes for everyone else, too."

She grunted in disgust. "My friend said that people keep dying around you. It's weird, that's all. I wanted to find out why it's happening."

"And I want to continue teaching this class. And since I'm in charge, I say we continue the class."

"But that's not fair," Amy whined.

"That's true of so many things," I said, trying not to go completely snarky. I took another quick look at Lucy, but she looked like she wanted to hide under the worktable. Honestly, I hoped she was embarrassed. I didn't enjoy feeling like I was under attack, especially when I was doing something I loved to do. I shifted my gaze back to her friend Amy. "As I said before, I'll understand if you'd like to leave. Or you can stay and we can talk after class."

She blinked, clearly shocked that I had made the offer. "Really? Um, okay. I'll stay and talk to you afterwards."

"Fine." I exhaled slowly. "Then let's get back to work. Where were we?"

Someone at another table spoke up. "You were explaining how to attach the next set of signature pages to the textblock."

"Right. Thank you." I walked back to the front of the room, taking more deep breaths as I went. That brief squabble had left me a little shaky, but I still had an hour left to teach these people two more bookbinding techniques so I straightened my shoulders and shook off the mood.

I tried to maintain a light, cheerful tone for the rest of the class, figuring that I wasn't the only one who'd been upset by Amy's oddly hostile questioning. At one point, Lucy raised her hand. "I don't want to bring up a sore subject, but you did mention that bookbinders use some dangerous tools. So I'm wondering if you've ever injured yourself while binding a book. And what do you do if you get blood on the pages?"

I took a breath in and out. *Okay, I could handle this.* I had a fleeting thought that I should've asked Mom and Meg to attend the class. They would've had some answers and kept things rollicking.

I smiled at Lucy. "Blood is a liquid, so that makes it an enemy of paper. It's also bright red, so it will stain the page. Therefore, my only rule when it comes to getting blood on a book is, *don't do it.*"

The entire class laughed and Lucy smiled.

By the end of the session, I was so relieved. As I was packing up my supplies, Lucy approached. I forced a smile. "I hope you enjoyed the class."

"I did. But I wanted to apologize."

"What for?"

She sighed. "My boss took your Book Lovers' Tour yesterday and she warned me not to bring up the topic of the murders. So I had already decided not to say anything. But Amy insisted on bringing it up. I'm sorry. I couldn't stop her."

I nodded. "I appreciate that. Thanks." I glanced around. "Did Amy leave?"

"No, she's still packing up her bag." Lucy lowered her voice. "After you got back on topic, she was starting to feel pretty stupid. Some of the people at our table were giving her dirty looks, and I was so annoyed with her I ignored her for the rest of the class."

"I hope she'll be okay."

Amy approached at that moment and waved her hand blithely. "I'm fine. I've got a thick skin. You probably noticed."

I considered what to say to the two women, then forged ahead. "I would like you to understand why I don't talk about these things. Coming across a dead body is not an uplifting moment. It's not cool or interesting or exciting. It's actually quite disturbing. And sad and painful, especially for the people who are going to be affected in a really horrible way for the rest of their lives. So I don't like being thought of as someone who attracts that kind of, you know, energy, or karma, or *vibe*. It's not fun for me. Do you get that?"

"Oh. Oh yes. God." Amy's eyes were awash with tears. She grabbed me in a hug and whispered, "I'm so sorry. I won't ever do anything like that again. I hope you'll forgive me someday."

"There's no need to forgive anything." When she let me go, I gave her a smile. "Don't worry, Amy. I know you're a good person. I really appreciate you coming to talk to me."

Lucy pressed her lips together, then blurted, "I was your biggest fan before and now I'm even more impressed."

I laughed. "Now you're just trying to butter me up."

"Absolutely," she said, and giggled.

"Brooklyn?"

We all turned at the sound of a man's voice. I suddenly lost my breath and I was pretty sure my eyes were as big as goggles. Rod Martin stood in the doorway next to an older woman who was trying to get his attention by reaching for his arm. He sloughed her off and stepped inside the classroom.

"Guess that's our cue to go," Lucy said amiably, and elbowed

Amy. They took off for the door just as Rod took a few more steps into the classroom.

I was still in shock. I wasn't even certain my voice would work, but I finally gave it a shot.

"Rod."

"Yeah." He grinned. "It's me."

"Uh, wow. Long time." I shouldn't have been so surprised to see him. After all, I knew Sara had brought him with her to the conference. And then there was that valuable book . . .

"Too long." He scanned me up and down. "You look amazing."

"Thanks," I said, although I didn't take it as a compliment. Rod Martin had always been a natural-born schmoozer, lest I forgot.

I had to admit, though, that he was even better looking than I remembered, and a little taller. His thin frame had filled out over the years and now he appeared to be happy, handsome, and prosperous. It just figured that his looks would only improve with age. Life could be so unfair.

"How have you been?" I asked. Not that I cared. Not really. I still wasn't ready to forgive him after he'd been the cause of so much misery between my two friends.

"Couldn't be better," he said jovially, clearly confident that his good looks and charm would get him whatever he wanted. And he was probably right.

The older woman appeared in the doorway. "Is that woman with you?"

He glanced over his shoulder and waved her away. "She's someone I work with. I'll see her later."

I didn't know what to say to him so I continued to pack up my supplies.

"Hey," he said. "I understand Sara gave you a little gift last night."

"She did." I smiled brightly while my brain calculated exactly what he would say and a hundred different responses I could make. I knew instinctively that he wanted the book back, but he probably wouldn't come right out and ask for it. No, he was too cool for that. He would try to cajole and flatter me to get it. And that wasn't going to work.

But hadn't I just been thinking that morning about whether I should return it or not? The rare book website I frequented had indicated that the book had been sold very recently. Had Rod sold it, thinking it was still in his possession? If so, he had to be panicking even as we spoke. I studied his jaw. Was it clenched? Was he starting to sweat around his hairline? Losing out on a seventy-four-thousand-dollar sale would cause me to sweat, just saying. But I couldn't see any outward signs that he was freaking out. He just kept smiling.

I made a decision in that moment, that even if he did ask for it back, I wouldn't give it to him. Maybe I would return it to Sara, but not to Rod.

"It was such a surprise," I continued, practically gushing. "I absolutely love it."

"Yeah, it's a beauty, all right."

"And the significance of the book is so touching, right? I mean, we were the Three Musketeers, remember? It just means a lot." I actually felt myself tearing up and tried to shake off the sentimental feelings. I didn't want him to think I was a wimp. On the other hand, maybe that could work in my favor.

Nope, I thought. There was no way I would deliberately act weak or fragile in front of him. I gathered my stack of endpapers and slipped them into my briefcase. "Sara seemed to think you could find another copy easily. I hope that's true."

"Oh yeah, no problem." He shrugged casually. "You know how it is with books. There's always another one coming around the bend."

"I do know books," I said, smiling. "And I recognized it for the generous gift it was. Sara was so sweet to think of me."

His smile was pensive. "I know she was hoping to patch things up with you. I hope the book helped."

There was no way he meant that, was there? So what was he really doing here? Rod was charming in a slippery kind of way, so it was hard to tell.

"The book was a lovely gesture," I said. "And it's been so great to catch up with Sara this week. I'm hoping we can keep in touch and remain friends after all this time."

His smile grew brighter. "Sara would love to hear that." He glanced around, seemed to realize the room was empty. "Well, I just wanted to track you down and tell you how pleased I was to hear that you're getting married. I wish you every happiness, Brooklyn."

"Thank you, Rod."

"Hey," he said. "If you're free sometime for coffee or a drink this week, let me know. I can even meet you tonight if you're available. I'd love to catch up on old times."

I almost rolled my eyes, but instead I just kept smiling. "I'd better check my schedule before I say yes."

We exchanged phone numbers, then he gave me a warm hug. It brought back so many mixed feelings from those times in school. I had loathed the way he treated Heather, and my feelings had lasted for so many years. Now I was finding it hard to switch them around. But if I was going to be friends with Sara again, I would need to rekindle my so-called friendship with Rod.

"This was really a nice surprise," I said. "Thank you so much for coming to see me."

"It was nice for me, too." He turned to leave, then glanced back over his shoulder. "Take care, Brooklyn."

"You, too."

That night, Derek was going out to dinner with his brothers, his partners from work, and some guy friends. It was as close as he was going to get to a bachelor party. I doubted he would tolerate anyone shouting "Surprise" and making him open twenty pink-wrapped gifts, but I hoped the guys would make sure he had a good time. Not that I was complaining about all those pink-wrapped goodies. My party had turned out to be awesome, once I got over my initial shock and befuddlement.

Since Derek would be out for the evening, I had decided to invite a few of my very closest girlfriends over for pizza and wine.

Robin and my sisters, of course, and my favorite neighbors, Alex and Vinnie and Suzie. I mulled over the possibility of inviting Heather and Sara. Granted, things had been pretty tense between them at the shower the night before, but at the last minute, I decided to text them both and invite them over. After all, if I really wanted to stay in touch with them, I needed to extend my own hand in friendship. If either of them decided not to show up, that was their choice. But I hoped that they would because, to be honest, I wasn't sure when I would ever see either of them again.

Heather texted me right back to let me know she would be here, but that she had a meeting and might be a little bit late. Sara texted a few minutes later to say that Rod was going out with a few associates and she would love to come over for pizza. I texted back my address and directions and she texted back a thumbs-up.

"Good," I murmured, and called to order the pizza.

An hour into my impromptu party, I realized that neither Heather nor Sara had arrived. I texted Heather first. "Are you lost?"

A minute later, she responded. "Sorry, I got stuck in a meeting. Will still try to make it if it's not too late."

"Okay. If not, let's do coffee tomorrow."

"Great!"

I took a sip of wine, then texted Sara the same message. "Are you lost?"

While I waited for her return text, I glanced around the room. Vinnie was showing everyone the latest pictures of Lily, who was rapidly growing into a beautiful little girl. I thought back to the night almost two years ago when the three of us and Gabriel were staying at a gorgeous old mansion near Lake Tahoe and got snowed in for a few days. It was on that trip that Vinnie and Suzie had found out that their best friends, Teddy and Maris, were killed in a tragic car accident and that their will stipulated that Suzie and Vinnie were to raise Lily as their own. The two women had accepted that challenging role and never looked back.

Robin was talking to Savannah about the gardens they had both planted in Dharma, London and China were laughing about the latest protection spell our mom had performed for Derek's parents, and Alex was passing around her freshly baked batch of red velvet cupcakes. I grabbed one just as my phone signaled an incoming text.

"Ugh, I'm stuck working!" Sara wrote. "I'll try to make it to your place, but it might be another hour."

"That's okay, come anytime," I answered. "What R U working on?"

"Cornelia shipped a ton of books out here and they're stored in the conference hotel basement. I have to bring them over to the convention floor."

"Sounds awful."

"Totally! She's trying to kill my girlish spirit."

"LOL. I'm so sorry. Hope you can make it."

"Me, too. I'll call you."

After that, I got wrapped up in the party, laughing and sharing old family stories along with plenty of anecdotes about Derek and his amazing brothers.

Almost an hour later, my cell phone rang and I answered right away. "Hello?"

"It's me, Sara."

"Hi. Everything okay?"

"I'm still working, but I should be finished soon."

"Are you all by yourself?"

"Yeah, but I can handle it," she said, then sighed. "I'm just so annoyed with my boss. She really has it in for me."

"I've got to meet this person. She sounds awful."

"Believe me, she's even worse than you can imagine. She's—"

She didn't finish the sentence so I waited. After a long moment of silence, I said, "Sara?"

"Sorry," Sara replied. "I thought I heard something. This basement is kind of creepy. Let me get off the phone so I can finish up and come over. Save me a slice of pepperoni."

"You got it." I rejoined my guests, replenishing everyone's drinks and bringing around more pizza. The party broke up around eleven o'clock and we never saw Sara or Heather.

The next morning Derek left early for a meeting at his office while I faced a shoe crisis. I couldn't say what got into me, but I had decided that with Derek out of the house, this was a perfect time to try on my wedding dress with my newly dyed white lace shoes.

I loved my dress, but it was impossible to slip into it without someone helping me zip up the zipper. Instead, I slipped my arms into the sleeves and held it in place around my waist, then slid my feet into the heels.

Staring in the mirror, I confess I really felt like a princess. But . . . something was wrong. My shoes felt way too loose. I had to sit down on the edge of the bed to take them off. I stared at the lacy style and remembered how I had fallen in love with them at the shop. These were definitely my shoes. I turned them over to look at the soles where the size was stamped.

"That's my size," I muttered. "But . . . oh God."

I felt as if I'd entered the Twilight Zone. Everything looked right, but something was very wrong. I tried them on again. Still too loose. "What am I going to do? I need new shoes."

"Meow."

I glanced down and saw Charlie staring up at me as if I was crazy or something. "Charlie, stop judging me and help. What am I going to do?"

"Meow," she said, and gave my pretty lace shoe a delicate lick.

"You're very cute but you're no help at all." Still uncertain what to do and feeling my heart rate climbing, I grabbed my house key and, clutching my dress so it wouldn't fall off in front of any neighbors who might be leaving for work about then, ran down the hall to Alex's apartment. She was my guru for all things related to clothing and shoes.

"What's going on?" Alex said, tying the sash of her silk bathrobe more securely.

"Please help me," I cried. "I tried on my wedding shoes and they don't fit anymore."

She smiled indulgently. "Well, you've been working out a lot. Maybe you've lost a shoe size."

"It that really a thing? I've never heard of losing weight in your feet."

"It can happen," she said enigmatically.

I was ready to start sobbing and she was going all inscrutable on me. "Alex, focus. I need new shoes."

She grabbed my hand and pulled me into her apartment. "It's going to be okay. Do you want a cupcake?"

"Of course I want a cupcake. And then I need new shoes."

Still holding my hand, she led me over to her kitchen counter, where a tray filled with newly frosted chocolate mint cupcakes sat. It was amazing. She must have started baking them at five o'clock that morning. "Sit," she said, slipping an apron on over my head. "Your dress is too beautiful to have crumbs falling all over it."

"Thank you." At least one of us was thinking clearly.

"Now have a cupcake and then we'll see if we can make those shoes fit."

While Alex finished dressing for work and I ate my cupcake, I texted both Heather and Sara, sending them each the same message. "Missed you last night. Can we get together sometime today?" I got no response from either of them. I wondered briefly if anything was wrong, but I couldn't worry about that at the moment.

Alex came out to the kitchen dressed to kill in a black-on-black couture suit with a cinched waist and epaulets, and shiny black stiletto pumps.

"You look like a sexy four-star general who's about to kick ass and take names."

"Just the look I was going for," she said with an impish grin. "Now let's see about those shoes."

"You're way too dressed up to deal with my silly shoe crisis. You should go to work. I can handle this. I think."

She rubbed my arm. "I'm never too dressed up to help you, Brooks."

I covered my mouth with my hand. "Now I'm going to cry."

She laughed. "Well, it's about time. You've been so calm and cool during all these months of wedding planning, it's downright unnatural. You haven't had one nervous breakdown or a screaming fit or even a little crying jag. You deserve to have a good cry over ill-fitting shoes, so go for it."

And so I did, briefly. She handed me a handful of tissues and I blew my nose a few times. But after another minute, I was completely bored with myself and my nose was stuffed up to boot. "Okay, I'm done," I said. "Let's go fix those shoes."

"That's my girl."

Within minutes Alex had assessed the situation and suggested that I buy a narrow inner sole and a set of heel cushions that would fit inside my white lace heels. "You can pick them up at any good drugstore."

"You think that'll work?"

"Yes. You're still basically the same shoe size. Your foot is just slightly narrower from all the working out. The cushions should solve the problem and they'll also help keep the shoes from rubbing against your heel. Shoe crisis averted."

"You saved my life," I said, giving her a hug.

"It's what I do," she said with a modest shrug, and took off for work.

I still couldn't believe I'd lost weight in my feet. I mean, I'd been watching my diet for months and exercising like a champ, but still. That was downright weird.

• • •

An hour later I was working on a special project, a beautiful little book of Shakespeare's sonnets that I planned to give to Derek as a wedding gift. When we first started dating, he had read a few of his favorite sonnets to me and I had almost swooned at the romance of it all. Maybe the British accent had something to do with it, but I knew he would love this book. I had asked my friend Genevieve Taylor of Taylor's Fine Books to keep an eye out for the perfect book and she had come through for me. It was small but lovely and in excellent condition with bright white pages and a number of charming colored illustrations throughout, each guarded by tissue. The book was covered in rich burgundy morocco leather with shiny gilding along the edges of the pages. I had tooled a pretty design of a stylized tree on the front cover and added gilding to the leaves. All that was left to do was construct a simple slip-case-style book box covered in matching burgundy linen with a ribbon pull.

I had just finished cutting the boards for the box when Derek arrived home. I tucked the book and materials away and joined him in the kitchen while he made himself a sandwich.

While we chatted about his office meeting, I texted Heather again. "Coffee today or tomorrow?"

She responded immediately. "Tomorrow better than today."

"Okay," I typed. "I'll check in tomorrow morning."

Then I texted Sara again but heard nothing back from her. I stared at my phone. "Hmm."

"What is it?" Derek asked.

"I never heard back from Sara last night and now she's not answering her texts."

"Did you try calling?"

"What a good idea," I said, smiling. I'd gotten so used to texting that the idea of actually dialing the phone and speaking to a person had become an odd concept. I pushed her number and waited. The phone rang six times and then went to voice mail. I left a quick message and ended the call.

"No answer?"

"No." I frowned at my phone. "I can't believe she would blow me off like this. We left each other on pretty good terms and then her husband, Rod, stopped by my classroom to say hello."

"How did that work out for you?"

I sat on the kitchen stool and watched him work. "It was weird, but not too bad. Of course, I don't trust him as far as I can throw him. I think he wants me to give the book back but he wouldn't come right out and say it."

"Where is the book right now?"

"It's in the safe."

"Good."

"I'll try Sara one more time." I dialed her number, but once again the call went to voice mail. I gazed up at Derek and shrugged. "I don't know why I'm worried. Her boss has been riding her pretty hard so maybe she's too busy working to check her messages."

"But you don't think so."

I grimaced. "I really don't."

"Would you feel better if we tried to track her down?"

Just another reason why I loved that man. He always knew the exact right thing to say.

"Yes. She might still be tied up with work, but I can't see her ignoring all those texts." I frowned. "Maybe she lost her phone."

"I'll finish my sandwich and then let's go find out."

We walked a few blocks over to the conference center and into the main exhibit hall. Dozens of organizations, publishers, bookstores, and vendors had rented booths where they were selling their products or giving away books and swag. The Glen Cove College Library, where Sara worked, had rented a small space to display the books published by the college press along with a number of favorite local authors and hometown memorabilia.

Sara wasn't in the booth, but another woman dressed in a business suit smiled at us. I got a quick look at her badge and saw that her name was Darla.

"Good afternoon," she said. "Are you looking for anything in particular?"

"Yes. Actually, I'm looking for Sara Martin."

"Oh." The woman glanced around nervously and lowered her voice. "I haven't seen Sara for hours. She didn't show up this morning for her shift in the booth. I tried texting but didn't hear back from her."

"Is she usually pretty responsible?"

"Are you kidding? *Responsible* is her middle name."

"When did you last see her?" Derek asked.

She leaned closer. "Last night. Our boss insisted that we cart all of our books over here before we could clock out for the day."

"Is that Cornelia?"

Her eyes widened. "How did you know? Oh wait, Sara must've told you about her." Darla shook her head in disgust. "She's a piece of work and she's been even worse on this trip."

"I'm sorry to hear that."

"Yeah. Well, that's why they pay us the big bucks." She snorted. "Anyway, we had to make a dozen trips last night carrying tons of books. By the end I was exhausted so Sara offered to finish up."

"What time was that?"

"About eight thirty or nine?"

I gazed up at Derek. "That was about the time I texted her to see where she was."

"If you see her," Darla whispered loudly, "tell her the boss is still cranky."

"Why is that?" Derek asked.

"Because we're still missing a couple of boxes of books." Darla shrugged. "I'm not sure how they went missing. It's not like Sara to miscalculate stuff like that." She grinned suddenly. "Maybe she did it to get back at Cornelia. The woman is the original grouch."

Despite my worry, I flashed her a friendly smile. "I'll give Sara the message."

"Thanks."

We started to walk away, but I thought of something else. It was probably a dumb question, but I wanted to know just how grouchy Cornelia could be. "Just curious. Did you have to move all the books by hand?"

"Oh, goodness no. We borrowed a hand truck from the booth next door. It wasn't industrial strength, but it helped."

"Okay, thanks."

Derek and I walked away. I glanced around, still hoping to catch a glimpse of Sara, but something told me I wouldn't have any luck. "Let's check her hotel. It's the InterContinental, right across the street."

When we reached the hotel lobby, I asked the clerk to call Sara's room. He didn't have any more luck than I'd had, so I pulled out my conference badge and showed it to him. "My boss wanted me to get some boxes that you have stored down in your basement and take them over to the exhibit hall. Can you point the way?"

"Yes, ma'am. In fact, I'll take you there."

"Thank you."

"It's a little tricky," he said with a grin, and led the way down the hall toward a bank of elevators. He walked past them to the far wall, where he pushed a door open and pointed. "That's the freight elevator. There are two basement levels. You want level two. That's where we store items that have been shipped out here for our guests."

"We appreciate your help," Derek said, and steered me into the elevator.

"Be careful," the clerk added. "It can get kind of dark and there's probably no one working down there at this time of the day."

"Okay. Thanks again."

I pushed the down elevator button and the doors slid closed. "Here goes nothing."

"He made it sound rather uninviting," Derek muttered.

"Yeah, not a place I'd want to hang out late at night." I shook off the spooky chills the clerk's words had left me with.

Derek wrapped his arm around my shoulders. "We'll just consider this an adventure."

"Seems our entire life is an adventure."

He kissed the top of my head. "Indeed."

"I'm afraid she might've gone home," I said, finally voicing what I'd been worried about all morning. "I wouldn't be surprised to find out that she and Rod had a fight and she just left."

"She probably would've told you that in a text," Derek said, which made perfect sense but did nothing to alleviate my concerns.

Something else occurred to me. "What if Cornelia fired her?"

"If Sara is doing all this heavy lifting, it wouldn't be in Cornelia's best interests to fire her."

"I guess not."

The elevator came to a shuddering stop and we stepped out into the second-level basement. As promised, it was a dark, massive space with a low ceiling. The air was dank and cold.

"Is there a light switch somewhere?" I asked.

Derek found the panel of switches, but none of them worked.

"That's not good." I felt those spooky chills return.

"No." His voice was pitched low and I could sense the tension in him.

"It's bad enough having to lug around a bunch of heavy boxes," I said, still trying to be upbeat about this whole situation. "I just hope she wasn't doing it in the dark."

"I've never heard of a hotel allowing their guests to work in a space like this without an employee supervising."

"It's odd, isn't it?" I shook my head. "Not one person working down here?"

"Perhaps they're on a break," he mused.

"Maybe. They could've left the lights on, at least."

"Let's remedy this state of affairs," Derek suggested, reaching for his cell phone and turning on the flashlight app.

"Much better," I said. "But I can't imagine Sara is working down here with all the lights turned off."

"Perhaps the lights were working last night." He swept his flashlight across the rows before us. "Let's do our due diligence and check each of those rows."

"Sara?" I called. The word echoed in the cavernous space. We started walking, searching up and down each long row. The shelves were stacked to the ceiling with boxes and crates.

"Sara?" I called again. There was no answer, but I didn't really expect one. "This place is huge."

We checked the next aisle. Nothing.

"She can't still be down here. For all we know, she's upstairs in her hotel room having a cocktail." I was grasping at straws. "Maybe she's sick or she pulled a muscle doing all this heavy lifting."

"Perhaps."

"She still would've answered her phone, though."

We kept going until we reached the end of the dark, creepy space. That was where I noticed pieces of several large crates scattered on the ground, cracked and broken.

"What a mess." I sighed, although it should have been expected, with so many wooden crates sitting on top of each other, filled with heavy books. A deserted forklift was parked in the middle of the aisle.

I nearly jumped when Derek grabbed my arm. "Darling, I don't want to switch off this light, so can you check your phone to see if you're getting a signal?"

"Sure. Man, this place is like a bunker." I pulled out my phone and checked my settings. "Believe it or not, I do have a signal. Why do you ask?"

"You need to call the police."

"Right now? Why?"

"In fact, let's go upstairs and call from there." As he spoke, he moved until he was standing in front of me.

"Why? Hey, you're blocking the light."

He sighed and squeezed my arm gently. "I'm sorry, love, but I'm afraid there's something disturbing at the end of this row."

I leaned over to see beyond him and stared into the darkness. "How can you even see down there?"

He turned. "I happened to aim the light right . . . there." His flashlight illuminated a pile of broken crates against the wall at the far end of the row.

"Oh." I began to walk toward the pile.

"Darling, wait. This would be better handled by the police."

"But we won't know what to tell them if we don't check it out."

Derek stayed right behind me, focusing his phone's bright light on the mess ahead of us. A huge pile of books towered over us as we approached. It had to be at least six feet tall. It looked as though three or four pallets of books had split open and spilled their contents. When I got closer, I hesitated, then stopped completely when I noticed someone's legs sticking out from under the massive pile of books.

I recognized those gorgeous boots.

"Oh no!" I rushed forward. "Oh God, no. It's Sara."

Chapter Seven

"She might still be alive!" I shouted, grabbing books and chunks of wood and tossing them off to the side. "Sara, hang on!"

Derek joined me, grabbing handfuls of books at a time and placing them only slightly more gently on the floor nearby.

"We can still save her," I whispered, lifting an armload of books and shoving them against the wall. I wanted to use more care with the books, but my priority was saving Sara. Later, I promised myself, I would stack them neatly.

"She could have been down here all night, love," he said. "If the full weight of these crates hit her in the head, it would be a devastating blow."

"Maybe she managed to block it enough to survive." I refused to believe we were too late. "Let's keep going."

"Absolutely."

"Maybe it's not even Sara," I muttered a few minutes later.

"Perhaps not," Derek said, his optimistic tone giving me the slightest thread of hope. Still, those boots . . .

We kept working for another ten minutes until we could finally verify who was buried under all those books.

"Oh my God," I whispered. Yes, it was definitely Sara. Still so beautiful. And horribly, completely dead.

Derek checked for a pulse, but gave up after a long moment. "She's gone. I'm sorry."

My throat closed up and tears began to flow. I sat cross-legged on the cold floor and used my fingers to brush Sara's hair back. "I shouldn't touch her, but she would hate having all this hair in her face."

Derek touched my shoulder in sympathy as he handed me his handkerchief. "I'm so sorry, love."

"Me, too."

An hour later the basement was lit up by a dozen portable spotlights. The air was still dank and cold, though, and I shuddered as I estimated at least a thousand books had been piled on top of poor Sara. Not to mention several heavy wooden crates that had broken apart in the fall.

"Books. It's always books with you," Inspector Janice Lee murmured next to me as she gazed upon the scene. I had called her immediately because, yes, I did have her number on speed dial. We were friends.

"With all due respect," I said. "It's usually just one book with me."

"True. This takes it to new heights." Shaking her head in dismay, she approached the body and stared at all the books and debris stacked around her. She took at least two dozen photographs from every angle and then turned to her officers. Even though Derek and I had managed to move the books off of Sara's body, she was still surrounded by hundreds more, making it difficult for Inspector Lee to maneuver around her. "Can we get these books and stuff moved out of the way?"

Two uniformed officers rushed over and began moving our piles of books farther away from Sara to allow better access for the police and medical examiner.

"Carefully, please," Inspector Lee cautioned.

I felt bad that I had thrown the books every which way and stepped forward. "I can help stack them against the wall."

"Thanks, Brooklyn," Lee said. "But my officers can take care of it."

The two men took the hint and moved the books away from the body, neatly stacking them along the wall. It took them nearly twenty minutes to clean up all the piles while Inspector Lee bent down to take a closer look at Sara's face and body.

"Will Inspector Jaglom be joining you?" Derek asked, when she stood up.

"Sadly he won't," Lee said. "Nate's actually contemplating retirement."

"Oh no," I said, thinking about the kind man with the wiry gray hair who tended to appear slightly rumpled, but always wore a smile on his face. "He's not that old, is he?"

"No, but he's discovered the joys of grandfatherhood," she

explained. "And since his wife is a doctor and loves her job, he's probably going to take his pension and run."

"I'll miss him," I said.

"Yeah, he's a good guy," Lee said. "I'm bummed."

"Please send him our best regards," Derek said.

"You bet." Lee continued to survey the area where Sara had died. While she worked, she took the opportunity to question Derek and me. "What made you two come down here?"

I explained the whole story. "I was having my sisters and a few friends over last night and Sara texted and then called me to let me know she'd be late. Her boss was making her bring all these boxes of books over to the convention center."

"I take it she didn't make it to your house last night."

"No. So I texted her a few times this morning to see if she wanted to meet for coffee, but I didn't hear back."

"What did you do next?"

"When Derek got home around lunchtime, he suggested that we walk over to the convention center to see if she was working in the booth she'd been assigned to."

"Which booth is that?"

I gave her the name of the small college Sara worked for and tried to describe the location of the booth on the convention floor.

"She wasn't in the booth, of course," I said. "Her coworker Darla said she hadn't seen her since last night and told us where the books were being stored. That's when we came down here on the off chance that she was still working."

"Did you have business with her or what? Why were you looking for her?"

I glanced up at Derek. "I guess you could say I was checking up on her. She and I . . . we had a falling-out back in grad school and I hadn't seen her since, not until two nights ago. I wanted to make sure she was doing all right."

Lee was gazing down at Sara's face as if studying her. "She was at your bridal shower."

"You remember her?"

"Sure. Tall, pretty, great hair. Great boots."

"That's her." It was suddenly hard to swallow around the lump in my throat. I took a few deep breaths to help maintain my composure. "I really appreciate you getting here so fast, but now that you've had a chance to check out the scene, I have to ask you something."

"Yeah?" She sounded suspicious, which, to be fair, was her natural state of being most of the time. Probably why she was so good at her job.

"Do you think this is a crime scene? Couldn't it have been an accident?"

"What do you think?"

"I just can't imagine someone thinking they could kill a person with a bunch of books."

Derek pointed out the shards of wood strewn all over the floor around Sara's body. "More likely she was killed by the weight of the heavy wooden crates that were dropped on top of her."

"Exactly what I was thinking," Inspector Lee said darkly. "Hardly sounds like an accident to me." She pointed back toward the elevator. "The light switch wires were cut. That doesn't sound accidental, either."

"But who would do that? This is all so random. She's not even from here, so why did someone pick this place to attack her? I can't imagine she made someone at the conference so angry that they followed her down here, jumped into the forklift, and tried to bury her in books. Most of the conference exhibitors are storing their books down here, so they're probably in and out of this room at all hours of the day and night. Why would a killer take a chance that someone might walk in and catch them in the act?"

Lee stared at her notepad. "So she worked at Glen Cove College. Where in the world is that?"

"It's in Indiana," I said, unsure where she was going with that question.

Lee shrugged. "She must have some coworkers who came out here with her."

I nodded. "She does."

"So she's not exactly alone in the big city, is she? No, she's here with friends and coworkers. Maybe there's a love interest. And maybe she's got an enemy or two. They're all here for a week of fun and games and good times. And one of those people might be thinking that this would be the *ideal* spot to do the dirty deed, far away from the prying eyes of everyone they know."

"Wow," I marveled. "That's both impressive and creepy."

"I amaze myself," she said, flashing me a crooked grin.

"I believe it." I let out a breath. "If you want to know all who traveled here from their small town, you could probably ask that woman we talked to, Darla. She might be able to give you a list."

Lee checked her notes. "Yeah, I've got her name written down."

I frowned, remembering something else that might be important. Duh. "Speaking of a love interest, Sara's husband came with her, too."

Lee's eyebrows shot up. "There's a husband. That might have been useful to mention right up front."

"You're right, sorry. I should've mentioned him first, but I got caught up in everything else."

"What's his name?"

"Rod Martin."

She wrote it down and circled it a few times. Probably because the spouse was usually the most likely suspect.

In this case, I had to agree.

"Tell me what you know about him."

"Well." *Where should I start?* I wondered. I gave her a brief history of our grad school days, explaining that he wasn't the most trustworthy, loyal guy in the world. "Even though he's officially a librarian, he actually works as an antiquarian book broker."

"Oh great, more book people," she said.

"It's a librarians' conference," I said mildly. "So yeah, we're everywhere. You can't escape us."

She grinned, then sobered. "What else do you know about Rod Martin?"

"I don't know him very well anymore, but I can describe him for you." I gave her the details and mentioned that he stopped by my classroom yesterday.

"Do you know why he stopped by to see you?"

"Yes, I'm curious about that as well," Derek said dryly.

Lee grinned at him, but I just gave him a look. "I told you about that."

"You did, but I'm at a loss as to his true motive for tracking you down."

"I think he came to see if he could coax me into giving back the book that Sara gave me the night of the shower."

"Why would he think you'd give it back?"

"Because it's currently worth seventy-four thousand dollars. And I have a feeling Sara wasn't supposed to give it away."

She was momentarily speechless, but quickly recovered. "Jeez, Brooklyn. How do you always manage to get involved with . . . Never mind. I know it's your business, but does there always have to be a book at the heart of these crimes?"

"Some books are worth killing over," I said with a shrug. "But I doubt this one was the catalyst for Sara's death."

"What book is it?"

"*The Three Musketeers*."

"Hey, I love that story."

"I do, too," I said. "The thing is, everyone at school used to call my two roommates and me the Three Musketeers because we were such close friends. So the book has a lot of nostalgia attached to it."

"Along with being ridiculously expensive."

"Right. But Sara told me that Rod would be able to get a new copy of *The Three Musketeers* anytime he wanted."

"Is that true?"

"No," I said with some confidence. "The book she gave me is very rare. I doubt there's another one like it on the market."

"I'll want to take a look at that book."

"Okay."

She glanced at her notes. "So what else did Mr. Martin say to you?"

"Once he realized I wasn't about to turn the book over to him, he was actually very nice. He wished me lots of happiness and good wishes. All that stuff."

"Okay." Lee blew out a heavy breath. "Okay. Have I got everyone's name now?"

Derek gave me an expectant look and I winced. "Oops. Did I give you Heather's name?"

"Heather Babcock is the other roommate?" Lee quickly flipped the page of her notepad and jotted it down.

"Right. She's the one who had the major falling-out with Sara over Rod Martin. They didn't speak to each other for twelve years. Until the night of my shower."

"She's the one with the short red hair, right?" She made a note. "Tell me more."

It didn't make me happy, but I went into even more gritty detail of the big fight twelve years ago and the forced reunion two nights ago.

Lee pursed her lips in thought. "So Heather has been carrying a jealous grudge against this woman for over a decade?"

I nodded reluctantly, then hastened to add, "Not that I think she killed Sara. There's no way. I mean, we haven't kept in touch so I don't know her as well as I used to. But still, it's impossible. She's always had a really good heart, and besides, what would she know about driving a forklift? I mean, someone would've had to have used the forklift to drop all those books and crates, right?

Heather wouldn't do that. I mean, who would? Not me. So really, it can't be Heather. But . . ."

Was I babbling? Yes. I clamped my mouth shut.

Lee waited. "But . . . what?"

My shoulders slumped. "But . . . yeah, okay. Heather had been miserable for a really long time and she blamed Sara for that."

Inspector Lee nodded slowly, still making notes.

"Oh. There's someone else you might want to talk to," I said. "I haven't exactly met her but apparently she was pretty tough on Sara."

Lee glanced up. "Who's that?"

"It's Sara's boss. Her name is Cornelia and she sounds horrible. Sara thought she was jealous of her. You can get more info about her from Darla—who seems terrified of the woman."

"Sounds like a peach." Lee made a few more notes, then closed her notepad and slid it into her jacket pocket. Kneeling down next to Sara's body, she stared at the scene for a long moment.

I signaled to Derek that we should leave her alone, but before we could walk away, she turned and glanced up at us. "Looks like we've got ourselves some good old-fashioned motives."

Derek and I hung around the chilly basement for another half hour, watching the forensics team spread out to gather any possible evidence. We stood over by the elevator, holding hands and talking quietly, staying out of the cops' way.

"Don't you think," I mused, "that it's possible that the forklift driver simply lost control? Maybe his foot hit the accelerator instead of the brake and the momentum caused his cargo to slide off and fall on Sara. So it could be an accident, not murder at all."

He squeezed my hand. "Even you must admit that's a stretch, love."

"I know," I mumbled.

"But all things are possible," he continued. "You can mention that to Inspector Lee."

"And watch her laugh at me? Always a good time."

"You never know. I'm sure she plans to speak to the hotel forklift driver eventually."

"Of course she will," I murmured. "You know, we should track down Heather and warn her."

"*Warn* her?"

I cringed and quickly checked to make sure that Inspector Lee wasn't nearby. "I mean, *tell* her that the police will want to talk to her. And she doesn't even know about Sara yet. I owe it to her to let her know before she hears it from the police."

His eyes narrowed in on me. "I think I'd better go with you."

I smiled for the first time in hours and pressed the elevator button. "That would be wonderful. You can meet her and judge for yourself whether she's capable of killing anyone."

"Everyone is capable of killing, given the right circumstances."

My smile faded. "Too true."

"But I would still like to meet her."

I hugged him. "Thank you."

The elevator arrived. Once we were inside and ascending to the ground floor, he gazed down and touched my cheek. "How do you feel about spending our wedding week dealing with murder?"

Sad to say, murder had become a part of our lives. As much as I hated to admit it, I was exactly what my mother thought I was. A murder magnet. How could I have expected our wedding week to be any different? But looking up into Derek's eyes, I knew another truth.

"As long as you're with me, I can handle anything."

I was surprised to find that it was still light outside. After spending several hours in that cold basement, it felt as if the entire world was a dark place.

I didn't know where Heather was or which hotel she was staying at, so I texted her. "Can you meet me for happy hour, like, right now?"

A minute later, she responded. "Yes! Where are you?"

"Across the street at McNally's Bar and Grill."

"I can be there in ten minutes."

"Awesome! See you then."

I smiled at Derek. "We've got ourselves a date."

When Heather walked in ten minutes later, we were already seated at one of the tall bar tables along the front window. I waved at her and she came right over and gave me a hug. "I'm so glad you texted me."

"Me, too."

"Oh. Hi." She stared at Derek and I remembered my manners.

"Heather, this is my fiancé, Derek Stone. I hope you don't

mind him joining us. Derek, this is one of my oldest friends, Heather Babcock."

They shook hands and then Derek stood. "The waitress seems a bit busy so I'll go get our drinks."

He took our orders and walked toward the bar.

"Oh my God, Brooklyn. He's gorgeous." Her gaze followed him. "And British to boot."

"Yes, he is," I said dreamily. "And he's kind and thoughtful and smart and brave and, well, I seem to have lucked out."

"I'll say you did." She chuckled, then added, "But I think he lucked out, too."

"Aw, thank you."

"If I had that drink, I would toast to your good luck and your happiness."

I squeezed her hand. "I wish the same for you, Heather."

"I'm going to be just fine," she said, wearing a smile that tugged at my curiosity.

"What's going on?" I asked, studying her. "You look . . . happy. Relieved, I guess. I don't know. Your mood just seems a little lighter than yesterday."

"And what's wrong with that?"

"Absolutely nothing. Just wondering what brought it on." *And please don't say Sara's murder*, I thought to myself and barely managed to keep from saying it out loud.

"I might as well tell you," she said shyly. "I mean there's nothing wrong with it, but some people might get the wrong idea. But then some people, well . . ." She waved that thought away.

"What are you talking about?"

"It's nothing," she insisted, and took a deep breath. "Okay. I met Rod for a drink last night."

"What?" I might've shrieked the word.

Derek walked up at that moment and gave me an odd look as he set our drinks down. "Here you are, ladies."

I grabbed my vodka gimlet and took a generous slug. "Holy moly."

"Thank you, Derek," Heather said, ignoring me. "What do I owe you?"

"Absolutely nothing. Drinks are on us tonight."

"That's awfully sweet of you. Thanks."

We held up our glasses and clinked them together. "Cheers."

I took another sip before I could manage to speak. "Heather had a drink with Rod last night," I said, flashing Derek a significant look. "Isn't that interesting?"

"Does he even know who Rod is?" Heather asked me.

"Oh, yeah. I've told him the whole story."

She smiled at Derek. "So now you know all the sordid details of our past."

He flashed a sympathetic smile. "Hardly. But it sounds as if you were all close friends once upon a time."

"*Once upon a time* being the operative phrase," she muttered.

I tried to get things back on track. "Heather, I wanted to see you tonight because I've missed you. But also, I just found out some bad news and I wanted you to hear it from me." *And to see your reaction when you hear it,* I added silently.

She set her wineglass down. "This sounds serious."

"It is." I reached for her hand. "I'm sorry."

She glanced down at my hand, truly worried now. "What is it, Brooklyn? What happened?"

"It's about Sara."

"Oh." Her look of concern turned to annoyance. "Now what's her problem?"

"It's not good."

"All right." Frowning, she rolled her shoulders and straightened her spine. "What is it?"

"Sara is dead."

She leaned in closer. "Sorry, but . . . what did you say?"

I repeated it and watched her mouth drop open. For a moment she looked as though she couldn't breathe. Then her eyes rolled back in her head.

"Heather? I didn't mean to spring the news on you."

But she clearly hadn't heard a word I'd said. Her head lolled and it was as if her entire body had turned to soft wax as she slid off the stool.

"Heather!"

She was about to hit the floor when Derek caught her and hoisted her up and into his arms.

I watched in horror, then shouted for a doctor. "Help! We need help over here! Is there a doctor in the house?"

There were a few screams and general confusion. Derek carried Heather over to the hostess podium, where there were several couches set aside for people waiting for tables.

"Clear this area, please," Derek yelled authoritatively, and everyone scattered.

The furor and confusion died down as a man from the bar rushed over. "I'm an EMT. What's wrong with her?"

Derek glanced at the guy. "Have you been drinking?"

He didn't seem to mind the question. "No, I'm the designated driver tonight."

"Good." Derek gave him a firm nod. "This is Heather. She just received some stressful news and fainted. She'll probably be fine in a few minutes, but we'd appreciate it if you could make sure."

"Did she eat or drink anything that might've caused her to pass out?"

"No," I said. "We just gave her some bad news."

"Okay, because I don't have any equipment with me, but if that's the only reason she fainted, she should be coming around in a minute. My name is Gus, by the way."

"Thanks for your help, Gus," I said. Staring at Heather, I had to wonder if she had actually fainted or if she was just pretending. Was this her way of deflecting suspicion? I had fainted a few times in my life and it was always at a traumatic moment. Would news of Sara's death be so traumatic for Heather that she would lose consciousness? Admittedly, she looked completely out of it, but maybe she was a better actress than I ever gave her credit for.

Gus knelt down next to the couch and leaned over close enough to make sure she was breathing. "Heather, come on now, wake up. You're going to be okay."

She stirred almost instantly but didn't open her eyes.

"Come on, Heather." He patted her cheek gently but firmly. "That's it. Wake up."

With a sigh, she whispered, "What happened?"

"You passed out for a minute," Gus said. "We were worried about you. How do you feel?"

She breathed in and out slowly. "A little spacey."

"That's okay. Take your time."

Her eyes blinked open and she frowned. "Who are you?"

"I'm Gus."

"Are you a doctor?"

"I'm an emergency medical technician."

She gazed around. "Am I in an ambulance?"

"No, sweetheart. You're in a bar."

Her lips curved. "Well, that's a new one."

"Yeah," he said, smiling softly. "It's a new one for me, too."

"Heather," I said, staring over Gus's shoulder. "Do you want to go to the hospital?"

"The hospital? Oh, no. I'll be fine."

We watched for another few minutes while she slowly got her bearings. She took a deep breath and appeared ready to sit up, but then her face crumpled and I thought she was going to burst into tears. "Oh God, Brooklyn. Did I really hear you say what I think you said?"

I nodded. "I'm so sorry."

She closed her eyes. "I don't believe it."

"Maybe we should get you back to your hotel," Gus said.

"No." She shook her head. "I'm a little discombobulated, but I'll be fine. I just need to sit up." She opened her eyes and gazed up at him. "Will you help me up, Gus?"

"I sure will." He eased her up to a sitting position and then sat down next to her.

Heather leaned against him for a long moment. I couldn't blame her. Gus was definitely hunky. "Thank you."

"You're welcome," he said. "Are you ready to stand up?"

"I think so."

"Let me help you get back to your table."

"Could you stay with me for a few minutes?"

"Of course."

Her eyes widened. "Oh, wait. I'm sorry. Are you here with someone?"

"Just a buddy," he said with a grin. "He'll survive without me for a while."

Her smile grew bigger. "Good."

Was she actually flirting with the man? Once again she looked happy, reminding me that she had gone out for drinks with Rod Martin last night while his wife, poor Sara, had suffered death by a thousand books and was now on her way to the morgue.

Within the span of a few hours, our lives had become completely surreal.

Back at the table, Heather wasn't letting her little fainting spell put a damper on her social life. We were on our second round of cocktails and Gus was still attending to Heather's every need when I received a text from Inspector Lee. "Can't find husband or girlfriend. Have you seen either?"

Admittedly, I was amazed that she had texted me for help. Glancing at Derek, I saw him observing me. "I've got to make a phone call."

He nodded knowingly. "It might be quieter outside."

I smiled at Heather and Gus. "Excuse me. I'll be right back." I walked outside to call the inspector.

"Inspector Lee," she answered after the first ring.

"It's Brooklyn. Derek and I are with Heather right now. I don't know where Rod Martin is, but she might know. Should I ask her?"

"I'd rather talk to her first," she said. "Where are you?"

"McNally's Bar. Do you know where that is?"

She snorted. "Of course. I'll be there in fifteen minutes. Don't let her leave."

"She won't." *Not as long as Gus sticks around*, I added silently.

Back inside, Heather was curious. "I didn't know where you went, but Derek said you had to make a phone call. Is everything all right?"

"It was nothing," I said breezily. "What did I miss?" I was trying to be nonchalant, but what would I say when the police arrived? Would Heather realize I had fingered her to the cops?

Fingered her to the cops? Suddenly I was in a noir movie from the forties? Could I be more melodramatic? Inspector Lee just wanted to talk to her. Shaking my head, I reached for my glass and took a fortifying sip of my vodka gimlet.

"Heather," I said, changing the subject. "I'd like to get in touch with Rod so I can tell him what happened to Sara. Do you know where he is?"

She let out a gasp. "Oh no! Poor Rod." She buried her face in her hands. Was she crying? Were they crocodile tears?

Gus exchanged looks with Derek and me. "Who's Rod?"

"Our friend Sara's husband."

He grimaced. "Sara's the one who died."

"Right."

He draped his arm around Heather's shoulders and gave her a light squeeze. "I think I should get going."

"Oh, don't go," she said, gazing up at him. "Do you have to?"

"Yeah. Will you walk outside with me?"

Her eyes brightened. "Yes." She jumped down from her stool and looked at me. "I'll be right back."

"Okay, good."

As soon as she left, I turned to Derek. "I don't want her to go too far. Inspector Lee will be here in just a few minutes."

Derek was watching out the window. "Then I'd better follow them because they just took off walking up the block."

"Oh, great." Inspector Lee would kill me if Heather disappeared.

Derek jogged out of the restaurant and I sat and cooled my jets. Where would Heather go? Maybe she just wanted to take a walk with her new friend Gus, who seemed like a really nice, smart guy.

I sipped my drink and lamented my questionable judgment. I should've told Heather that I had spoken to the police and that they were on their way to talk to her. Sure, that might've spooked her, but at least she would know what was happening. On the other hand, if she knew the cops were on their way, would she make a run for it?

Make a run for it?

And there went my imagination again. But then, who knew what someone might do if they were feeling guilty enough?

Why would Heather be feeling guilty? The only possible reason was that she had something to do with Sara's death.

And I hadn't even started to grill her about Rod. Was that why she was feeling guilty? Because she'd been in a bar with Sara's husband around the same time the woman was murdered? And how had Heather and Rod wound up having a drink together last night? I couldn't believe they had simply run into each other at the conference.

Although, come to think of it, that was exactly what had happened to me and Heather. We had literally just run into each other. So it could've happened again, I suppose.

And on a different note, why had she gone for a drink with him in the first place? How could that be a good idea? She had suffered through a bitter breakup with him and the betrayal had haunted her for twelve long years. So now they were all friendly and cozy again?

But wait. Maybe Rod had set the whole thing up. I wouldn't put it past him. And I was much more comfortable thinking it was his idea rather than thinking Heather had sought him out.

My mind was going in a hundred different directions and I was starting to get a headache. I glanced out the window, but didn't see Derek anywhere. It didn't matter, though, because I had complete confidence that he wouldn't let Heather slip away. I sipped my drink and tried to relax.

"There you are," Inspector Lee said from right behind me.

I flinched. "I didn't see you coming."

"I'm like the stealth bomber."

I rolled my eyes. "Right. Do you want a drink?"

"Nah. I'm on the clock." She glanced around. "Where are your friends?"

"Didn't you see Derek outside?"

"No. Why isn't he in here with you?"

"He went outside to make sure Heather didn't disappear."

"She's trying to disappear? From me? I'm hurt."

"Don't be," I said. "I didn't tell her you were coming, so I think the reason she left has more to do with the nice guy she met tonight."

"Ah, young love."

"It's a beautiful thing." I grabbed my purse and pulled out a credit card. "I'm going to pay the bill. If you want to go outside and look around for Derek, I'll be out in a minute."

"Sounds like a plan."

She took off and I signaled the waitress. As she walked away with my card, I wondered again how Heather would react to the fact that I'd brought the police here. She shouldn't be angry with me. After all, an old friend had been murdered so, naturally, the police would want to interview everyone who'd seen her over the past forty-eight hours. And furthermore, Heather had been with the victim's husband at roughly the same time that Sara was killed. Even if she was completely innocent, she might know something that could help Inspector Lee solve the crime. Maybe Rod mentioned something crucial when they were together.

And why did I even care what Heather thought? At this point, all that mattered was finding justice for Sara.

The waitress returned with my credit card. I signed the receipt, shoved my copy into my purse, and walked to the door.

Once again it felt like I'd been here for hours, but I checked my watch and saw that it was barely seven o'clock.

Out on the sidewalk, I looked up and down the street, trying to spot Derek and Inspector Lee. But now they had both disappeared. Lee couldn't have gotten too far because she was only a minute or two ahead of me. I took off down the street toward my house, thinking they might be on the nearby side street.

Summer weather was coming soon, but for now, the night was cool enough that I wished I had thought to bring a jacket. I zipped my hoodie up and shoved both hands in my pouch pocket for warmth. I smiled at the sound of the roaring crowd watching the ball game at the Giants' stadium less than a quarter mile away.

There was a dark, narrow alley at the end of the row of buildings, and when I peeked down there, I could see Inspector Lee talking to Derek. Heather stood off to the side. Where was Gus?

I walked toward them and spoke to Heather. "Did Gus leave?"

"I'm not sure I'm talking to you," Heather said, tossing her hair back. "Why would you think I know anything about Sara's death?"

"I never said I did," I said calmly. "But the police will want to talk to anyone who knew Sara. Plus you were with her husband last night and the police are trying to find him. I thought you might know where he is."

"Rod didn't kill Sara," she insisted.

"But the police still need to talk to him. He's Sara's husband." *In case that detail slipped your mind,* I thought. I didn't ask her why she was so adamant that Rod was innocent. Why, all of a sudden, was she his staunchest ally? I didn't get it.

She huffed. "Maybe so, but you could've warned me that the police were coming."

"You just fainted, Heather. I didn't want to freak you out all over again."

Inspector Lee had been silent during our brief discussion, but now she spoke up. "Why don't we go somewhere more conducive to carrying on a conversation?"

"What a good idea." I rubbed my hands together to warm them up. And why were we in an alley in the first place? I would have to ask Derek later.

"Our place is just a block or so away from here," Derek suggested.

I slipped my arm through his. "Perfect solution."

"I'm not sure that's a good idea," Heather said, frowning. She was clearly not ready for what she anticipated would be a tough police grilling.

"Beats taking you down to the police station," Inspector Lee said, her cheerful tone belying her steely determination to interview Heather tonight.

Heather gulped, seeming to finally grasp the situation. Glancing at Derek, she said, "Your place sounds great."

With a satisfied gleam, Inspector Lee met my gaze. "I'll get my car and meet you all there."

Chapter Eight

On the way back to our place, I made a special effort to explain things to Heather, who was still treating me like the plague of doom. "I didn't mean to spring Inspector Lee on you, but when I found Sara's body, I had no choice but to call the police."

"Wait." She grabbed my arm and pulled me to a stop. "What? *You* found her body? Brooklyn, that's awful. Why didn't you tell me that? How did that even happen?"

Her shock brought it all back to me and I had to take a moment to compose myself. "You're right, it was awful. She was supposed to come over last night, too, but never showed up. So this morning I started texting her to make sure everything was okay, and she never responded. I was getting worried so I went looking for her. And I found her."

"That's terrible." But her pouty lip was showing again. Was she jealous that I didn't try to hunt her down, too?

"I went looking for you, too," I assured her, as we started walking again.

"To turn me in to the police," she muttered.

"No," I insisted. "I wanted to tell you about Sara. I would've called you sooner, but I was stuck in that cold, ugly basement for hours."

She must have realized how petty she was starting to sound because she sidestepped closer and wrapped her arm around my waist as we walked. "I'm an idiot. You poor thing. I can't even imagine. That must've been horrifying."

"It was. Look, back in school the three of us didn't end things on a very happy note, but you and Sara were once my best friends. I absolutely hate that this happened."

I didn't mention the alarming fact that this wasn't the first time I had discovered a dead body. *Wait until my mother hears about this*, I thought, as the words *murder-magnet* reverberated around my head. I quickly shook away the thought and kept walking.

Once we were home, I poured a glass of water for each of us and changed the topic of conversation. "Do you think you'll see Gus again?"

"We're going out tomorrow night." Heather gave a shy smile. "He's a really nice guy."

"I agree. Plus he's an honest-to-goodness hero."

"I know." She stared off at nothing in particular, obviously brooding. "Of course, I'll never see him again after Sunday, but it'll be nice while it lasts."

"He really seemed to like you, so you never know." That was me, the eternal optimist.

She gave a grim laugh. "Yes, actually I do. He lives here, I live in Wisconsin. Two different worlds."

"Hello? Telephones. Email. Airplanes."

She smiled a little but I could tell she was already saying good-bye to Gus.

The buzzer rang.

She glanced around. "Is that a signal to let me know that I'm being a total buzzkill?"

I laughed. "If it works, yes. And also, it's our security system." I walked into the kitchen and checked the screen to see who was at the door downstairs. Inspector Lee was waving to the camera so I dialed the number to open the door.

Heather had begun pacing in front of the kitchen bar and I grabbed hold of her hand.

"Don't be nervous," I said. "Inspector Lee is a good friend and I trust her. She just wants to ask you a few questions."

"Famous last words," she mumbled, but sucked in a breath and straightened her shoulders. "Here goes nothing."

Heather survived Inspector Lee's interrogation. I sent the two of them off to talk in my workshop studio while Derek and I hung out in the kitchen. Forty minutes later, Janice was ready to leave—I still had a hard time calling her anything but Inspector Lee—and I walked her to the door, but stopped when I remembered something.

"Did you want to take a look at that book I was telling you about?"

"*The Three Musketeers*? Sure. I was going to give you a call tomorrow, but if you're up for it now, let's have a look."

I led the way down the hall to the closet where I kept my book safe. The square cubicle had originally operated as a dumbwaiter back in the eighteen hundreds when this building was a corset factory. The dumbwaiter rope-and-pulley mechanism had long been removed and I had recently installed an old jewelry store safe in the space in order to upgrade the security level as well as my peace of mind. It was steel-lined and impenetrable—so far.

I picked up the book, unwrapped the cloth cover I had used to protect it, and handed it to her. "Here you go."

"Whoa. I can see why someone might spend a lot of money on this one." She turned it over and examined the workmanship. She ran her hand across the smooth leather cover and stared closely at the illustration. "It's a beauty."

"It is." I felt a little burst of pride and happiness that Inspector Lee could recognize and appreciate the qualities of a rare book and hoped that it had something to do with her association with me. True, she was usually resistant to the idea that any book might be worth killing over, but this time I happened to agree with her. I couldn't see how this particular book might have led to Sara's death.

"Here," she said, handing it back after a quick inspection of the inside cover and the title page. "I'd rather have you keep it in your safe than gamble on it surviving the police station."

"Okay, thanks. It'll be here if you need to see it again." I wrapped the book up in the soft cloth and slipped it back into the safe, pitifully grateful that she hadn't insisted on holding on to it for evidence.

I walked her out into the hall.

"So did Heather tell you where Rod was staying?" I asked as we strolled to the elevator.

"He's been sharing a room with his wife in the conference hotel," she said. "But Heather doesn't think he was there much."

"Interesting," I said, frowning. "So he and Sara may not have been getting along. I wonder what Heather thought about that possibility."

She scowled as the elevator door opened. "Clearly I've said too much. Good night, Brooklyn."

"Good night, Inspector." I wore a grin all the way back inside.

Once Janice was gone, I asked Heather to stay awhile longer. Derek poured three small glasses of wine and we spent another hour chatting. I was determined to keep it light, so I asked all about her job and her life back in Valley Heart, Wisconsin. She managed to relax and even admitted that the so-called grilling by Inspector Lee wasn't all that bad.

Something hit me in mid-sentence. "Wow, I completely forgot that you fainted just a few hours ago. You recovered so quickly." *Too quickly?* I wondered. "How are you feeling? Would you rather have a glass of water?"

"I'm fine," Heather said, waving away my concern. "I forgot about it, too. I've never fainted before in my life."

"I'm glad you're okay." But I wondered all over again if she had really fainted or if she had been faking it. Had my sad revelation about Sara's death been that traumatic for her? Or was guilt the real reason she had reacted so oddly? I took a sip of wine, then ventured into new territory. "So how was it seeing Rod after all these years?"

She sighed. "You know, after all these years of tormenting myself over our breakup, I was expecting a major confrontation."

"I've got to admit that I was, too."

"But it was fine." She stared at her wine as though she were replaying the scene in her head. "Don't get me wrong, I gave him plenty of grief when we first saw each other. I had to say something, right? I mean, he broke my heart, the jerk."

"I'm glad you said something."

"But you know, once I called him on it and he admitted he was a major jackass, I was ready to let it go." She swirled her wineglass. "After that, we laughed a lot. It was fun. We took a selfie."

"Ooh, let me see."

She pulled her phone out and showed me a photo of the two of them sitting at a bar, grinning into the camera. I examined their smiles and especially their eyes, looking for what, I didn't know. It wasn't like I'd be able to tell from a photograph whether one of them had just murdered Sara and then rushed to the bar in order to establish an alibi.

"You look really good," I said. "Will you send this to me? I'd love to have something to remind me of you."

"Sure."

I handed the phone back to her and she pushed a few buttons. "You should have it now."

"Thanks." I gazed at her for a moment. "Okay, I've got to ask. Are you going to see him again?"

Her eyes widened in surprise. "Are you kidding? No way. I wouldn't trust him as far as I could throw him."

I grinned, having recently expressed the same feeling about Rod. "I'm so happy to hear you say that."

She sighed. "I'll admit he's still as cute as ever."

"Yeah, that was always a problem."

"Oh, I would call that a major problem." She gave a firm nod of her head. "But I'm happy to say without a doubt that I am completely over him. Finally." She finished the last sip of wine and then set down her glass.

"I'm proud of you." *I just hope you didn't kill his wife,* I couldn't help adding.

She smiled. "Yeah, I'm proud of me, too." She stood and reached for her purse. "I should get back to the hotel. I have a seminar in the morning."

Derek stood. "We'll walk you back."

"You don't have to," she protested. "I can call a cab."

"It's barely four blocks," I said. "We can use the air."

As we walked, we chatted about the conference and the seminar Heather was attending the next day. We walked with her all the way to the door of her room, then said good night.

Derek and I strolled home holding hands. Despite all the turmoil and tragedy swirling around us, I experienced a few moments of peace.

"This time next week we'll be in Paris," I said, and made a mental note to check the weather report for Paris tomorrow. Not that I needed the reminder. I'd been checking every day for the past month.

Derek smiled. "Just to warn you, I plan to spend the first few days sitting on a park bench with a book, a fresh baguette, and a hunk of cheese."

I squeezed his hand. "If there's wine in that scenario, I'm so there."

He chuckled. "Definitely wine."

"I'll be there even without the wine," I amended.

He smiled and we walked in silence for half a block, enjoying the clear dark sky and chilly air.

When we reached the stoplight at Brannan, I said, "I'd like to track down Rod Martin tomorrow. I want to see how he's doing."

"Because you care?" Derek asked. "Or because you suspect him of murder?"

"Part of me would love to see him carted off to jail, but I'm afraid he's got an airtight alibi, thanks to Heather meeting him for a drink last night."

"Yes." He frowned. "Convenient, isn't it?"

"I know she was happy tonight, but it still seems odd that she would've agreed to spend time with him."

"Definitely odd. I'd be interested to hear how they got together."

I wished I'd brought that up with Heather earlier. All she had said was that they ran into each other, but I wanted more details. "I'll text her tomorrow and see if she'll meet me for coffee."

"Excellent."

His face was partially illuminated by the streetlamp and I recognized that look. "You're thinking Rod set her up."

"What do you think?"

"It's possible. The timing is just a little too perfect, isn't it? They were drinking together in a bar the same night and at almost the exact same moment that Sara was dying under a huge pile of books."

Derek frowned thoughtfully. "Are we certain they met for a drink? Or could that be the story they conjured up for the police?"

"I saw the picture of the two of them together."

"The police can check her phone for the time and date the photo was taken."

"Oh, good idea." I thought about it for a moment. "Isn't it also possible that Heather was setting up Rod? Maybe Heather was the one who arranged for them to have drinks so that *she* would have an alibi."

Derek smiled. "I love it when you start rounding up suspects."

I sighed. "I would like to be proven wrong."

He shrugged philosophically. "Heather had a dozen years to think about what she would do if she ever ran into Sara or her husband again. Maybe Sara's death was years in the making."

The thought depressed me. "The one thing I can't believe is that Heather would knowingly agree to provide Rod with an alibi." I took that idea and expanded it for a moment. "That would require them to have been in contact with each other before they even arrived for the conference."

"Stranger things have happened." Derek smirked a little. "Usually to us."

"Good point," I said, smiling. "You know, Inspector Lee should check their social media pages. People say all kinds of stuff out there."

"Not a bad idea, darling." We waited for the light to turn green at Fourth Street before crossing.

"She's probably already doing that," I said. "It's amazing how people post the most revealing information, never realizing that someone out there might connect the dots."

He shook his head. "*Amazing* is one word for it."

"Yeah. *Idiotic* is another."

He tucked my arm through his. "You'll call Inspector Lee in the morning, just in case?"

"Absolutely. She loves getting advice from me."

He was still chuckling as he keyed in the security code and we walked into our building.

"I wonder if Heather called Rod to give him a heads-up that the police are looking for him."

"If they're in cahoots, she probably did."

"I just hope Inspector Lee went straight to Rod's hotel room when she left our place."

"That's what I would do," Derek said. "I wouldn't want to give him too much time to plan his escape."

"You're assuming he's guilty."

"I'm not assuming anything. It's equally possible that Heather killed Sara. Or that they were working together. If they have, in fact, rekindled their love affair."

"Well, for now, they both have an alibi."

Derek pondered that as the elevator shuddered to a halt and the door opened. "Again, it all seems a bit too tidy, doesn't it?"

I scowled. "Yes, it does." We stepped inside and the thing began its slow climb to the sixth floor. "But I still can't see how Rod could've arranged for his wife to die at almost the exact moment he was meeting Heather for a drink."

"We don't know the time of death yet."

"True. Only that it was sometime after she called me." I thought about it. "You know, if Rod and Heather were both in the bar when Sara died, maybe someone else killed her. She and her boss had some serious animosity for each other, from what I heard."

"The elusive Cornelia," Derek said.

"Exactly. I hope Inspector Lee tracks her down."

"Of course she will."

"I've still got too many questions about Rod and Heather."

"I do, too," he said. "We don't know what time Sara died, only that it was after she called you. We don't know what time Rod and Heather met at the bar, nor how much time they spent together."

"I could ask Heather, but she might get a little defensive."

"Rightly so."

With a sigh, I admitted, "I'm circling back around to Rod. Was he angry with Sara? Did her giving me that book seal her fate? Maybe if I'd given Rod *The Three Musketeers*, Sara would still be alive."

"No. You mustn't think that, darling." Derek gazed at the

rough-hewn walls of the freight elevator, thinking for a moment. "I don't know the man, but from everything you've told me about him, it sounds as though he has a rather healthy narcissistic streak."

I stared up at him. "You could call it that. He was always so sure of his own awesomeness. It's entirely possible that the book had nothing to do with anything. Rod could have set this whole thing up ahead of time and then sat back like some potentate and watched it play out."

"Perhaps."

The heavy door stuttered open and we walked down the hall to our apartment.

"On the other hand," Derek countered as he slipped the key into the lock, "we may be giving him too much credit."

I laughed despite my frustration. "Probably so. Because honestly, he's not all that awesome."

"Good to know."

"So until Inspector Lee actually confirms that his alibi is a sham, we'll need to look elsewhere to find justice for Sara."

It was Friday morning and I had no more conference obligations. However, I did plan to run over to the venue to meet Heather for coffee, and I was also anxious to track down Rod sometime today. I hadn't seen him since he walked into my classroom a full two days ago.

Other than that, I could do anything I wanted to do. Veg out, sleep in, or read a book. It all sounded like heaven.

Unfortunately, though, I had awakened with pre-wedding jitters. I couldn't sit still. Maybe I was conflating my wedding anxiety with worries about Sara's murder, but I kept jumping up to check my wedding list, then staring into space, then pouring more coffee while I berated myself for having jitters in the first place.

Derek had left early for yet another office meeting. So much for taking the week off, but that was what happened when you owned the business. Today they would be discussing everyone's assignments while he was out of the country for ten days. So I was on my own.

I ultimately decided that I would spend a little while finishing up Derek's special gift and then devote an hour or so to my new books from Heather and Sara, examining them and making any fixes that were needed. Work always helped me focus on something other than the multitude of crazy ideas zipping through my brain.

"I'll need more coffee for that," I said out loud to no one in particular. And for my own peace of mind I pulled out my wedding list one more time to check that everything was handled.

To call it a checklist was a little deceptive, I thought as I lugged out the six-inch-wide binder filled with everything you could ever hope to learn about putting on a wedding. It was both daunting and miraculous at the same time.

I quickly scanned the list and got to item number eight, subsections (a) through (cc), before I cringed. "Our families. I don't even know what they're doing or if they're on schedule."

I hoped everyone was playing nicely, having fun together, frolicking in Dharma and exploring the wine country. Tomorrow they would all pile into cars and drive into the city, where they would check into their hotels in time to relax and dress for the rehearsal dinner tomorrow night.

"I can't take the pressure," I muttered, pressing my hand over my heart. Would they make it in time? Were they all getting along? Why did I feel like there might be problems? Maybe I was connecting psychically to someone in the family because I just knew something was going wrong in Dharma. I grabbed the phone and called my mother.

"Sweetie!" she cried. "Is everything all right?"

"That's what I was about to ask you."

"Oh." She sighed softly. "This is so sweet. Meg, come quickly. Brooklyn is having a bridal moment."

"I don't even know what that means," I grumbled.

She laughed. "It means you're freaking out, kiddo."

"No I'm not."

"Of course you're not," she said soothingly, although I sensed an undertone of mockery. "Take some deep breaths. I already did a cleansing ritual but I'll do another one at the rehearsal dinner Saturday night."

"And I'm going to assist," Meg said chirpily.

"Hot diggity dog." I giggled nervously. My mother had found her soul mate in Meg. I couldn't be happier for them both, except for the part where they faithfully supported each other's whack-a-doodle eccentricities. Seriously, if Derek and I ever did have kids, we had some truly interesting genes to look forward to.

"I'm really chuffed that I can help," Meg said, then grew serious. "Now, about your jitters."

"I don't have any jitters," I said. I thought about Sara's murder and sighed. There was no way I could keep that news from my mother. And she was going to flip out when she heard it.

"Wait, what is it?" Mom said suddenly. "What's going on? I'm getting a vibe."

"Oh, I'm feeling it, too, Becky," Meg whispered. "Brooklyn, something happened. Tell us, dear."

"Actually," I said with a sigh, "something did happen and it's pretty bad. Sara, my old friend from college, was found dead yesterday."

"By you," Mom said. It wasn't a question.

"Derek was with me."

"Oh, that's good," Meg said. "I'm so sorry, Brooklyn. That must have been devastating for you."

"It was pretty awful."

"She was murdered," Mom said flatly.

"How did you . . . Never mind." I shook my head. She must've heard something in my voice. I would have to be more careful next time.

Next time?

I shook that thought away and took a few deep breaths to shake away this mood. "Anyway, I called because I was thinking about all of you and hoping you were enjoying yourselves."

"Oh, we are living the good life, no question," Meg said, picking up on my need to change the subject. "The weather is beautiful and there's so much to see and do."

"I'm glad." Feeling better, I sat down on the couch to enjoy the conversation. "And how are your boys doing?"

Meg referred to her five grown sons as "the boys." Never mind that each one was bigger and hunkier than the next, or that all of them worked in seriously scary fields like counter-espionage and foreign intelligence. To her, they would always be her "boys."

"They're having a whip-bang time up here," Meg exclaimed. "My goodness, they've been working in the fields like seasoned farmhands and they've helped repair some of the barrels in the cave. And of course they've helped pour the wines in the tasting room."

"Good for them," I said.

"To be honest, Brooklyn," Meg said, her voice lowering conspiratorially, "I believe they've been *sipping* more than simply pouring. But I'm assured that it helps with the sales."

"We call that quality control," I said, and Meg laughed.

"Austin and Jackson love having them around," Mom added. "They're already like one big happy family."

"Your brothers have been more than welcoming, Brooklyn," Meg said. "I'm starting to feel as though I have seven sons, not just five."

"Good grief, bite your tongue," Mom said, chuckling.

I laughed as I wiped away tears. "It's so good to talk to you both. I feel so much better."

"I'm glad, dear," Meg said. "It helps to step outside your world to get a little perspective once in a while, doesn't it?"

"It certainly does." I finished my last sip of coffee. "I'll let you go. I just wanted to check up on everyone. I'll see you all tomorrow."

"We're so looking forward to it, Brooklyn."

"Me, too."

Mom piped up. "Me, three."

I disconnected the call and sat back on the couch. The anxiety churning in my stomach a few minutes ago had calmed down. Still, I jumped up and ran to the kitchen island, where I scanned my list again.

Cake, check.

Photographer, check.

Flowers, check.

Dress, shoes, veil, check.

Weather. I frowned. Was it going to rain? I didn't think so, but I turned on the Weather Channel just to make sure. The forecast for Saturday and Sunday was blue skies, low seventies, slight breeze off the ocean. In other words, a perfect San Francisco day.

The wedding ceremony was to be held in the beautiful garden of the Covington Library. I had agreed to have the wedding on a Sunday because Ian had offered to close the library for the day, just for us. There was no way I could turn down such an incredible offer. The caterers would begin setting up and decorating late Saturday and the ceremony would take place Sunday afternoon. We would have an open bar and a band for the cocktail hour and then go inside for dinner and dancing. For that we had hired the most fabulous, talented DJ I'd ever heard.

On paper it all sounded so normal and maybe even a bit, well, ordinary. Typical. But to Derek and me it meant that we would be married in a breathtaking location with a beautiful view, surrounded by our wonderful friends and family. We would all enjoy a memorable evening filled with good food, good wine, and good music, and if that was typical, I didn't care. I was thrilled with our plans.

I continued down my list until I got to item number twenty-seven. Gifts for the bridesmaids. I had a vague memory of seeing that item before, but I had to rub my eyes to make sure I was seeing it now. Because the fact was, I had completely spaced on buying the gifts. I had nothing!

"Oh no!" How could I have forgotten gifts for my bridesmaids? How?

"Calm down." I tried to look on the bright side. My best friend Robin and my three sisters were my bridesmaids. We were all so close, they would probably forgive me, right?

"Are you nuts? They'll never forgive me." I buried my face in my hands. "You are the worst bride in the world."

I took so many deep breaths trying to calm down that I was now in danger of hyperventilating.

"I've got it!" I shouted, pacing back and forth in front of the kitchen island. "Problem solved. I can give each of them one of my pretty handmade books."

I paced back and forth, picturing the books in my mind. I still had some left over from the Book Lovers' Tour. Everyone loved them!

Seconds later, I stopped mid-pace. "You dolt. They'll never speak to you again if you give them those books."

I began pacing again. "You do realize you're talking to yourself, right?"

With a shrug, I muttered, "Yeah. So what?"

"Meow."

I glanced down and found Charlie staring up at me and shaking her head. Or maybe that was my imagination.

"I wasn't talking to you. I'm perfectly sane." I picked her up and held her for a long moment. Holding Charlie was an instant calm-me-down solution, not that I needed such a thing. I wasn't usually so panic-prone, but this week it seemed to be my semi-permanent state of being.

Calming my mind for that moment helped me realize there was only one thing to do. After my mani-pedi on Saturday, I would swing by Tiffany in Union Square and buy jewelry for everyone. Things were more special when they came in a little blue box, right?

I supposed I could've jumped in the car right then and rushed over to Tiffany, but this was supposed to be my day to relax. Shopping would be the complete opposite of relaxing so I decided to put it off until the next day when I would be in run-around-town mode anyway.

"Another crisis averted," I said, exhausted by my own foolishness. "Thank you, Charlie."

I set her down on the floor and petted her soft fur one last time. Then to divert myself, I washed out my cup and cleaned the coffee machine. Good times. When I was done, I decided I would take an hour or two and work on books as I had initially planned. Work always made me feel better.

Opening the safe, I pulled out the two books I'd received from Heather and Sara. Then fortifying myself with chocolate-covered almonds, I went into my studio. I took the book of Shakespeare's sonnets from my desk and checked my work. The pretty little book still gleamed from some leather polish I had applied the other day. The gilded leaves on the front cover looked beautiful. All that was left to do was to finish constructing the box.

First I cut out the pieces of burgundy linen and carefully glued them to the boards. It only took a few minutes for the glue to dry completely. Then I carefully measured, cut, and glued beautifully patterned endpapers to the interior sides of the parts of the box. Once these were dry, I glued a satin burgundy ribbon securely to one side. And finally, I glued the main pieces together to form the slip case. Using a hands-free magnifying glass, I trimmed the linen right to the edges and used a toothpick to glue the material until you couldn't tell where the seams ended.

I took a quick minute to admire the book and the box. The burgundy shades blended perfectly and together they looked so handsome and elegant—much like Derek Stone himself. I felt a tingle in my heart at the thought of him and then chuckled at my own giddiness.

With a happy sigh, I set the box aside to dry completely.

Riffling through my paper drawer, I found a piece of black and gold handcrafted Nepalese paper and a length of gold ribbon. As soon as everything was dry, I would wrap the gift and wait for the perfect moment to give it to Derek.

With that job done, I brought Sara's and Heather's books over to the worktable. Pulling a pair of thin cotton gloves out of a drawer, I sat down and slipped them on. The gloves would protect the books from scratches or fingerprints as well as any oil or dirt or excess chocolate my hands might've picked up. Then I grabbed my most powerful magnifying glass and began to examine the books more closely.

"Talk to me," I murmured. It wasn't my imagination; books really did talk to me. Not the words on the paper, but the paper itself. The cracked leather, the fractured spine, the torn pages. I heard them calling my name. The severed hinge, the shredded headband, the faded gilding. They whispered, *Help us, Brooklyn Wainwright, you're our only hope.*

I felt their pain. Really. I didn't make this stuff up.

I started with *The Three Musketeers*, first studying the leather cover from all angles. The workmanship was exquisite, especially the beveling around the colorful painting of the book's main characters. The gilding on the spine and both covers was still intact and I wondered if the book had been refurbished lately. It was almost too good to be true.

As I scrutinized every inch of the rich leather and thick, soft vellum, I had to admit that I was starting to feel guilty for keeping the book when I knew that Rod wanted it back so badly. Clearly, Sara had had no business giving it to me, but she had, and now that she was gone, I was determined to keep the book as her last treasured gift to me.

Was that wrong? Was I just getting back at Rod for screwing up our lives all those years ago? Probably. But I wasn't about to tell him that, no matter how guilt-ridden I might feel about keeping it. Because frankly, the book didn't mean anything to him—except a hefty amount of cash. But to me *The Three Musketeers* was a symbol of a happy time in my life when Sara and Heather and I were the best of friends and inseparable. Those days were gone, of course, but the memories were still vivid.

Didn't friendship weigh more than money in the greater scheme of things? Of course it did. That was my story, anyway, and I was sticking to it.

I opened up the book and gazed at the endpapers, which featured a fascinating, colorful illustration of Paris in the 1600s. In those days, the government and much of the town centered in and around the *Île de la Cité*, the island in the middle of the Seine. It showed a heavily fortified drawbridge and high-walled buildings along the shores of the river.

Turning to the title page, I studied the information listed there.

I hadn't noticed it last time, but the title page felt slightly thicker than the page before it. That happened once in a while with old books that contained illustrations. The illustration page might be slightly more fragile than the pages with print on them, depending on the type of picture and the method used to transfer it to the page.

I stared more closely at the title page through the magnifying glass. Frowning, I removed the cotton gloves and walked over to my workshop sink to wash my hands. I wanted to actually feel the pages and I couldn't do that while wearing the gloves. Returning to the book, I stared at the page again, then ran my fingers over the paper, comparing the thickness of the title page to the ones on either side.

"Something's wrong." I set the book down on the table, still open to the title page. Lifting the magnifying glass again, I examined the inside margin, or gutter. Without taking the book apart, this was as close as I could get to where the pages were sewn together.

And then I saw it.

My cell phone rang suddenly and I checked the number before answering. "Inspector Lee. Just the person I was about to call."

"Interesting," she said. "I've got some questions for you, but you go first."

"Okay. I was just examining my copy of *The Three Musketeers*, the book I showed you last night."

"What about it?"

"It's a fake."

Chapter Nine

"What?" Inspector Lee shouted into the phone.

"A forgery," I repeated, praying that my hearing would return soon. I couldn't blame Janice for being shocked. So was I. "A fake. They did a really good job and the book is beautiful regardless, but it's been altered to show an earlier date."

"Which would make it more valuable."

"Exactly."

"You're sure?"

I frowned. "Uh, yes."

"Sorry," she said quickly. "I should know better than to question you. But damn, Brooklyn."

"Yeah, that was pretty much my reaction, too." And now I wondered if Sara had done the forgery work herself or if Rod had paid to have it done. Or had they purchased it that way? Had the two of them been duped as well? Maybe Sara didn't realize it was fake when she gave it to me.

I hoped that was the case because I hated to think that she had deliberately altered a nearly impeccable work of art, just to raise the price even more. Never mind that it was a criminal offense.

I quickly calculated how much the book would be worth, given that it was a forgery. Everything about it was still beautiful, and if I had enough time, I could track down the provenance of the book and determine its actual value. Off the top of my head, I guessed it would be closer to the forty- to fifty-thousand-dollar range, maybe less. Since I couldn't be sure and since I was leaving on my honeymoon in a few days, I decided that the best thing to do would be to leave the book with Ian McCullough at the Covington Library. He would be able to arrange an appraisal faster than I could.

Another question occurred to me an instant later. Was *this* the reason Rod had tried to get the book back? Had he known it was fake all along? Had he lied to Sara about it?

An additional thought chilled me to my bones. Was the forged book the motive for Sara's murder?

I shook off the chills and came back to the conversation with Inspector Lee. "So why were you calling me?"

"Oh, yeah," Inspector Lee said, apparently just as sidetracked as I was. "Not sure it's still relevant now, but it's important that we investigate every possibility."

"Of course."

"So I'd like you to tell me everything you know about Heather Babcock."

"Heather? So you think she's—"

"A suspect," she said flatly. "Everyone is until further notice.

I promise I'll try to clear her as soon as possible, but for now, I've got to do the groundwork."

"I know, I know." I rolled my shoulders to shake off the tension. "I think I've already told you everything I know about her. She works for the city library in Valley Heart, Wisconsin. She does everything for them. Preservation and conservation, book restoration, collections, archiving. She probably reads stories to the children on Saturday mornings."

"Did she ever mention anything about an anonymous donor?"

I felt the lines on my forehead furrow in confusion and quickly changed expressions. My mother's warning from a few days ago was still hanging over me. "No. She's never said anything about a donor, anonymous or otherwise."

"Apparently they've got someone sending anonymous cashier's checks directly to Heather."

I stared at the phone for a moment. "I have no idea what that means."

"An anonymous donor is someone who donates money anonymously."

I smiled. Inspector Lee could be such a smart-ass sometimes, but it was part of her charm. "I know what it means in terms of an organization, but what you're saying is that Heather herself has an anonymous donor. All her own?"

"She doesn't keep the money," Janice explained. "But she gets credit for it, which translates to a small check to Heather at the end of each year. The donor has told the city that the only reason she's giving them money is because of Heather, so this person insists that Heather gets a piece of the action."

"That's nice."

"Yeah. Except that a while back, the city was concerned enough to call in the local cops. They looked into it for a while, but finally closed the case. Couldn't see any evidence of her stealing money."

"But they had to make a point of telling you," I muttered.

"Hey, we cops stick together."

"Yeah, yeah. Meanwhile, Heather's under suspicion until proven innocent." But I was getting ahead of myself. Heather *was* still under suspicion until we figured out who killed Sara.

"Everyone's under suspicion at this point," Janice said, echoing what I'd just been thinking.

Something still bothered me about Heather's situation back home. "Don't you think it's weird that her city library would call in the cops? Maybe Heather was simply helping this donor person on the side and they took a liking to her."

"What kind of stuff would she be doing?"

"I don't know." I waved one hand in the air as if she could see me groping for an explanation. "Maybe she was repairing their books. Or calling them whenever a new book came in so they could get first dibs. Heck, maybe she was mowing their lawn."

"Yeah, maybe. But . . . Just a sec, Brooklyn," she said as someone in the background spoke to her for a minute. Finally she said, "Sorry, I've got to go."

"Wait. When will we talk again?"

"Yeah, I'll miss you, too."

"You know you're crazy, right?"

"Funny. I wasn't before I met you." She chuckled, obviously

cracking herself up. "I'll call you in a while. I want to see that book again."

We hung up and I went back to work on the book, where my resentment over the forgery began to fester all over again. But before I could begin to deal with it, my phone buzzed. It was Heather texting me back. "Finally," I whispered.

"I can meet you at the coffee kiosk in fifteen minutes," she texted.

I replied, "I'll see you there."

I quickly cleaned off my table, then grabbed the books and returned them to the safe. I ran to get dressed and was out the door in under ten minutes.

Heather took a sip of her vanilla latte and slowly shook her head. "I still can't believe she's gone. It's just surreal, isn't it?"

"That's a good word for it," I agreed. Heather had begged to hear more about how Derek and I had found Sara under the books in the basement. I hadn't given her all the gory details but it was enough for her to realize how awful it was.

She rubbed her arms. "Thinking of her in that cold dark room. It gives me the chills."

"Yeah, me, too." But I forced a smile, more than ready to change the subject. "So how did you and Rod find each other the other day?"

"I literally ran into him inside the book room. I was browsing, walking up and down the aisles, and suddenly he was standing in front of me. It was such a shock."

"That's amazing. You keep running into people by accident. That's how we found each other."

"I'm so glad we did," she said.

"Yeah, me, too." I took a sip of my decaf latte. I didn't dare order more caffeine after all the agitation I'd gone through earlier today. "So anyway, I'm dying to hear more about your conversation with Rod."

She smiled and I could tell she was in a reminiscing mood. "It was great, Brooklyn. He's been really successful as a book dealer."

"That's what I understand."

"He said that he fumbled around with different jobs for a few years. Worked in a couple of libraries. You know how it is."

"I sure do," I said with a grin.

"But as soon as he started buying and selling books, he found his calling. So that's nice."

"I'll say. Did you talk about the old days?"

"Only enough to give him grief for dumping me the way he did." She glanced around, then lowered her voice. "He told me that he and Sara almost got a divorce more than once. She was very suspicious and jealous of anyone he was friends with, especially women. Obviously."

"Right. Can't blame her for that."

"I know, right? I call it poetic justice. I mean, because she was constantly jealous. It's only fair that she would mistrust every other woman since she was so untrustworthy back then." She frowned guiltily. "But now that she's dead, I feel bad for thinking that about her."

"I know." I sighed. "I have those same sorts of thoughts about her, too. Basically, I blamed her for everything that happened. Don't get me wrong; I blamed Rod, too. But she's the one who destroyed our friendship and she hurt you so badly. The entire thing was really painful."

"I'll tell you a secret," Heather said. "For years I dreamed of running into her and smacking her right across the face. And then we'd have this knock-down, drag-out fight, and finally we'd start laughing and end up friends again. Now that'll never happen. And that makes me really sad."

My own eyes were tearing up and I was having a hard time picturing Heather as a killer. Still, it would be smart to keep some perspective. Nevertheless, I reached out and squeezed her hand. "That is so sweet. Not the part about smacking her, but about being friends again."

She sniffled, then gave a short chuckle. "I know. I'm really bummed."

"Yeah."

She gazed at me. "Let's not talk about it anymore, okay?"

"Agreed." We sipped our drinks for a long moment, then I said, "So. Have you heard from Gus yet?"

"I have." And just like that, her expression changed completely. She was radiant. "I saw him for breakfast this morning."

"Breakfast." I smiled. "The guy moves fast."

"He does. I can hardly believe it's happening so quickly, but it's wonderful. He told me he's never felt like this before."

"After one day? Wow. What about you?"

Heather took a deep breath as if trying to settle herself. "Honestly, Brooklyn, I've never felt this way before, either. We're going out again tonight and spending Saturday morning together. Saturday night he has a thing with his parents so I won't be able to see him. But he's promised to call me."

"That's really nice, Heather. He seems like a good guy."

"I know." She took a deep breath. "Brooklyn, he wants to visit me and see what Valley Heart is like."

"Whoa. Forget about moving fast, this guy is moving at warp speed." *Maybe a little too fast?* I wondered.

"I know." Heather looked as concerned as I felt. But she deserved to meet someone fabulous and have some happiness in her life. Unless of course she was guilty of murder, in which case she deserved to spend her life in prison.

"He's a great guy," she continued, "but I'm a little scared. Mainly because I feel the same way. I just want to spend all my time with him."

"I know exactly how that feels," I said, thinking of Derek. "It's a wonderful feeling, isn't it?"

"The best in the world." She flashed a shy smile. "He says he doesn't mind moving to Wisconsin if it means he can be with me. He says he can work anywhere and make a good living."

"That's true enough." Paramedics would be welcomed into any town.

She laughed. "So in case it didn't sink in, let me repeat that I'm free tomorrow night. What are you doing? Can you get together?"

"Oh, Heather, I'm so sorry," I moaned. "It's the rehearsal dinner."

"Oh, no, I'm a space cadet. I totally forgot about your wedding. Sorry." She laughed. "I'm so happy for you."

"Why don't you come to the dinner? You know some of my family and I would love to introduce you to the rest of them. And it would give you something to do while you pine away for Gus."

She swatted my arm. "It's not so bad that I'm pining. Oh, all right, it is that bad. But I would love to come if it's not too much trouble."

"No trouble at all. I'll text you the directions and we'll see you at six o'clock."

"Thank you so much, Brooklyn." Heather jumped up from the table and grabbed me in a warm hug. "Can you believe how much our lives are changing? I'm so happy I came to the conference and found you. And Gus."

"Me, too." And I would be a lot happier when I was certain she wasn't Sara's killer.

As I walked home, my phone dinged, indicating a new email. At the stoplight I checked and found a group message from the Librarians Association announcing that there would be a memorial service for Sara in the conference center at three o'clock that afternoon.

What a nice idea, I thought, and picked up my pace. I had almost two hours before I had to be back for the service and I wanted to take a shower and dress nicely.

On a whim, I called Inspector Lee back to tell her about the service, just in case she wanted to observe any buggy behavior.

"Buggy?" she said.

"You know," I said. "People get buggy when they're guilty, haven't you noticed? It's possible that the murderer could show up and completely flip out after hearing Sara's eulogy."

"You're the only one acting buggy," she said, snickering. "But that's part of your charm."

Smiling to myself, I said, "I know there's a compliment in there somewhere."

She laughed, and after we agreed to meet at the designated time, I disconnected the call.

I arrived home just as Derek drove into the garage. We road in the elevator together and I told him about the service. He offered to go with me.

"I would love that," I said. "You're my hero."

I dashed off to take a shower and was ready in record time. But while I'd been showering, Derek had gotten caught up in a conference call with his office. As I waited for him to finish, I strolled back to my studio to spend a few minutes on my computer, checking out all the photos that my bookbinding students and tour participants had sent me.

There were some great shots of the bookbinding class I'd taught and a few of me during my speech on book conservation. I must admit I looked quite professorial. There were some selfies taken by the Purple Sweater Woman on the bus tour, who also took a beautiful shot of my mom and Meg laughing. I caught myself sniffling sentimentally at the two of them looking so happy and so pretty. I copied that photo to another file and wrote myself a note to make copies for both of them. I wouldn't have time to do it myself and also frame the shots before the wedding, but I would send one to each of them after the honeymoon. I knew they would love it.

I began arranging the pictures in chronological order, and as I opened up more photos and lined them up on my screen, a strange pattern began to emerge. Or maybe I was just too suspicious for my own good.

Wherever the wariness came from, the fact was that I kept seeing the same two men show up in the background. I probably wouldn't have noticed them, except that they were in so many shots, and more importantly, they just didn't look like librarians. To be honest, they looked more like thugs.

"Sorry, love," Derek said from the hall archway. "I'm ready to go now."

"Will you come look at this?" I asked.

He walked over and stared at the images on my computer screen.

I glanced up at him. "Do you see what I'm seeing?"

"Of course. The same two men appear in the background of many of these photos, yet they weren't all taken at the same time or in the same place."

I smiled. I should've known he would pick up on it.

"I don't know what to think," I said. "Were they following me? I don't recognize them from any of my classes or the Book Lovers' Tour. So who are they?"

"This bald fellow looks vaguely familiar," he said, and pointed to one particular photograph that showed both men's faces clearly. "Will you send me a copy of this one?"

"Sure." I clicked on the photo and emailed it to him.

A second later, his phone beeped and he opened up the picture to study it for another minute. He tapped his screen a few times and then closed the program and slid his phone back into his pocket. "Ready to go."

"Did you send it to your office?"

"Yes. Corinne will run both of them through our facial recognition program and we should have our answers shortly." He held out his arm. "Shall we go?"

I beamed at him. "You are a genius."

"Thank you, darling. But you're the one who pointed me in the right direction."

"They probably thought they were being discreet, but neither of them look like librarians." I held up my hand. "I'm not saying that librarians have a look, per se, but . . . you know what I mean."

He chuckled. "Of course."

We crossed over to Fifth Street and walked the few short blocks to the conference center. There was still plenty of time to get seats in the large auditorium where the service was being held. We sat next to the aisle near the back and I turned to watch the doorway, hoping to catch Inspector Lee. As soon as she walked in, I waved her over.

"We saved you a seat."

She nudged me with her elbow. "You're a peach, Brooklyn."

The crowd settled down and the head of the librarians' association walked to the podium. A librarian herself, she presided over the service and gave a touching tribute to "one of our own."

Several more speakers said lovely things about Sara and I was glad I'd slipped several tissues into my bag. Then the dreaded Cornelia Jones, the head of Sara's college library, was introduced. She walked to the podium and I realized that I had seen her before. She was the woman who had followed Rod into my classroom the other day. She was probably in her forties, tall and full-figured, with dark hair she wore pulled back in what my mother would call a French roll. She was attractive in a matronly sort of way, but the permanent frown lines around her mouth and across her forehead detracted from any beauty she might've once claimed.

Cornelia's speech was an odd combination of complaints and praise—given begrudgingly. For some reason, instead of celebrating Sara's life, she painted a dour and depressing picture of life back in their small town. It probably wasn't meant to be a downer, but I could tell from her face that she had lived her life in that gloomy state of mind. Her words had more to do with her own personality than with Sara or with their hometown. Cornelia was a real sourpuss.

"I suppose Sara got along well with everyone," she continued, her voice a monotone. "And we will miss her." She coughed self-consciously and added, "I confess I, er, don't know too many of the details of her death, but I know that, um, dear Sara died as she lived, buried in books."

"Buried in books," I murmured. "Strangely apropos." *And how would she know that little detail if she wasn't involved in Sara's murder?*

The room burst into thunderous applause, which shocked the heck out of Cornelia. I couldn't blame her for being surprised at the outpouring, because she was a downright drudge. I had a feeling Sara had gotten along well with everyone *except Cornelia.* But that line about being buried in books was a definite winner with the librarians.

I leaned closer to Inspector Lee and whispered, "She's the one who forced Sara to move all those boxes of books. I'll bet she did it out of spite."

"What makes you think so?"

"When we met Darla in the booth, she was visibly frightened of being caught talking to us. And she admitted that Cornelia had it in for Sara. And I told you that Sara thought Cornelia was jealous of her. What a horrible boss."

Lee weighed my words as she studied Cornelia. "She reminds me of an angry dog. Constantly growling."

"That about sums it up." I wondered if Inspector Lee had already interviewed Cornelia, but I knew that if I asked her, she would avoid answering.

The applause died down and Cornelia continued speaking.

"She should've quit while she was ahead," I murmured.

Inspector Lee snorted.

Cornelia continued taking subtle digs at Sara. She moaned that the library budget was going to suffer because they had paid for Sara to fly out for the conference, and now that she was dead, it was a wasted ticket. She blamed Sara for all the extra hours Cornelia would have to work. She sniffed contemptuously. "It's not fair to be saddled with all of her work just because she's dead.

But . . . I suppose she did the best she could. My thoughts and prayers are with her family today."

"Ugh," I muttered.

Cornelia had lost any goodwill she might have garnered from the audience and a few minutes later she left the podium accompanied by silence.

"Wow, Debbie Downer," Inspector Lee whispered. "She really didn't like our victim. I'm looking forward to hearing her alibi for the other night."

My eyebrows shot up. So Inspector Lee hadn't interviewed Cornelia yet. I was glad she'd heard that speech before meeting with the woman. It would give her more perspective on Cornelia's personality—or lack thereof.

"She's awful," I said. "And stupid." I hadn't met many stupid librarians in my life because they were usually the smartest people in the room. But Cornelia qualified for stupidity award of the year. And as long as I was handing out awards, she also won in the mean-spirited and passive-aggressive categories.

Happily, the last speaker gave a rousing, upbeat eulogy, and by the end of his speech the crowd was cheering and shouting, "Amen!"

I had to dab my eyes again, it was so moving. Sara and I hadn't spoken in over a decade, but reconnecting this week had been really great. Whether she had intentions of defrauding a book buyer or not was for the police to figure out, but we had once been friends. This whole mess was breaking my heart.

I glanced around at all the smiling, tearstained faces, relieved that the service had ended on a high note. I wondered why Rod didn't speak, and I suddenly realized that I hadn't seen him here at all. I stood and scanned the room, trying to spot him.

"Looking for someone?" Derek asked.

"Seems weird that Sara's husband wouldn't be here."

"Perhaps he has a reason to avoid being seen."

I nodded intently. "Perhaps he does."

Inspector Lee glanced at Derek, her eyes narrowed in speculation. "That's an interesting point. Why would he not attend his wife's memorial?"

As Derek stood, his phone beeped.

"That might be Corinne," I said.

"It *is* Corinne." He tapped the screen and stared at the results.

"What's going on?" Inspector Lee asked.

Quickly and quietly, I explained about the two men who'd appeared in so many of the photographs my people had sent me by email. The inspector was watching Derek as closely as I was.

Derek's assistant, Corinne, was a lovely older woman who had followed him here from their London office to help open their San Francisco branch. She was as smart and efficient as any of the special investigators in Derek's offices and her loyalty to him was beyond question, a quality I particularly appreciated.

"My suspicions were correct," he murmured, angling the phone so that I could see the screen. "This fellow here, the one I thought I recognized, is former FBI, now working as a private detective. His name is Roy Mattingly."

"What's a private detective doing here?" As soon as the words were out of my mouth, I shook my head. "Never mind. Dumb question. We've got murder and possible criminal fraud, for starters."

"For starters." Derek opened another screen on his phone, but closed it after a few seconds.

"More interesting information," Inspector Lee mused. She wrote down the name of the FBI guy, then glanced around the room as if expecting to see the man.

"Any news on the other guy in the photo?" I asked.

Derek shook his head. "No word yet on him."

"Too bad." Derek's facial recognition system was the most sophisticated in the world. If Corinne couldn't track down the other guy, he might be completely off the radar.

"Do you have a picture of the other guy?" Inspector Lee asked.

"Absolutely," Derek said, and brought the photo to his phone screen. "Let me send it to you."

"Thanks," she said. "And keep me posted. If you find out who he is, I want to know."

"Definitely."

Gazing around the room, I caught sight of Heather speaking to another woman. Seeing her reminded me of something and I turned back to Derek. "I hope you don't mind, but I invited Heather to the rehearsal dinner tomorrow night. I know she's a suspect, but we're still friends until further notice."

"I don't mind at all," he said. "It was kind of you to invite her."

"I would hate to think of her all alone in her hotel room."

"I'll contact the restaurant to add an extra seat at the table."

"Thank you."

He glanced around. "Darling, if you don't mind, I have a few more questions for Inspector Lee."

"I'm in no hurry to leave," I said. "Unless you'd rather talk to her alone."

"Of course not. I'll just—"

"Brooklyn."

I whipped around and saw Rod walking toward me. I looked back at Derek and Inspector Lee. "Can you wait a minute? I want to introduce you to Rod."

"Certainly," Derek murmured.

I watched Rod approach and wondered, where had he been? I hadn't seen him during the memorial. Something told me he had heard some of it, though, because his face was pale and his eyes were bloodshot. Had he been crying? Was he really upset about Sara, or was he putting on a show for everyone here? I couldn't help but be suspicious of him, even if he had a perfectly legitimate alibi for the night of Sara's death.

Rod came within a few feet before realizing that Inspector Lee was standing with me. His eyes widened and he might have bolted, but I grabbed him before he could take off.

"Rod." I forced him into a tight hug. "I'm so sorry."

"I still can't believe it."

"I know." After a moment we broke off the hug and I said, "I'd like you to meet my fiancé, Derek Stone. Derek, this is Rod Martin, Sara's husband."

They shook hands and Derek commiserated with him for a moment. Then I said to Rod, "I tried to look for you yesterday to tell you, but I didn't know where to find you."

He frowned at me. "Tell me what?"

Derek gave my arm a subtle squeeze before he and Inspector Lee walked off and began talking in hushed tones. I was bummed not to be in on their conversation but I would pester Derek for the details later.

I turned back to Rod. "I—I wanted to catch you before the police found you. To tell you that Sara was, you know, dead." My throat suddenly dried up. It was still hard to say it.

"Oh." He blinked a few times, but was still frowning. "I don't understand. Why would you be the one to tell me that?"

"Because I'm the one who found her."

His mouth dropped open. "You? Oh, wow. Okay. Sorry, I didn't realize. That must've been horrible for you."

"It was." An image planted itself in my brain, of Sara buried alive in that pile of heavy books and broken crates. I shook my head to get rid of the grim picture, but it refused to leave.

"When she didn't show up in our hotel room, I thought she was just in a snit," he said. "Figured she would show up eventually when she got over whatever was bugging her."

"You weren't worried about her?"

"She's done this before. Sometimes when she's really ticked off, she'll spend the night at a girlfriend's house. So no, I'm sorry to say I wasn't worried. But now I feel like an idiot for not going after her. Instead I spent all day in the exhibit hall, doing my schtick."

"What schtick is that?" I asked, but I had a feeling I knew. And meanwhile, I wondered what he had done to put Sara in a "snit."

He managed to smile. "Buying and selling books. Wheeling and dealing. That's my schtick. My job. My company has a booth on the exhibit floor. Number 1274. If you have time, please come by and browse."

"I'll do that." Was he still going to be working in the company booth? Even after his wife's murder?

He winked at me. "I'll give you a nice discount."

This was just creepy. Discounts. Work talk. His wife hadn't even been dead twenty-four hours. But I smiled and played along. "How can I say no?"

"Great." He sobered quickly and gave my arm a warm squeeze. "Look, Brooklyn, I know you didn't want to give up *The Three Musketeers*, but now that I've lost my sweet Sara, I'd be willing to beg to have that book back."

I sighed. It was so hard to believe anything he said. "I understand your feelings, Rod. I have a lot of sentimental feelings about the book, too, so let me think about it, okay?"

But he was staring at something over my shoulder and whatever he saw did not make him happy. Without warning, he covered his face and began to sob like a baby. Grabbing my arms, he yanked me close and buried his face in my shoulder.

The shock I felt must have shown on my face because Derek took one step closer, grabbed Rod from behind, and jerked him away from me.

"Watch yourself, mate," Derek said, taking the friendly approach as opposed to punching him in the face.

"Oh. Uh, sorry," Rod muttered, still sniffling and snorting. "I'm a little overwhelmed." He pulled a handkerchief from his pocket and blew his nose, then glanced around as though he were embarrassed about his crying jag. But it didn't feel authentic. I remembered just how good he had been at feigning emotions he wasn't really feeling, so I was less than moved by the outburst. Rod's scans of the room were too furtive and I got the feeling he was looking for someone. Or *hiding* from someone?

"Are you waiting for someone?" I asked, trying to sound casual—as opposed to confrontational.

"Who, me? No." He raked his hand through his hair. "To tell the truth, I don't know whether I'm coming or going. I'm sorry I broke down there, but I can't seem to control myself. Whenever I think about Sara, I just lose it."

At that moment, Derek leaned in to whisper in my ear, "Wait here, love. I'll be right back."

Surprised, I watched him stride off and saw Inspector Lee jog after him. Where were they off to? I didn't follow because I still had a few issues with Rod.

"Anyway, I'm sorry," Rod said, still sniffling.

I gave him a moment to pull himself together, then said, "I know you're feeling pretty awful right now, but I have to tell you some more bad news."

He seemed to brace himself. "What is it?"

"*The Three Musketeers* book is a forgery."

"What?" he shouted, then instantly cringed. I almost laughed because it was the same reaction as Inspector Lee's.

"Sorry for yelling," he said. "But what in the world are you talking about?"

"I was examining the book this morning and found that the title page had been replaced and the publication date was altered. The book is lovely, but it's not worth what you thought it was."

"You've got to be kidding me," he cried. "Are you accusing me of trying to sell a fake book?"

"Not at all," I said, keeping my voice calm. He was good at feigning emotions, but he didn't seem to be pretending now. But how could he not have known all along that the book was a forgery? He was supposed to be an expert. And so was Sara for that matter. "I'm just telling you what I discovered."

I was so wrapped up in Rod's emotional swings that I hadn't noticed that Derek had returned. I flashed him a questioning look, but knew better than to ask where he'd gone while Rod was standing here listening. Derek moved closer and casually draped his arm around my shoulders and I recognized it as a purely protective move. I had to admit it felt pretty great to have the man I loved standing at my side.

"I'm a reputable bookseller," Rod continued, growing more upset. "And I'm completely shocked by this."

"I don't blame you," I said. "I was pretty shocked when I realized it."

"How could something like this have happened?"

"You'd know more about that than I would. Did you buy the book from another reputable bookseller?"

"No, I—" He gasped. "Oh my God. Oh no. It was Sara."

"Sara . . . what?"

"Sara found the book and brought it home to me."

I flashed him a look of disbelief. "She *found* it?"

"I mean, she, uh, bought it. In an old used bookstore. They didn't know what they had, but she recognized its value."

"Hold on," I said. "Are you saying—"

"No, you hold on," he snapped. "Are you accusing Sara of breaking the law behind my back?"

"Calm down, Rod. I don't know who was breaking the law. It could've been the used bookseller." I was a little affronted that he would instinctively push the blame off on a wife who was no longer here to defend herself. And frankly, I didn't believe his story that Sara had found it in an old used bookstore. Anyone, especially a bookseller, could see that the book was extremely valuable. "I just know that the book was altered and I'm assuming it was done in order to sell it for a lot more money. And that's very likely a criminal offense."

He seemed to mull my words over for a moment, then shook his head numbly. "I'm at a complete loss. I can only surmise that it was Sara who forged the book."

"Wait. So it wasn't the bookseller, it was Sara. Was she familiar with the process of forging a book?"

"Of course not. I mean, I don't know." His eyes widened with another realization. "Oh no, I've got to call her office to let them know. She was the head of the book restoration department. If she did it for one book, she might have done it for others. They need to know."

I was still angry that he was putting all the blame on Sara. But I had to admit he was right to notify Sara's college. "That's a good idea, but can't Cornelia do it?"

He blinked, apparently surprised that I knew the name of Sara's boss. "Cornelia is the head librarian but she isn't in charge of restoration and conservation."

"I see."

"I'll have to take *The Three Musketeers* back to them," he said reasonably. "They'll need to hunt down the original owner and make sure they know exactly what the story is. I'm happy to swing by your place later and pick it up."

Inspector Lee returned and joined the conversation. "That's not an option. The book is part of our investigation and will stay in San Francisco until further notice."

"What?" he demanded. "Why?"

"That's police business," she said enigmatically.

I always hated it when she said that to me, but today I rather enjoyed hearing it.

Rod turned to me in confusion as if I might be the one to explain and fix everything.

"The forged book could've been the motive." When my words didn't seem to register, I added softly, "For Sara's murder. Remember?"

"Of course," he said testily, but just as quickly he began to choke back tears. "How can I ever forget she was murdered? I'll have to live with her loss for the rest of my life."

"I'm sorry, Rod." I patted his shoulder. "Look, it's true that

Sara and I didn't talk to each other for years, but I felt like we were finally starting to connect again. I'll miss her, too."

"She would've loved to hear you say that."

"I know. Oh, hey, Heather told me that you two had a drink the other night."

He gave me a cautious look. "Yeah."

"She showed me the selfie you took together. That's a great shot."

"Thanks." Rod sighed. "I'm really glad we reconnected, too, Brooklyn."

"Me, too." I wasn't sure that was true, but I didn't intend to ruin the moment. Rod gave me a quick hug, then eyed Derek and took a few steps back.

"I'd be happy if we could make up for lost time," he said. "Why don't I take you and your fiancé out to dinner tomorrow night? We could clear the air and really talk."

"That's such a lovely offer, Rod. Thank you. But we're not available tomorrow night." I hesitated, then added, "We're having the rehearsal dinner for our wedding."

He slapped his forehead. "Of course. My mistake." He grabbed hold of my hand and clutched it tightly. "I'm so happy for you. Both of you. I wish I could be there to wish you well."

"Thank you, Rod."

"Yes, thank you," Derek said blandly. "Darling, we should go."

I gazed up at him. I had the feeling he was hoping to get me out of there before I invited Rod to the dinner and wedding. But he didn't need to worry about that.

"All right, love." I turned and gave Rod an encouraging smile and a hug. "Take care of yourself, Rod."

"You, too," he said, and once again, I caught him glancing anxiously over my shoulder.

Maybe Rod was just one of those people who was always looking for someone more interesting to talk to. Or maybe there was somebody here who scared the bejeezus out of him. I figured that was the more likely scenario because I really got the feeling that he'd been trying to hide behind me earlier. Which was ridiculous since he was several inches taller and at least fifty pounds heavier than me.

As he walked away, I realized that none of it mattered, because I would never see him again. I turned to Derek. "Where did you two dash off to?"

Derek shot a glance at Inspector Lee first, then said, "When Rod burst into tears and grabbed you, I happened to see Roy Mattingly standing by the door on the other side of the auditorium."

"The FBI guy? I'll bet that's who Rod was staring at over my shoulder."

"Quite possibly," he said. "But oddly enough, as soon as Mattingly saw me coming, he took off."

"So you didn't catch up to him?"

"Not yet," Inspector Lee said, a dangerous edge to her voice.

I clutched Derek's arm, feeling a bit shaky. If Derek had recognized the FBI guy, then surely the FBI guy knew who Derek was. So why did he run away from him? The possible answers to that question did not exactly fill me with tranquility.

"Darling," Derek said. "Why did you tell Rod about our rehearsal dinner tomorrow night?"

"I was just making small talk."

"So you weren't inviting him to break into our home and steal the book?"

"What? Me? No."

He pursed his lips as he considered my evasive gaze. "Just checking."

"It did sound like an invitation to commit burglary," Inspector Lee mused. "If he were so inclined."

I gave an uncertain shrug. "Depends on how desperate he is to get that book."

"I don't like the odds on this one," Inspector Lee said.

I slid my arm through Derek's. "But wouldn't he assume that the police have the book? Especially after what you said to him."

Inspector Lee shrugged. "I didn't exactly admit that we have it. And he might be desperate enough to try to break in anyway."

I gazed up at Derek. "Our house is impenetrable, right?"

"Nothing is impenetrable," he said, so casually that I knew I'd blown it.

"Your place comes close, though," Inspector Lee pointed out.

But Derek's tone said it all.

"Shoot," I grumbled. "I screwed up, right?"

He gave me a comforting squeeze. "We might be able to remedy it."

I took a moment to rethink the problem. "If I ask nicely, Inspector Lee, would you consider assigning someone to watch our place?"

She laughed. "Brooklyn, you're so entertaining. But sorry, I can't justify the man-hours on a hunch."

Derek smiled. "No need, Inspector. I'll have one of my men keep an eye on things."

"That's handy," she said, grinning. I had to agree.

"Thank you." I reached up and kissed his cheek. "And I'm sorry, I wasn't thinking. Blame it on wedding jitters."

But Derek's attention was diverted elsewhere. I turned to see what he was looking at and saw Rod Martin talking to Cornelia, Sara's boss. They both looked furious and Rod was jabbing his finger at her. She shoved him and he grabbed her arm.

"Whoa, what's that all about?" I wondered.

"Two angry people blaming each other for a crime?"

"Think I'll go find out," Inspector Lee said, and took off across the room.

Derek and I glanced at each other and immediately followed, approaching from behind so Rod wouldn't see us. The crowd had thinned out, so we could get close enough to hear them clearly.

"She hated you," Rod was saying. "And I know you hated her, too. You were practically giddy when you sent her down to that basement to get those books."

"That doesn't mean I killed her."

"With Sara out of the way, you stand to—"

"Why would I kill the golden goose?" she hissed.

Inspector Lee strolled up, stopping the conversation. "Everything okay here?"

"Who the hell are you?" Cornelia demanded.

"That's just rude," Lee said, grinning.

I almost laughed and whispered to Derek, "This is not going to end well."

He just shook his head.

Lee flashed her badge and then took Cornelia's arm. "I'd like you to come with me."

"What? No! Why aren't you taking him?"

"I already spoke to Mr. Martin. Now I want to talk to you."

"I didn't do anything!" she wailed.

As Inspector Lee passed us, she rolled her eyes. "This day just keeps getting better and better. I've got to play the lottery."

It probably wasn't funny, but we both laughed all the way home.

Back home, we settled down at the kitchen bar. Derek pulled out a bottle of wine, but then stopped. "Darling, do you realize we have neglected to choose our cocktails for the wedding?"

"I didn't want to say anything," I said coyly.

He studied me for a moment. "You forgot as well, didn't you?"

"Yes." I grinned, then shrugged. "I'm afraid we've become slipshod in our wedding preparations."

"It's disgraceful." He opened the cabinet in the dining room and removed a shaker and two martini glasses. "Let's get this done and try not to be distracted again."

"You're right." I sighed. "If we don't have a signature cocktail at our wedding, people will talk."

"I couldn't live with that," he said, and began concocting the first drink. "And I don't want you to lose sleep so I will admit that I emailed the caterers to let them know our two choices."

"So they'll be prepared with whatever choice we make?"

"Exactly."

Derek knew that, besides being delicious, I had only one other requirement of our signature cocktail and that was that it had to contain light-colored liquids. I hated the thought of someone spilling a Tequila Sunrise on my pristine white wedding dress.

"Now this first one is a light amber shade, but I think you'll find it delicious." Derek dipped the rims of the two martini glasses in white sugar, poured the liquid into the glasses, and handed one to me.

"It's pretty. What is it?"

"Essentially it's a sidecar, but with several twists. We start with a good cognac, add simple syrup made with honey instead of sugar, add in a shot of orange liqueur and a generous squeeze of fresh lemon juice. Then shake vigorously and garnish with a good-sized lemon twist."

After one sip, I said, "I choose this one. It's just as delicious as you said it would be. Does it have a name?"

He grinned. "Why don't you name it?"

I thought for a moment. "Honey, lemon twist, cognac. How about Twisted French Honey?"

"A bit complicated," he said with a laugh.

"Okay. We can shorten it to Twisted Honey. It's quirky yet romantic. I like it."

"Then it's perfect."

"Are you going to make the second drink?"

"My second choice starts with a base of ginger syrup that involves a lot of peeling and chopping and then boiling and steeping the ginger root to draw out its rich, peppery flavor. So for the caterers' and bartenders' sake, I suggest we stick with the Twisted Honey, if that works for you."

"It works great for me." I took another sip and smiled.

He leaned over and kissed me. "I'll email the caterers to let them know what we've decided on."

"So except for a quick trip to Tiffany tomorrow, we are officially done with all the wedding preparations. Hallelujah." I took the last sip of my drink and set my glass on the bar. "I think we should have another round, just to be sure."

Despite overindulging on two Twisted Honeys the night before, I woke up without the jitters and that put me in a good mood right from the start. The entire day ran like a well-oiled machine. All my plans fell in line perfectly, a miracle after the last few days of internal chaos and missteps. My sisters and Robin were on time for our mani-pedis at the spa, and Alex, my mom, and Meg joined us, too. We laughed and chatted and had the best time together. Now that my sisters and Robin lived in the wine country, I missed hanging out with all of them, so we vowed to do this more often.

Afterward, I broke away from the group and stopped at Tiffany to pick out gifts for my girls. I found the cutest silver bracelet with one tiny dangling heart and ended up buying six of them. One for me, one for each of my four bridesmaids, and one for Alex, who had been such a great help to me.

The shoe crisis solution alone had made Alex's gift worth it, but she had also been an awesome self-defense instructor for the past year and had helped me get my arms in shape for my wedding dress. And she did actually save my life at least twice. She was dating my darling, dangerous friend Gabriel, which provided me with good gossip and intrigue. Plus, cupcakes. Alex had become very dear to me and I wanted to make sure she knew it.

I had to admit I was a little anxious as I dressed for our rehearsal dinner. Not because of the dinner, which would be wonderful; and not because of the guests, some of whom I had never met; but because I was worried that our house might be broken into while we were out.

"I never should've said anything to Rod," I muttered to myself in the mirror.

"Meow," Charlie said in agreement as she took two turns around and then plopped down on top of my feet.

I smiled and lifted her up to snuggle for a minute. "I love you, Charlie Cupcake."

I had never known a cat to be this affectionate, especially after my experiences babysitting Vinnie and Suzie's two cats, Pookie and Splinters. Those two had always been properly disdainful of everything I did for them. But Charlie was a sweet creature who seemed to love me as much as I loved her. She made me happy. It helped that she had been a gift from Derek, which meant that I cherished her all the more.

Derek checked his phone as he walked into the room. "Mitch is in place, parked across the street," he announced. "So along with every high-tech security gadget known to man, our home is being monitored by a real live human who is trained to kill."

"Wonderful." I wasn't sure if he was kidding about the "trained to kill" part, but I was happy to hear that Mitch was on duty.

"Ready, love?" Derek asked.

I set Charlie down and grabbed my small clutch purse. "Whenever you are."

We had rented a private room in our favorite restaurant near the Embarcadero. The cozy terrace offered a view of the Bay Bridge and the Berkeley Hills beyond. The weather was temperate enough to have cocktails outside and that was where I was introduced to the rest of Derek's family.

Seeing Derek chatting with his four brothers took my breath away. One man was more gorgeous than the next, and all of them had a dangerous streak that added to their attractiveness. Naturally, the most gorgeous and dangerous of them all was Derek, although any of his brothers' wives might have argued the point.

I was about to take a sip from my second glass of champagne when Heather walked in.

We gave each other air kisses and I laughed. "I'm so glad you could make it."

"Thank you so much for inviting me. This is so special." She looked a little hesitant. "I hope you don't mind, but I brought a guest."

"Oh." I was shocked, but recovered quickly. "That shouldn't be a problem."

She was watching the door. "Here he is."

I was thinking how happy I was that Gus could see her tonight after all. But then I spun around to greet . . .

"Rod?"

Chapter Ten

Derek recognized my distress and instantly alerted the maître d' that with Rod's unexpected arrival we would need one more additional place setting. The man handled the news with complete aplomb, which was so much better than the way I was tempted to handle it. I had never been prone to tantrums, but this latest surprise was putting me to the test.

"Rod," I said tightly. "What a surprise." Coldly furious, I looked from him to Heather and back again. This was beyond rude. Tonight was about Derek and me and our family and close friends. Rod had no business being here and everyone knew it.

"I know I'm imposing," he said sheepishly, clearly aware that he never would have been invited if not for Heather. "But I happened to run into Heather and she insisted. I hope you don't mind."

He knew I minded, and I seriously doubted that Heather had insisted. I gave Heather a quick glance and her face was a mask of serenity. That was her *tell*, I realized. Way back when, if Rod was up to something, Heather would maintain a façade of eerie calm, as if mentally distancing herself from the situation. Clearly nothing had changed, so I knew there was more to the story than what Rod had said.

I couldn't help but wonder if they were sticking together in order to provide another alibi for each other. But then, I couldn't think of anything going on tonight that would necessitate an alibi. I chalked it all up to my being utterly annoyed with both of them and vowed to ignore them as much as possible.

"Wonderful," I said finally, unwilling to make a scene. "Please have a cocktail and enjoy yourselves." I would've loved to have taken him by the arm to the door and told him to get out. But I knew that would've upset my mother and Meg. Things were awkward enough without adding to my real guests' discomfort. Rod was here and we would all have to play nicely together. Or die trying.

Rod gave a thumbs-up and strolled toward the bar. I grabbed Heather's hand before she had a chance to follow him. "You *insisted*?"

She rolled her eyes. "He's so full of it. He almost started crying until I broke down and agreed to bring him with me. I know I shouldn't have but, honestly, Brooklyn, I didn't think you'd mind that much. After all, he just lost Sara. And you know me. I'm such a sucker for a sad face."

I slid a glance at the man in question, who was smiling at the bartender. As for Rod being the grieving husband, he was showing no signs of it tonight. "Yes, you're a sucker," I said, forcing myself to smile.

"Don't worry. I'll make sure he behaves."

Derek would make sure the man behaved. I had no doubt about that. I glanced around. "I have to get to know my future in-laws, but give me the high sign if you need anything."

"I'll be fine. And I really am sorry." She gave me a hug.

I sighed. "Just have a good time." I watched her wander off. I supposed that if Rod was here at the restaurant, he wouldn't be trying to break into our home. So I decided to relax and enjoy myself.

The evening turned out to be so much more fun than I could've hoped. Rod and Heather were both polite and friendly to the other guests, and the rest of Derek's family members were as charming and smart as his parents. His brothers were all gorgeous, as I might have mentioned before, and my cheeks hurt from smiling and laughing so much at their adorable ways of flattering the bride—that would be me—and teasing the groom, their brother. Each of his brothers' wives greeted me with open arms and graciously welcomed me into their ranks. And their darling children were so well behaved, it was scary.

Our two families seemed to fit together as though we had always been friends. I'd heard enough stories over the years about nightmare in-laws that I knew I was lucky to have these wonderful people.

The dinner itself was phenomenal, as we had known it would be since this was one of our favorite restaurants in the city. Dad had brought the very best bottles of wine from Dharma to serve the guests. The service was wonderful and I told myself that after the week we'd had, Derek and I deserved a smooth, lovely evening.

Then halfway through dinner, Derek's father, John, decided to drop a bombshell. He stood up and tapped his wineglass with his spoon. "I know we're celebrating a wedding, but I have an announcement to make."

Everyone made a point of mimicking him, clinking their glasses with their utensils until we were all laughing again.

"Go ahead, Dad," Derek said when the commotion died down.

John cleared his throat. "I'm thrilled to tell you that your mother and I are in the process of buying a house in Dharma."

Beside me, Derek jolted and I looked at him. It was so unusual to catch him off guard at all. I sort of enjoyed seeing the flash of emotions dart across his face. Pleasure, worry, and maybe just a touch of fear. I almost laughed, really. He'd seen me dealing with my own parents all the time and now he'd be having the same experiences.

When the applause and laughter died down, John continued. "We plan to live half the year in Cambridge and the other half in Dharma. And of course, both of our homes will always be open to any of you who would care to visit."

I thought it was wonderful. Mom and Meg had mentioned going house hunting in the wine country, but I never thought Meg and John would actually find a place and want to buy it.

"Wait a minute," Dalton shouted. "No, no, no!" Since he was now living in Dharma with my sister Savannah, his parents' decision seemed to be hitting him the hardest.

"What Dalton meant to say," Dylan interjected quickly, "was congratulations, Mum and Dad!"

There was more cajoling and laughter as my own father draped one arm around John's shoulders. The two of them looked so pleased with the announcement, it was hard not to grin back at them. My mom and Meg were sitting close together, looking so happy, it was as if they were long-lost twins suddenly rediscovering each other.

"Then why is his face so red?" Douglas asked, chuckling at his baby brother's discomfiture.

"I believe Dalton turns red when he's happy," his father said drolly. "Just as Derek does."

I stared at the love of my life and noticed that he was still a little wild-eyed as well. But the smile curving his mouth told me he liked the idea of having his parents living closer half the year—he was just going to need a little time to get used to it.

"Derek's face is red because he's flushed with eagerness to take his bride. Dalton, on the other hand, must be delirious with joy, since Happy is his middle name," Duncan said.

"Huh," Dylan said. "I thought his middle name was Berk."

Even I laughed at that one, having learned a while back that *berk* was British slang for *idiot*.

Dalton wasn't taking any of it. He stood and shook his finger at Derek. "My parents are moving in practically next door to me. This is your doing. Admit it."

Derek laughed even harder and was joined by his other brothers. He took my hand under the table and gave it a squeeze. I shot a look at my own parents, who were clearly thrilled at having their new friends move into the neighborhood.

Dalton scowled at his mother. "I move ten thousand miles to

get away from you, and now you're going to move in next door? I'm not sure I like that."

"Ten thousand miles isn't nearly enough when a boy misses his mum." Meg giggled. "You silly goose. You're not fooling anyone. We all know you love the idea."

Dalton rolled his eyes, but his mouth was quivering as he tried not to smile. "At least promise me you'll only be here half the year."

She tossed a chunk of her dinner roll at him. "We promise. For now."

"And she attacks me with bread products," Dalton griped. "Do you see why I had to move?"

"You poor bugger." His oldest brother, Douglas, clapped Dalton on the back. "The good news for us is we'll all have a place to stay in the wine country."

"Hear, hear," Duncan cheered. "And the parents will be out of our hair for six months at a time. Sounds like a win-win to me."

"Oh, come now," John balked, though I could see a twinkle in his eyes. "When have we ever been *in* your hair?"

"What an unsavory image," Daphne proclaimed, to more laughs. She was happily married to Duncan and came from a fabulously wealthy family who built jets for the British government. She insisted she was a simple wife and mum, but I had a feeling her security clearance might have been higher than any of the men's.

Derek and his brothers continued to chuckle and tease each other and tell wonderful stories throughout the meal. I was proud to say that my family members held their own. More than once I noticed Savannah's eyes glistening with happy tears and I knew she was thrilled with the news that Meg and John would be spending more time in Dharma. Ever since Dalton moved halfway across the world to live with her, Savannah and Meg had become such good friends, I was actually a bit jealous of her.

My younger sister China and her husband, Beau, sat with their adorable daughter seated between them. Hannah was clapping and giggling, clearly loving the laughter and good-natured shouting at the table.

London, our baby sister, sat next to her charming husband, Trevor. We often teased him about being a slacker because he was not only a brilliant physician but also a renowned wine expert. They had left their twins, Chloe and Connor, at the hotel with a babysitter because, as London had stated when she walked in, "I'm going to party all night."

I caught John's eye and we both smiled. When he winked at me, I fell in love all over again. The man and his wife had raised a beautiful family who loved and joked with each other as much as my family did, and I couldn't be happier knowing I was about to become a part of it all.

I gazed around the table, hoping everyone here shared my happiness. When I got to Heather, she blew me a kiss, making me laugh. Rod sat next to her and the look on his face in that moment gave me a chill. He wasn't looking at me, thank goodness, because he wasn't smiling at all. In fact, he wore a look that was so sinister I wouldn't have been surprised to learn that he was planning my demise right here at the table.

As soon as I had the thought, I wondered if maybe I was just being paranoid. After all, his wife had just died a horrible death. It could be that he was simply in mourning. But since overhearing his conversation with Cornelia yesterday, I had my doubts.

Derek's phone beeped and he stole a look at the screen. Standing, he murmured, "I'll be right back."

"What is it?" I asked. "What happened?"

He scowled. "It's Mitch. Someone tried to break into our building."

"Sorry he got away, boss."

Derek and I stood next to Mitch's car on the opposite side of the street from our building.

"Don't worry about it, Mitch," Derek said. "I'm just grateful that you prevented him from getting inside."

Mitch was grumbling and the scowl on his face could have frightened small children. "Your building security is pretty tight, boss. He probably wouldn't have made it inside anyway. Still, I'm pissed at myself for letting him escape."

"But you got a look at him and that's important."

"Not much of a look, but I'm hoping what I saw might help."

Earlier Mitch had insisted that we not rush to leave the party because the excitement had blown over and our apartment was still safe. So we stayed for another hour and managed to thoroughly enjoy ourselves and our guests. Some of the heartier folks were going back to the hotel bar to continue the party while others were off to bed. Heather and Rod both hugged me and thanked me again. Rod even apologized for crashing the party but said he was glad he did because he had a great time. I was in too good a mood to be angry and wished them a safe trip back to their hotel.

When we finally got home, I was happy to see Mitch still sitting in his car across the street from our place.

"No more activity tonight, boss."

"Can you describe what the guy looked like?" I asked, rubbing my arms to ward off the cold night air.

"He was wearing a baseball cap, so his face was in shadow," Mitch said. "All I could tell was that he was tall and heavyset."

"Was he bald?" I asked.

"No, he had a full head of hair."

"But you said he was wearing a baseball cap," Derek said.

"Right, but his hair stuck out around his ears."

"Dark hair?" I asked.

"From what I could see, thanks to the light above the front door, I'd say yes, it was dark brown."

We thanked Mitch and said good night. Once we were inside the building, I said, "I guess we can't blame this on Rod."

"Not unless he's in cahoots with someone else."

"It wouldn't be the first time Heather was on hand to provide him with a perfect alibi for the evening."

"Or vice versa, darling."

I frowned. "That's right. Seeing Heather stroll in with Rod tonight made me so angry, I wondered how I could've forgotten that she was still a murder suspect."

"After carrying a grudge for twelve years, she certainly has motivation," he said.

"I'll say." The elevator door opened slowly. We walked inside and I pushed the button for the sixth floor. "You know, I was thinking that Mitch's description sounds a lot like Thuggy Guy. I mean, you know, the other guy in the photos. When I first saw his picture, I thought he looked like a thug."

"Yes, I know who you're referring to," he said, smiling. "And you're right, the description does sound like him. I think I'll look at our security camera footage tomorrow to see if we can get a better shot of whoever tried to break in. And Inspector Lee took a copy of his photo and she's running it through their law enforcement systems as well. I can't see that her system would yield anything that ours didn't, but you never know. I'll give her a call in the morning."

"That all sounds really good," I said, as we stepped out into our hallway. "But we may have a little scheduling conflict if you were planning to wait until tomorrow to work on this."

"Ah, yes." He nodded somberly. "Tomorrow is our wedding day."

"I'm happy you remembered," I said, slipping my arm through his. "But we have an even bigger problem if we were hoping to wrap up this murder investigation soon. The librarians' conference ends tomorrow and anyone who might be considered a suspect will be going home. So we'll lose our best chance to get any more answers from Rod or Cornelia or Heather. Or even Thuggy Guy. I doubt he's a librarian but he showed up for the conference so he might be planning to leave tomorrow."

Derek's jaw was clenched as he nodded. "Then I'll take care of this tonight."

• • •

True to his word, Derek rolled up his sleeves and got to work while I made him a cup of coffee. He called up the security camera video, but couldn't get a good look at our would-be burglar's face. Then, on the off-chance that his company's facial recognition program had hit a snag, he spoke with the analyst working the night shift at his office. The guy was happy to run Thuggy's photo through the system again.

He also texted the original photo of Thuggy Guy to Mitch, hoping he might be able to say whether this was our intruder or not.

On a hunch, I put in a call to the Glen Cove College Library, where Sara had worked. Thanks to their automated system, I was able to get the number for the librarian in charge of collections. Naturally she wasn't in her office at ten o'clock on a Saturday night—actually midnight her time, I realized—but I left a detailed message asking whether Rod Martin had called them regarding his wife, Sara, and the altered copy of *The Three Musketeers*. I requested that the woman call me back at her earliest convenience, and figured I would hear from her sometime on Monday. That was okay, I thought, since we weren't leaving for Paris until Tuesday. Rod had probably called to give them the information, but I felt better for having followed through with the college myself.

I didn't know what to believe about Rod, but I hadn't appreciated him throwing Sara under the bus as soon as I told him about the forgery. I wasn't buying his innocent act, especially after catching the angry words he had exchanged with Sara's boss, Cornelia.

On the other hand, it was just weird the way Sara had given me that rare though forged book. She had admitted that she wanted to upstage Heather, but besides that, I had to wonder if maybe she just wanted to get rid of it. She had to have known it was forged. Was Rod right? Was Sara a little shady, too?

I was too tired to think about Sara and Rod so I turned off my brain and just relaxed on the couch with Charlie and Derek, who sat with his computer on the coffee table, drinking coffee.

I tried to stay awake until he was done but ended up dozing on and off for the next hour. At one point I heard him speaking French to someone on the phone and wondered if he had also sent the photo to Interpol. I spoke a little bit of French but I was so sleepy I couldn't be sure if he was talking about killers and thieves or making restaurant reservations for our honeymoon in Paris.

I woke again when he lifted me up and carried me to bed.

"Did we get him?" I mumbled.

"We got him," he said, as he reached to turn off the lamp on my night table.

"I'm so proud of you."

He kissed my cheek. "I love you."

"Mm. Me, too. Are you coming to bed?"

"Yes." He tucked the sheets around me. Seconds later, he climbed into bed next to me and I was sound asleep again before he turned off his light.

. . .

We both awoke early the next morning, and after washing my face and brushing my teeth, I raced to the coffeepot. The sun was shining, the sky was a brilliant blue, and I blessed the weather gods who had given us such a beautiful wedding day.

"Good morning," I said, greeting Derek who was already busy in the kitchen. "Thank you for making coffee."

"It's the least I can do on our wedding day."

"Aww, happy wedding day," I said, and wrapped my arms around his waist. "I love you."

"Same to you, darling." He kissed me soundly and we clung to each other for a long moment.

After a while, I sniffed the air. "Is that bacon I smell?"

"Yes, it's staying warm in the oven."

I gazed up at him. "Have I told you lately that I love you?"

"It's been several seconds," he murmured.

"I do. I love you so much."

"You love bacon."

"It's sort of the same thing, right?"

He laughed. "Go sit down and drink your coffee or I'll make you help me cook something."

"We both know what a bad idea that would be."

"You're right. I rescind the threat."

"Good thinking." Because breakfast would take some time, I retrieved my computer from my office and set it on the island counter. While I drank coffee and watched Derek, I checked out the newest batch of selfies my students had sent from the conference. Selfies. For heaven's sake, I'd completely forgotten about the picture Derek had identified in the middle of the night. In my defense, I was half asleep when he mentioned it.

Meanwhile, Derek separated an English muffin and slipped both halves into the toaster. Then he began chopping up shallots and chives for the scrambled eggs.

"Tell me what you found out about Thuggy," I said, having grown fond of that name.

"He's a book collector from Prague," Derek said as he scooped up the minced chives and dropped them into the scrambled egg mixture.

"A thug from Prague?"

He smiled. "We don't actually know that he's a thug."

I glanced at the computer screen. "Oh, here he is again in this photo." I tapped the screen. "Looks like he's talking to someone, but it's not the FBI guy."

"I'll see it in a minute," he said as he buttered the English muffin. "Tell me about the guy he's talking to."

"Okay. He must be short, because Thuggy towers over him in this shot. He's completely bald and wears little John Lennon glasses. He looks very intense and angry, like a Trotskyite."

Derek wrapped the buttered muffin in foil and stuck it in the oven to stay warm. He began to heat up the frying pan, then turned and smiled. "Have you seen a Trotskyite before?"

"Sure. Mom and Dad's friend Leon was a Trotskyite. He used to bring over copies of *People's World* for us to read."

Derek frowned. "I'm not familiar with *People's World*."

"It emerged from what used to be called *The Daily Worker*. You know, the Communist Party newspaper?"

"You used to read the Communist Party newspaper?"

"Well, Leon asked me to, and he was Dad's friend. The articles were impossible to understand so I had a hard time. Of course, I was six years old at the time." I shrugged and smiled.

"A budding Bolshevik."

I laughed. "Oh sure, that was me. Anyway, Leon would quiz us on the articles, but if we got something wrong, he would get angry and lecture us. I used to cry and Dad finally asked him not to come over anymore. I can still remember how Leon called Dad a deluded Menshevik just before he slammed the door. And we never saw him again."

"Deluded Menshevik." Derek grinned. "Harsh words."

I smiled at that. "Oh yeah, it was quite the smackdown. I had no idea what any of it meant, but to my six-year-old brain it sounded as if he had cursed my father to the devil. It made me really mad, but Dad just laughed it off. Told us Leon's name wasn't really Leon, after all. It was Archie. He changed it to Leon because that was Trotsky's name. So basically he was just a fanboy. From then on we referred to Leon as Archibald." I shook away the memory and turned back to the photo on the screen. "Anyway, come look at this guy."

Derek poured the egg mixture into the frying pan, adjusted the flame, and walked over to look at the photo. "They are certainly talking intently. They must know each other."

"I think so, too."

"This one is a little out of focus. Does he show up in another shot? Maybe one that shows him head-on?"

"I'll keep looking." I pulled up six more photos. "Here's Thuggy again, but . . . oh, good, here's Leon again. And this is a perfect shot."

"Leon," he said. "That's what we're calling the bald guy?"

I smiled. "It suits him." I scanned the other photos. "Oh, and here they are again, but look how they're pretending to ignore each other in this shot."

Derek took a look at both photos and pointed to one of them. "Send me that shot, will you, love?"

"Sending right now." I clicked on it and forwarded the shot to Derek. "Done."

A moment later, his phone beeped. "Message received." He checked the eggs, then picked up the phone, typed out a text, and sent it on to someone in his office. A moment later he was back at the stove, resuming his duties as breakfast chef as though he weren't a high-powered security expert trying to solve a brutal murder as well as a rare-book forgery on his wedding day.

I poured us both more coffee, then said, "So let's go back to Thuggy."

Derek played along. "We've assumed all along that he came here looking for a book."

"Should we assume something else besides that?"

"Perhaps he came here looking for a book *seller*."

I gazed at him, then nodded slowly. "You mean Rod? Do you think Thuggy is after him? Is that why Rod keeps freaking out whenever he sees the guy?" I stared at the photo again. "He is pretty scary-looking, thus the name *Thuggy*."

"I have no idea, but it's a possibility. Perhaps Rod promised him a book and hasn't yet delivered on the promise."

"If that's true, then it's all about *The Three Musketeers*."

"We don't know that for sure," Derek said, obviously trying to soften the blow.

"He wants that book," I said flatly. "And Sara gave it to me. Doesn't that make me a target?"

Derek's gaze hardened. "I won't let anything happen to you."

Strangely enough, I wasn't comforted. "So you really do think I'm in danger."

He turned the heat off. "I don't, actually. But I do think there are several people out there who are desperate to get their hands on this book."

"What can we do?"

He raised one eyebrow. "Shall we make it available to them?"

I stared at him. "You mean, like an enticement? We tell them we have the book, we lure them out into the open, and then . . . what? Sell the book to the highest bidder? Have the police arrest them?"

"Perhaps Inspector Lee will have some ideas."

"I'm sure she will." I let out a short chuckle. "But what exactly do we tell her? And if we do entice one of these buyers to show up, do we first let them know that the book has been tampered with?"

"No."

I smiled. "I agree."

"Call it a hunch," Derek said dryly, "but I doubt that Rod has mentioned that minor detail to the prospective buyers out there."

"Of course not, because that would deflate the price."

Either way, I had made up my mind that Rod was not a good guy. At best he was a grifter, and at worst, a vicious, clever killer. Had he and Cornelia been operating a book forgery ring behind Sara's back, or was she involved as well? The thought actually depressed me. If our hunch about Rod was true, then Sara, who had lived with him all these years, had to have known he was a con artist. Was it easier to go along with him than fight him? Or was she the one who ran the grift?

Derek scooped the eggs onto our plates, gave us both two slices of bacon and half of the English muffin, grabbed jam and salsa from the fridge, and came and sat down across from me.

"This looks wonderful, Derek."

"It should fortify us for a few hours."

We enjoyed our meal in silence for a minute or two, then I glanced up at him. "Based on Mitch's description, we're assuming the guy who tried to break in was Thuggy."

"That's safe to say."

"So how does he know I still have it? I might've already given it to the police."

Derek looked at me. "But more importantly, why did he pick last night to try and break in? Did he know we wouldn't be home?"

Disgusted, I set down my coffee mug. "If he knew that, then Rod had to be the one who told him. I knew it. I knew he was trouble from the very start. And now he's trying to get me killed! We have to call Inspector Lee."

"I called her last night and told her what I'd learned—which wasn't much. I also mentioned that if she didn't put a tail on Rod, then I would."

"My hero."

"And you're mine," he said simply.

I beamed at him. "Let's call Inspector Lee right now. I'll tell her I'm bringing the book with me to the Covington, which is what I was planning to do anyway. I don't have time to appraise it so I'm going to ask Ian to do it. I want to know what it's worth after being tampered with."

Derek called on his phone and she picked up after the first ring. "Don't you two have better things to do with your day?"

"We do have some plans for later this afternoon, but right now we wanted to let you know that we're bringing the book with us to the Covington."

"Planning to use it as bait?"

"Well," I said, taken aback. "Sort of."

"That's a really bad idea, especially on your wedding day."

I explained that I had already decided to ask Ian to appraise the book while we were on our honeymoon. But just how we would actually bait the hook would take some planning.

She sighed. "Look, I have the afternoon off because I'm going to the wedding of two crazy people. But I'll try to get a patrol car over there, just to be safe. Just, you know, don't do anything stupid."

We talked for another few minutes, then Derek thanked her and ended the call.

I glanced at my wristwatch. I had planned to give Derek the Shakespeare book this morning, but now I realized it would be better to wait and give it to him tonight after we got home. After we were married. The thought made me smile.

"Is it getting late?" he asked.

"Yes. It's almost nine and I have to be at the Covington at noon. It'll take me at least an hour to get ready, so realistically we have about one hour to figure out how to bait the hook." I looked at him. "Is that enough time to catch a killer?"

"When it's us doing the catching, my love," Derek said, lifting his coffee cup in a toast, "more than enough."

After I cleaned up the kitchen, I made a few phone calls. First I called my mother to make sure the family was awake and feeling good.

"We're in the hotel coffee shop with Meg and John and we're all perfectly healthy and happy. You should be soaking in a tub and fluffing yourself up, not worrying about us."

"Mother, I've never fluffed myself up in my life. I don't even know what that means. But look, making sure you're happy is one of the things that helps me relax. So actually I'm doing both."

"That makes perfect sense in the weirdest possible way. I love you, sweetie. See you soon."

Next, I contacted my bridesmaid wrangler and best friend, Robin. "Everything okay with you guys?"

She laughed. "Austin and I are sitting in the booth next to your parents. I know you must be freaking out because you're wasting precious time making dumb phone calls."

"They're not dumb," I insisted. "They're important to my peace of mind."

She snorted. "Hang up the phone and go do something fun. Like pack for your honeymoon."

"I'm already packed."

"I've never understood how we got to be friends. You're such a pain. See you later."

"Love you. Don't be late. You're in charge of everything."

"I know. I've already talked to the caterers and the flower people. Ian was there early to open up the Covington and let them into the garden and the kitchen and the banquet room. The cake is there, too, sitting on a shelf in the walk-in refrigerator. Laura, our hair and makeup lady, will meet us at noon in Ian's office, hereinafter known as the girls' dressing room. The photographer and his crew will also be there at noon to start shooting ambient shots of the grounds and the views, then he'll come to the girls' dressing room at one o'clock. The musicians will set up at two o'clock in the garden and the DJ will show up promptly at four."

"So you've been slacking off." I smiled as I pictured her rolling her eyes.

"Yes. That's why I have to hang up now."

"I love you."

"Shut up. I love you. Good-bye."

I took a quick moment to remember everything Robin had just said. She had been my best friend since we were eight years old and I couldn't have loved her more than I did right at this moment. This was going to be the most beautiful day ever.

After that I started on the not-so-fun calls. First I contacted Rod and left a message for him. Then I reached Heather's voice mail and left a similar message. My hope was that in case Rod didn't get the message, Heather might run into him and tell him.

I checked my watch again and walked into Derek's office, where he was staring at some diagram. San Francisco sunshine streamed in through the windows and lit the room up like a painting. While I studied Derek, I noticed what *he* was studying. It had taken me a moment to realize it was the layout for the Covington Library.

"Are you really memorizing the layout of our wedding venue?"

"Of course. You never know when you'll have to access a different route in or out."

I tipped my head to one side and smiled. "This is just something you do, isn't it? You never know when someone will attack. Did you do it for our dinner last night?"

He smiled blandly, but said nothing.

Of course he did and of course he wouldn't admit to it. Derek was all about security—especially when it came to me. And I loved that about him.

"That's okay," I said. "I don't want to know. I mean, I do, but . . . never mind."

"Did you need something, love?"

I had to think. "Oh yeah, I was thinking we've got just enough time to run over to the conference center and see if Rod is working in his booth. I left him a message but I'd really like to see him in person so we'll know that he took the bait, and then wait for him to contact Thuggy and Leon."

He grinned at my nicknames, but then sobered. "I'd rather not take a chance on being late for our own wedding. Why don't I call Inspector Lee and ask if she has time to pay Rod a visit?"

I frowned. "But will she agree to bait the hook for us?"

He set his cell phone down. "Good question. She already knows what we plan to do and she doesn't approve. So whether or not she'll agree to take an active part in the deception is an uncertainty. But it doesn't hurt to ask."

"And maybe she'll come up with a better idea."

"Excellent point." He picked up his cell phone again. "Let's see how she reacts."

He placed the call and she answered right away. Derek explained our idea and she started laughing.

"So is that a no?" I asked.

"No, that's a *big, fat no.* Let me explain. First of all, I'm a cop. So there's no way in hell I would ever go along with this. And second of all, you're my friends. I'd never want to be responsible for sending a possible killer to your wedding. Do you get that?"

"We do," Derek said amiably. "Thank you for being sensible."

She laughed. "You guys don't make it easy."

Derek and she talked for another minute and then he ended the call. "She's right, love. Let's not incite any negativity on our wedding day."

"You're right and so is she. Besides, I already left cryptic messages where I could, so that'll have to do."

Derek stood and gave me a kiss and we held each other for a moment. "We're going to have a wonderful day."

"I know." I checked my watch for the hundredth time and

winced. "I don't know why I thought we'd have plenty of time to visit Rod. If I don't go take a shower right now, I won't be ready in time." Mainly because I knew I would come up with a dozen other things I needed to do before we finally left for the Covington.

He gave me another quick kiss. "Go ahead and get ready."

"Okay." I started to stroll out, then snapped my fingers. "I almost forgot the book. I'll go get it."

I jogged down the hall to the closet safe and pulled *The Three Musketeers* from the inner chest. Dashing to my workshop, I found a padded envelope and slipped the book into it, then returned to Derek's office. "Here you go. Will you be sure to ask Ian to put it somewhere safe?"

"Yes, love." He checked his phone for the time.

"I'm going, I'm going."

"Good," he said, grinning, then pushed a button on his phone. "I'll just check in with Corinne one more time."

I walked out of his office shaking my head. I still couldn't believe we were trying to solve a murder and get married at practically the same time. Was this really how I wanted to spend my wedding day? Was I staring into the future? Would our lives always be like this?

I turned and gazed at Derek, sitting at his desk talking intently to his assistant, Corinne, while looking so smart and masculine and dangerous and sexy. And my only thought was, *I wouldn't have it any other way.*

Chapter Eleven

My friend Ian and the Covington Library had pulled out all the stops for our wedding. The rose garden was more lush and verdant than I'd ever seen it before. Flowers were bursting into bloom everywhere you looked, and I wondered if Ian had secretly brought in hundreds of extra plants just for the occasion.

Months ago, Ian and I had spent an afternoon strolling around the extensive grounds and we had agreed that the Shakespeare herb garden, with its winding brick paths, wooden benches, wonderful Celtic knot shrubbery, and perimeter of bay laurel trees, would be the perfect spot for afternoon cocktails and hors d'oeuvres following the ceremony in the rose garden.

Checking it out now, I was pleased to see that the caterers had set up two full-service bars on either side of the garden. There were small tables with chairs scattered throughout the expanse. Later on, a phalanx of servers would be circulating through the crowd carrying trays of yummy appetizers along with our signature cocktail—Twisted Honey—as well as glasses of champagne and white wine. The red wine would be served later at the sit-down dinner, thereby decreasing tenfold the chances of having someone spill red wine on my white dress. I had to admit that the red-wine-spillage scare was a particularly chilling wedding nightmare that I'd experienced twice now. I had seen so much wine spilled in my lifetime, I knew it could happen anywhere, anytime.

It was noon and the weather was still wonderful. I gazed out at the views of the Golden Gate Bridge, the bay, and the green hills beyond, and didn't catch a hint of fog. I didn't know how long that would last, but I prayed that the blue skies would hold out until the weather cooled and we all went inside for dinner.

I took a deep breath and felt myself tremble. Everything was so beautiful, simply perfect. My stomach tingled at the thought and I immediately wondered if I was jinxing anything by being so utterly happy for this day.

I didn't believe in jinxes, did I? Of course not.

Reluctantly I left the gardens. Pulling open the heavy iron door, I walked back through the elegant side foyer with its wide black-and-white-checkerboard marble floor and entered the main exhibit hall. It was empty now, so I stole a moment to enjoy the quiet and visit a few of my favorite displays. Walt Whitman's handwritten letters to his publisher. The vibrantly illuminated manuscript of Chaucer's *Canterbury Tales*. John Lennon's original drawings.

I'd spent so many wonderful hours in the Covington Library that it felt exactly right for Derek and me to start the next chapter of our lives here. I sighed a little at the wealth of knowledge and beauty within these walls. The room was a stunning tribute to books and ephemera as well as to architecture, with its deeply coffered ceiling, its Frank Lloyd Wright–inspired sconces, and its floral-patterned wrought-iron railings that lined the second- and third-floor walkways.

"Visiting old friends?"

I turned. "Ian." I ran and gave him a big hug. "Hello, old friend."

"Hey, I'm not that old."

I laughed. "No, you're not. You look like a teenager."

"Let's not get carried away."

"But it's true."

He looked so handsome in his suit and tie. I had ordered a yellow boutonniere for him and it looked wonderful with his gold-and-green-striped silk tie. Ian had been my brother Austin's friend all through college. At some point, the two of us met and decided we were perfect for each other. We started dating and even got engaged for a brief time, until we realized we were great friends, but not in love. A few years later, Ian announced that he was gay and now he had a wonderful husband and was blissfully happy.

I slipped my arm through his and we strolled down the hall. "I love it here. Thank you so much for doing this for me and Derek."

"I couldn't be happier that you wanted to have your wedding here."

We walked down the wide corridor that led to Ian's suite of offices. I was pleased to see that a no-nonsense security guard was posted and waiting by the door at the end of the hallway.

"Hello," I said.

"This is Gerald," Ian said.

"Good afternoon, Miss Wainwright." He pushed the door open for me and tipped his hat. "I hope you have a wonderful day."

"Thank you, Gerald." Ian walked with me inside the large outer office, where we bypassed all the desks and office equipment and headed for Ian's private office. This was where my girlfriends and I would spend a few hours before the ceremony dressing and fixing our hair and makeup.

He gave me a kiss on the cheek, wished me all the happiness in the world, and walked out as I entered his personal sanctum sanctorum. I was still amazed and very grateful that he had so willingly turned over his office to me and my bridesmaids. There were priceless works of art everywhere you looked and a floor-to-ceiling bookshelf holding the most rare and expensive books imaginable. I had a feeling if you tried to walk out with just one of those books, mild-mannered Gerald would have you facedown on the floor and in handcuffs in seconds.

The room was large enough that two separate sets of comfortable couches and chairs had been grouped together for conversations or interviews or for guests to sit and chat. There was also room for a small conference table and a huge mahogany desk, of course, where Ian plotted daily to collect the great books of the universe.

There were two doors subtly disguised in the richly paneled wall. One was a small closet and the other led to a large executive bathroom with full-length mirrors, several vanity tables, and even a fainting couch. Ian had explained that his office was occasionally the scene of intimate parties for the library's biggest donors. Thus the vanities and fainting couch. I once asked him if rich people fainted when they gave away money, but he wouldn't explain.

But this was the first time Ian's office would be used by a bridal party for a wedding. He seemed perfectly happy knowing that his sacred office space was about to be transformed, as he put it, into the Girl Zone.

I found my dress and veil hanging in the closet. My suitcase was on the floor and I dragged it out to the coffee table and opened it. Inside I found my carefully packed shoes, my jewelry, boxes of goodies for my bridesmaids, and all the other necessities I would need for the day, along with my makeup and some clips for my hair. I gave a silent prayer of thanks that Robin and Alex had accomplished so much while I was busy giving speeches at the library convention.

Alone for the moment, I thought back to Derek kissing me good-bye at our front door less than an hour ago.

"I won't see you again until I walk down the aisle," I'd said wistfully.

"I can stop by Ian's office to say hello."

Alarmed, I said, "No, you really can't. You're not allowed to see me in my wedding dress until the ceremony. It's bad luck."

He gave me his most tolerant smile and ran his hands up and down my arms. "That's ridiculous."

"My mother will be there, you know. Do you really want her waving a smoldering sage stick at you to clear the vibes?"

"You make a good point, love."

"Let me paint a clearer picture." I took a deep breath and let it out slowly. "You only have brothers, so maybe you weren't aware of this hard-and-fast rule. So here's the deal. You don't get to see me in my wedding dress because my mother will kill you."

"Ah." He grinned and kissed me again. "Now that makes perfect sense."

"Thank you." I kissed him back. "I love you."

I heard someone laughing outside Ian's office and I went to see who it was. Robin and my sister China were just walking into the outer office, followed by my other two sisters, London and Savannah. London looked petite and polished, as always. Savannah was bald and beautiful, as always. A few years ago she had shaved her hair in solidarity with a girlfriend who had cancer and the look suited her so well that she kept it. I was almost certain that her bald noggin was the reason Dalton fell in love with her at first sight.

"Hi, girls," I said. "Come on in."

"It's like we haven't seen you in hours," Robin said, smirking.

Savannah gave me a hug. "You do know that we've been here for two hours, right?"

I blinked. "Where have you been?"

"Robin had lists for all of us," London said. "I worked with the flower people, making sure all the flowers had arrived, and arranged the boutonnieres and bouquets in the refrigerator."

"And I was forced to approve the cake and other desserts," Savannah explained with a world-weary sigh.

Robin was gleeful. "There were cookies."

"And they needed taste-testers," China added with a grin.

"You give and you give," I said, laughing. "Thank you for helping."

"Don't close the door," Robin said. "Your mom and Meg are right behind us."

I snuck a peek out the door. "Did you see Alex out there?"

"She'll be here in a few minutes," Robin said. "She's handling the guest book, right?"

"Right. With Gabriel." I had made the guest book by hand and it was beautiful if I did say so myself. I had even gone so far as to coordinate the book cover with the color of Alex's dress, which she seemed to get a kick out of.

"I hope they won't have to work too hard to get people to sign it," I added. "I would hate to see Gabriel having to strong-arm someone who neglects to sign their name."

"Guest book duty is harder than it sounds," Robin warned. "Some people will pick up the book and carry it around with them. It's like they can't think of something pithy to write on the spur of the moment so they want to keep it with them until brilliance strikes." She had married my brother last year so I suppose she knew what she was talking about. She glanced around the room. "I think we need champagne."

As if on cue, Meg walked into the room carrying two bottles of lovely French champagne. "Good morning, ladies!"

"This is going to be too much fun!" Mom said, holding up a shopping bag filled with snacks and chocolate bars.

I had to laugh as I set out the piles of goodies on the sideboard. London found glasses in one of Ian's elegant cabinets and began to pour.

"Should we lock the door?" China asked. "The men are just down the hall."

I grinned. "No, Gerald the guard will protect us."

Within a few minutes, as always happened when more than two women got together with a couple of bottles of champagne, the decibel level rose to ear-bleed levels. I wasn't about to say anything because Mom was right, I was having too much fun. I just hoped the walls were soundproof because the poor dogs in this neighborhood were going to go crazy if they had to listen to us shouting and shrieking with laughter for the next hour.

My hairdresser, Laura, arrived and set up shop at the bathroom vanity. We propped the door open so everyone could walk in and out and watch if they wanted to. After touching up Mom and Meg's makeup, Laura went to work on me. She fashioned a soft braid across the back of my head, pulling selected strands out to curl and fall around my neck in sexy profusion. Those were her words, but they were pretty accurate, if I did say so myself. She tucked tiny bits of baby's breath through the braid and added a diamond barrette on one side. I would wear a veil for the ceremony and then remove it for the party, but for now, I was beyond thrilled.

"Wow." I stared at myself in the mirror. "You are an artistic genius."

"Thank you for noticing." Laura smiled. "Yes, I am."

I was starting to wonder where the photographer was, when I noticed that my mother was crying.

"Mom, what's wrong? What happened? Are you in pain?"

"Oh, Brooklyn. You look stunning," she said, sniffling.

"Don't cry, Mom. You're going to ruin your pretty makeup." I grabbed a tissue and handed it to her. "More importantly, you know that if you keep crying, I'll be forced to join you. And that would be disastrous."

She dabbed her nose with the tissue. "You were always a beautiful girl, sweetie, but now you look like a fairy princess come to life. Simply breathtaking."

"I don't even have my dress on."

"It's your hair," Meg said, and now she was sniffling, too.

"Thank you, Meg. But don't you start crying, too."

I was afraid there might be a chain reaction so I looked around for Robin. My best friend from age eight would have a good laugh with me over all this tear-jerking nonsense. I spied her sitting on the couch, bent over, slipping on her high heels.

"Hey, Robin," I called. "Can you come in here?"

She didn't sit up, wouldn't make eye contact. "Not just now."

I was taken aback. "Why not?"

Then I heard her sniffling.

"Oh no. No, you can't be crying." It was frankly horrifying. The natural order of life on the planet had gone dangerously askew. "Stop that."

She smiled through her tears. "It's just . . . you look . . . really great."

"You're just upset because I didn't wear my Birkenstocks like I threatened to do." I tapped my champagne glass and raised my voice. "Attention, everyone, I have an announcement to make. We have hired the most expensive hair and makeup artist in San Francisco, and once she's finished with your makeup, you are not,

I repeat, *not* allowed to cry. Or make me cry." I wagged my finger at Robin. "That goes double for you, missy."

Robin chuckled and sniffled at the same time. "It's okay, I haven't had my makeup done yet."

"Fine," I said imperiously. "You may cry."

Now she laughed. "Thank you, Princess."

My hairdresser grinned. "I'm not the most expensive in town, but I'm close."

"You're worth it. I look amazing."

"Yes, you do." She began to apply a thin layer of foundation on my cheeks. "I think I've only got a few more of the ladies to make up. Once I'm finished with everyone, I'll help you put your dress on."

"Thank you, Laura. I need all the help I can get." My dress wasn't particularly elaborate or heavy, but I knew I needed help with the zipper. And I was liable to rip it to shreds if I stepped into it the wrong way. And then I would be the one crying.

Fifteen minutes later, Laura gazed at me in the mirror. "Wow, you should wear makeup more often, Brooklyn. You look like a beauty queen."

I stared at myself. The makeup had been applied subtly, just enough to highlight my best aspects and give me a bit of what she called her patented "blushing bride glow."

"This is mind-blowing," I murmured.

"My work here is done," Laura said with a laugh. "Who's next?"

I heard my cell phone ringing and glanced at the screen to see who was calling. It was an out-of-state number but I recognized the area code. "Hello?"

"This is Virginia Hawthorne, the collections librarian at Glen Cove College, returning your call."

"Thank you so much for calling me back, Ms. Hawthorne."

"I was in the office catching up on some paperwork, otherwise you wouldn't have heard from me until Tuesday."

"I'm grateful for this chance to talk to you. You've probably already heard from Rod Martin, but I wanted to follow up just in case."

"No," she said. "I haven't heard from Rod, but Cornelia called to tell me about poor Sara. She was one of my dearest friends and I still can't believe it."

"I know. I'm so sorry."

She took a deep breath. "Thank you. But about your message. It left me with a few questions."

I scowled. "I'll bet it did." I explained that I was a librarian, too, and a bookbinder. I told her that Sara had given me a finely bound copy of *The Three Musketeers* as a bridal gift and what I had subsequently discovered inside the book.

I could hear her typing on her computer. "If it's the book I'm thinking of, it's been missing from our collection for over a year."

"Oh dear," I said, stunned. After I assured her that the book would be returned to the college once the murder investigation was completed, Virginia thanked me.

"We've had an alarming number of antiquarian books stolen in the last few years," she explained. "We finally narrowed down the possible suspects and, unfortunately, Sara was one of them. We hired an investigator to look into it, but we haven't received his report yet."

Hmm. That was interesting. "Is your investigator an ex-FBI agent named Roy Mattingly?"

"That's his name although I don't know his background. He was hired by our head of campus security."

"Ah." I thought for a moment. Was there something else the investigator was looking into? "I know it's an imposition, but would you mind calling me when you get the results of his investigation? I feel as though I have a connection to the case now and I would love to know the outcome."

"I don't mind at all." She chuckled. "We librarians have to stick together, right?"

"That's right," I said, pleased with myself for mentioning that I was a librarian, too.

She sighed. "I would hate to think that Rod had anything to do with this. He's such a nice guy."

I rolled my eyes. "Yes, isn't he?"

We finished the call and I absently reached for my champagne glass. I went back over everything Virginia had said, and knew that Derek would want to hear about it. I set the glass down. "I've got to talk to Derek."

"Sweetie, no," Mom said. "It's bad luck. You'll see him soon enough."

"Okay, Mom, you win." I stared at my phone and realized that I could text Derek, but that seemed like a waste of time.

There was too much to tell him and I would see him in a little while anyway. The information could wait.

He's such a nice guy.

If you only knew, I thought. Would a nice guy kill his wife? Not that I had any proof that he was the culprit yet, but it seemed like the most likely possibility.

But again, I had to wonder why. Why would Rod kill Sara? I suppose there were plenty of reasons for a husband to kill his wife, but if the conversation he'd had with Cornelia was to be believed, Sara might have been at the heart of the whole forgery thing.

I perched on the arm of the couch and sipped champagne while Laura finished touching up everyone's hair and makeup. When she was ready to help me with my dress, I opened the hanging bag and fell in love all over again. It was lace with a bateau neckline and lacy cap sleeves that barely covered my shoulders. For some reason, I found those little cap sleeves the most adorable thing. The dress was fitted from the neckline to the waist, where hundreds of tiny crystals gleamed and reflected the light. From there it flowed to the floor in thin layers of lace and chiffon satin.

The girls oohed and aahed enough to convince me that I'd made the right choice.

I had never thought much about wedding dresses until around six months ago when I was forced to try on at least three dozen. Until then, I had been certain I didn't even want a white dress. So much for thinking I knew what I wanted. It was true what they said, that you would know the perfect dress as soon as you slipped it on.

Staring at myself in the mirror now, I acknowledged that this was indeed the perfect dress for me. And I smiled at the thought that Derek would freak out when he got his first look at me. And wouldn't that be a nice moment? I couldn't wait.

Alex walked in just then and stared at me. "You are stunning. Look at those arms. I am so proud of you."

I tried not to tear up as I gave her a hug. "I have you to thank for these arms. And the fact that my shoes fit."

"Hallelujah," she said with a laugh.

"Wow," London said, turning to Alex. "I want arms like hers. How do I sign up with you?"

"Me, too," China said. "You need to open a gym in Dharma." She held her own arms out to examine them. "My arms look like chicken legs. I want some definition."

"I'll give you the names of a few trainers up there."

"Bless you."

Alex glanced over at me. "I'm going to go check on things out there. I'll report back."

"Thank you," I said, relieved that someone was willing to keep me posted.

The photographer arrived and started snapping pictures with me and my bridesmaids. He took some with my mom and some of me with Mom and Meg. They had both chosen dresses in shades of dark blue that complemented each other perfectly. And I was thrilled with how gorgeous my bridesmaids looked in their dresses. Naturally I'd had some help with that from Robin and my sisters. In other words, they had chosen their own dresses rather than leaving it up to me. I understood, having lived most of my life in a fashion-free zone. All I had asked was that they stick to the silvery blue shade I'd fallen in love with at the bridal shop.

So Savannah had chosen a short, sexy, sleeveless lacy sheath while China and London's choices were more ethereal with a layer of soft chiffon flowing from the waist to the knee. China's version was short-sleeved while London's featured long lacy sleeves that hugged and silhouetted her supple arms. Both of them looked simply beautiful.

Robin's dress was something only she could've pulled off. The top was form-fitting knit in the same silvery blue color and the matching short taffeta skirt was flouncy and adorable. "The better to dance all night," she'd said when she chose it.

Together we had accomplished the impossible, because somehow the same color flattered everyone and it warmed my heart to see my sisters and best friend so happy wearing the styles they preferred.

The florist came into the room with our bouquets and corsages and there was more cooing over the beautiful job she had done. I was carrying a cascading white bouquet of ranunculus, peonies, roses, calla lilies, and orchids with bits of greenery for contrast. My bridesmaids held smaller arrangements with the same white flowers with a sprinkling of pale blue sage buds that looked perfect with their blue dresses.

Meanwhile, the photographer was shooting candid shots of the group, so I took a moment to rummage through the closet and pull out my cell phone to check the time—and yes, check for messages. We still had thirty minutes before we were to head for the side foyer, where we would wait for the ceremony to begin. Time was beginning to slow down.

"Getting antsy?" Robin asked.

"I guess so. It's the calm before the storm, right?"

"Yep." She grinned. "The whirlwind is about to begin. Might as well chill for a few minutes, because you won't be able to relax until much later tonight."

"I guess it's time to take care of a very important bridal obligation."

She frowned. "What are you talking about?"

I walked over to my suitcase and pulled out a little shopping bag. I reached in, pulled out a little blue box, and handed it to Robin. "Don't open it yet." Then I went around the room and gave my three sisters similar blue boxes. "Okay, you can open them."

"I'm just happy to have this little blue box," China said.

"It's pretty special," I said, grinning. "But what's inside is even better."

They opened their gifts at the same time and I was thrilled when they all started squealing with joy.

"It's beautiful."

"I'm going to wear it right now."

"This is so sweet," Robin said, and gave me a little peck on the cheek. "Thank you."

"You're welcome. Wear it in good health and happiness."

London held up her hand to admire the bracelet. "This is so lovely."

I laughed. "You sound surprised."

She winced a little. "I sort of thought you might give us books."

My mouth gaped open. "Would I do that to you?"

"Uh, yeah," Savannah said.

I chuckled. "I thought about it, but I knew you would take turns stabbing me if I showed up with books."

"True."

Alex walked back into the room. "Everything is running like clockwork."

"Wonderful." I pulled another blue box from the bag and handed it to her. "Thank you for everything you've done for me."

"What? No. I'm not . . ."

"You have been my savior and my friend."

She sniffled as she stared at the little box.

"No!" I cried. "No tears. Especially not you. Remember your black belts."

She laughed. "All right." She sniffed one last time and opened the box. Lifting the delicate silver bracelet, she whispered, "Oh, Brooklyn. It couldn't be more perfect."

She slipped it on and gave me a careful hug. "You didn't need to . . ."

"Shh," I said. "Yes, I did. Thank you."

Mom was sniffling again. "I'm going to need to redo my makeup."

"I'm standing by," Laura called from the other room, and we all laughed.

After the gifts were all distributed, we still had some time to kill. Since I didn't want to sit down in my dress, I nudged Robin. "Walk with me."

The two of us paced slowly around the spacious room. "You hit a home run with those bracelets," she said. "They're perfect."

"I'm so glad. I'd been thinking about them for a long time and I'm happy everyone likes them."

"Really? A long time?"

I sighed and hung my head. "I ran out yesterday and found them. My original plan really was to give everyone books."

"That's the girl I know," she said, laughing.

We strolled another few steps around the room. "Have you been down the hall to see Derek or Austin or any of the men?"

"Not since we waved good-bye to each other out in the hallway." Robin stopped, reached for my hands, and gave them a squeeze. "Won't be long now."

I laughed. "You make it sound almost ominous."

"Oh, no. It's going to be the most wonderful day you've ever had."

I laid my head on her shoulder. "Thank you."

There was a sudden spurt of shouting outside the door and I heard the sound of heavy footsteps running down the hall. Then a voice shouted, "Hey, don't go in there! Stop!"

I straightened up. "What in the world?"

Chapter Twelve

"What's going on out there?" I said, feeling a cold chill that had nothing to do with the weather.

Alex came running over. "I'll check it out."

She would know what to do, I thought. Alex had served in the Balkans during her time in the military. "Good. We need to—"

All of a sudden the door was thrown open and two men stormed in carrying guns. They were dressed in the same security guard uniforms that Gerald wore. How they'd managed to find the uniforms was a good question, but I guessed that they had probably snuck in through the service entrance and found a utility closet filled with them.

"Stay calm," the taller one shouted, "and no one gets hurt."

My sister London screamed, then slapped her hand over her mouth. Her eyes were so wide and filled with fear I instantly regretted thinking we would all be perfectly safe here—or anywhere.

"What do you want?" Robin yelled, her outrage overcoming her fear in the moment.

But I knew what they wanted. I recognized them both. It was Thuggy and Leon—and they wanted the book.

I scanned the room quickly, trying to make eye contact with everyone, willing them all to stay quiet and remain as calm as they possibly could. I looked around once more and realized that my mother and Meg were gone. Had they slipped away while I was pacing the floor with Robin?

I'd definitely heard shouting in the hall, but had it been loud enough for Derek and the other men to hear? Was Gerald the guard hurt? What about Mom or Meg?

The two men glanced around the room and zeroed in on me.

"She's the one," Thuggy said.

"Don't shoot the bride!" London cried.

"It's okay, honey," I said, trying without much success to soothe my sister's nerves. "Everyone stay cool."

"Listen to her," Thuggy said menacingly.

"What do you want?" I asked, stalling because I knew very well that they wanted the darn book. And I knew why they had come to the Covington to look for it. Because Rod had taken the bait and told them I would be bringing the book with me. *But you left the same message with Heather,* I thought suddenly. What if she was the one who told them?

"What do you think?" Thuggy said. "We want the book."

"I don't have it here." I waved both of my arms at myself. "I'm getting married."

"Whatever," he groused. "We know you brought the book with you. Just hand it over and nobody gets hurt."

"I told you I don't have it with me. Why would I?"

Thuggy looked at Leon, who shrugged and waved his gun, trying to look more dangerous. He succeeded.

"You do realize that my fiancé is right down the hall. He is licensed to kill in twenty-seven countries and is the premier security expert in the world." I was making a few of those numbers up, but they didn't have to know that.

Leon looked worried now and elbowed Thuggy. But Thuggy wouldn't be dissuaded. His teeth were clenched. "Just give me the book."

"I told you I don't have it. Look, just let everyone go, and I'll take you to my house and give it to you myself."

His laugh was raspy. "We aren't that dumb. We know you have the book and nobody leaves this room until we get it."

"Yeah, it's like you're all collateral," Leon said with a snicker.

"Collateral, really?" Savannah plopped both hands on her hips. "What's the plan? Hold us hostage until someone brings you the stupid book?"

"Savannah . . ." I didn't need my sister giving these two any ideas.

"Your timing sucks, by the way," Robin said defiantly. "She's getting married in an hour."

"And like she told you, her fiancé is deadly," London said.

"And two of his brothers are British spies," China added. "Derek used to be one, too, right, Brooklyn?"

"And there's Dalton," Savannah chimed in. "He's Derek's brother and my partner and he's got the head of the CIA on speed dial."

Thuggy stared at her and shook his head. "You're bald."

"You must be the brains of the outfit," Savannah said, her voice dripping with scorn. "Yeah, I'm bald, but I can grow my hair back and you'll still be stuck in Stupidville."

"For heaven's sake," Robin snorted, "did you really think you'd waltz in here and have a bunch of poor, cowering women at your feet?"

Leon snorted. "She got you good, man."

"Shut up," Thuggy snarled.

I glanced at Alex, saw her grinning, and almost laughed out loud. I had thought I would need to calm them down, but it turned out that my bridesmaids had nerves of fricking steel.

Thuggy waved his gun at me. "And all you women can just clam up now, except for you." He sneered at me. "Give me the book. Did you hide it in here somewhere? Is it in your purse or something? Where is it?"

"Maybe you should search the room," Savannah suggested sweetly.

China added, "Yes, we can wait."

"I told you all to clam up."

"And we all take orders so well," Robin said drolly.

Leon glanced around nervously. "Hey, man, she didn't tell us we'd be barging in on a wedding."

She? I stared at him, dumbfounded, wondering if I'd heard him correctly. But I knew I wasn't mistaken. So it was Heather all along. She had to have been in cahoots with Rod this whole time. It made me sick, but I had to maintain my cool.

"Who cares?" Thuggy growled. "I want that book."

"Look around you," Robin said. "There are hundreds of rare, expensive books in this room. Grab a couple and get out of here."

I almost gasped at the idea, but she was right. "Yes, take whatever you want. Just please leave us alone."

"Come on, man," Leon whined. "The big mouth has a point. Let's do what she says and go. It's gotta be some kind of bad luck to shoot a bride."

"Big mouth?" Robin echoed. "He called me a big mouth?"

"I'm sure it's not personal," China said, grinning.

"I paid good money for that book," Thuggy insisted, "and I don't like being swindled."

"You were more than swindled, pal," I said, gulping down the bile that my anger was stirring up. "Rod Martin had that book altered to look older and more rare than it really is. He charged you more money than it was worth and now you're out both the money and the book."

Robin almost looked impressed. "Wow, looks like you've been conned times two."

"But fine," I said with a shrug. "You still want the book. My fiancé has it. I'll just text him and he'll bring it."

Leon smacked Thuggy's arm. "The book's a fake. Now what?"

"It's still worth money," Thuggy insisted. "So we get it from the fiancé and then we track down that double-dealing louse, Martin. He's going to pay for this."

"Did y'all forget the part where Derek is licensed to kill?" Robin asked.

I sighed and walked over to the sideboard, looking for my phone and silently cursing Heather and Rod. They had taken our bait, but instead of showing up themselves, they had sent these creeps to find me. I could see how these two clowns had gotten into the library in the first place in those security guard uniforms. But I couldn't worry about that now. I just wished I had something I could throw at them, because there was no way I was going to let them walk out of here and get away scot-free. I would make sure they paid for scaring us half to death, waving guns and making threats. I stared at my phone, then back at Thuggy. "Shall I text my fiancé?"

He scowled. "Just wait a minute."

I shot a look at Alex and then gave the bookshelf a sideways glance. Did I dare throw books at them? I just needed to divert their attention long enough for someone like Alex to run out and get help. I could always repair the books if the spines were severed or the covers broke off.

Without warning, two streaks of blue came charging out of the bathroom, whooping and shrieking as they attacked both men from behind. Thuggy was pushed to the floor and my mother began to pistol-whip his head with a hair dryer.

"Mother!" London screamed.

China shouted, "Hey, that's Mom. Give 'em hell, Mom!"

Robin jumped in to help Meg take down Leon, while Savannah kicked Thuggy.

"Be careful, Meg!" I shouted, then cringed at the way she was beating Leon with a shower brush. When he managed to roll over, she used some of Lauren's fabulous hairspray, got him right in the eyes, and he screamed like a little girl.

I tried to step in and help her, but then a gunshot went off and I shouted, "No!"

For two seconds we all held our breath in silence, then Mom pushed herself up off the floor and straightened her dress. "I think he shot himself in the foot. What a dope."

"Oof!" That came from Leon, who was still tangling with Meg. The rest of us jumped to her defense and began hitting him with anything we could find. Tears poured from his eyes thanks to the hairspray, but he was still fighting. Alex grabbed the brass bust of Mozart from Ian's end table and brought it down on Leon's head, finally knocking the guy out.

He was still writhing, though, so Savannah pulled up her sexy sheath dress and sat down on Leon's back to keep him on the floor. China grabbed the gun off the floor and pointed it at Thuggy, who was groaning from the bullet wound in his foot.

I looked around for Robin. "Go get Derek."

"No!" Mom shouted. "He can't see you in your wedding dress."

Meg grabbed hold of my arm. "We've got this, dear. I'll call the police. You needn't bother Derek."

I patted her shoulder. "You and Mom were awesome, Meg, but Derek will want to know about this." I met Robin's gaze. "Please?"

"Right." She headed for the door, but turned and glared at me. "Try to stay out of trouble while I'm gone."

Derek had heard the gunshot and arrived in seconds. He sounded as panicked as I'd felt a minute ago. Unfortunately I couldn't *see* him because my mother had banished me to the restroom and closed the door.

I could hear him, though, swearing furiously at the two men who had dared to attack us on our wedding day. His brothers and Gabriel were right behind him and helped carry the two bad guys out to the hall. Robin reported that Gerald had been knocked unconscious by the barrel of Thuggy's gun, but he would be fine. He apologized for not coming to our rescue but the crooks had bound and gagged him and shoved him into a closet. The police were on their way to drag the two men off to jail.

I shouted to Derek through the door. "The librarian from Sara's college returned my call. Rod never called her and they hired an investigator to look into a rash of missing books from their collection. She said that Sara was one of the suspects. And Heather is involved. I don't know how, but she is."

"So Rod lied about calling the school," Derek mused. "And Heather is somehow tangled up in it, too? Fascinating. I'll get Inspector Lee on the phone to track them down."

"Good," I said. "Because they're grifters *and* they're liars."

"And quite possibly murderers."

. . .

Once Derek left the room, Laura was called back to touch up our hair and makeup. After she was finished, I stared into the mirror to make sure my veil was straight.

"That was rather invigorating," Meg declared.

"It was," Mom said. "Although truth be told, I've never been so scared in my entire life."

I didn't care about my dress as I grabbed her in a ferocious hug. "If you ever do anything like that again, I'll . . . well, it won't be pretty."

"Oh, sweetie. Promise me that'll never happen again."

"I promise."

I saw tears forming in her eyes and shouted for Laura. "Makeup! Don't leave yet!"

"I'm right here," Laura said, waving a hairbrush in the air. "And I'm not leaving. This is the best wedding I've ever worked on."

"Yeah, we try to keep things exciting around here." I sighed as the adrenaline rush subsided.

"You do lead an interesting life," Robin admitted.

"What a day," I muttered, glancing in the mirror again. "And it's not even half over."

"Look on the bright side." China plucked an infinitesimal piece of lint from my shoulder. "The part where dangerous criminals attack the wedding party? You got that out of the way, so it should be smooth sailing from here on out."

I laughed. "You always were a glass-half-full kind of gal."

London sighed and rested her head on my shoulder. "You look so pretty, Brooklyn."

I was grateful for her changing the mood. "I think we all look fabulous."

"Can you believe I just sewed my hem this morning?" Meg said. "I'm lucky I didn't tear it out, tangling with that scoundrel."

"You and Mom were so courageous," I said, and gave her a big hug. "But don't you ever do that again. I'd much rather give up some silly book than have anyone get hurt."

She took a deep breath and blew it out. "Oh, but I feel revitalized. That was fun!"

"Oh, no," I moaned. "You and my mom really are twins separated at birth, aren't you?"

Everyone laughed and London said, "Tell us what happened, Meg. How did you decide to attack those two men?"

"We hid in the bathroom stall," Meg said. "We could hear every awful thing they were saying to you." She turned to me. "Honestly, Brooklyn, we couldn't let those horrible men have their way, so we plotted our attack."

"Wow," China said admiringly. "You really do sound just like Mom."

"That is a wonderful compliment, China." Meg patted her cheek. "Your mother is the best person I've ever met."

China's eyes began to water. London sniffled a few times and grabbed a tissue.

"Stop!" I said, feeling my own eyes about to fill with tears. "I can't take any more crying. Let's not talk about any of this until after I'm married."

Chapter Thirteen

"Don't be nervous, Brooklyn," London said, giving me a quick hug as we waited in the side foyer for our cue to start walking out the door to the ceremony.

I smiled. "I'm not nervous at all."

This was, without a doubt the most *right* thing I'd ever done in my life. It felt as though I'd been moving toward this moment with Derek since the first time I met him. He was perfect for me and I knew that our life together was going to be amazing. So nerves had no place here. All I felt was eager anticipation.

"I know," my sister said, a puzzled frown on her face. "There must be something wrong with you."

"It's a little irritating," China admitted. "When I got married I threw up all morning."

"Trust me," Savannah told her, "we all remember."

"And Brooklyn is so calm and cool. It's unnerving," China mused, watching me.

"Welcome to my world," Robin muttered, then grinned and grabbed my hand. "You ready, kiddo?"

"More than ready," I said, and laughed. I felt downright joyful. I couldn't wait to marry Derek.

My mother and Meg had already gone out to the garden to take their seats. Dad would be standing behind the chairs to walk with me down the aisle.

"May I have a moment with the bride?"

I whipped around. "Dad!"

"Hi, honey." He wrapped his arms around me and gave me a gentle squeeze. "I've never seen a more beautiful bride in my entire life."

I glanced around and noticed my bridesmaids had slipped into the hall to give me and Dad a few minutes alone. I chuckled. "Good thing no one else is around to hear you say that."

He gazed down at me. "All of my girls are beautiful, but I've honestly never seen anything more exquisite than you today."

"Dad, don't make me cry." I laid my head on his shoulder for a long moment.

"I'm afraid I'm making myself cry a little," he said, pulling a handkerchief from his pocket. "Your mother told me I would need this." He blew his nose and laughed. "She's always right."

"I love you, Dad."

"I love you, too, my darling girl." He grinned, his eyes still gleaming from the tears. "What do you say? Let's get this party started."

Dad walked out to the garden, and a minute later, the door opened again. At this rate, I would never be married.

"Hello, gracious."

I turned. "Oh, Robson. I'm so glad it's you."

Robson Benedict was my parents' guru and the head of the commune in Dharma where I had grown up. As a child I had called him Guru Bob, but now he was Robson, my good friend and a kind, lovely man. I was so happy that we had chosen him to perform our ceremony today.

"I had to take my turn wishing you well and happy, my dear." He gave me a warm hug and then gently held me by my shoulders. "I couldn't be more pleased that you and Derek have found joy together."

"Thank you, Robson."

After another quick hug, he said, "You look beautiful and the day is glorious. Savor it all."

"I will. Thank you."

He winked and turned to leave. "See you soon."

I smiled as Robin and my sisters joined me again. We heard the music begin and they all gave a little squeal.

"That's our cue," London said. She went out first, followed by China ten seconds later and then Savannah.

Robin turned and gave me a quick kiss on the cheek. "I'm so excited for you and Derek."

"Thank you, Robin." I pressed my forehead against hers. "I'm so happy you married Austin and officially became my sister."

She sniffed. "Oh great. Thanks for making me want to sob."

"No crying! Remember the makeup!" We both laughed, then Robin took a breath and squared her shoulders.

"Uh-oh, it's been more than ten seconds," she said. "Gotta go. See you soon."

I gave her a thumbs-up. "I'm right behind you."

As soon as the door closed behind her, I counted to ten slowly as I'd been instructed to do, then pushed the door open and walked out into the warm sunshine. Standing on the landing, my gaze went directly to the ribbon-and-rose-bedecked arbor at the other side of the garden, where Derek stood waiting. Over the heads of all our guests, I saw him staring back at me, looking a little dazed. I gave silent thanks for the beautiful dress and my pretty hair and everything else that had helped put that stunned look on his face. Even from this distance, I could see the love shining in his eyes and I knew my love was reflecting back at him. I was willing to bet we had never been happier than we were in this moment.

Gradually the rest of the scene came into focus and I glanced around at all the guests, who were standing and watching me, smiles lighting up their faces. My friends and family members all looked so happy to be sharing this moment with me, and I knew it was impossible for anyone in the world to be more overjoyed than I felt. I couldn't wipe the grin off my own face even if I tried.

I knew I had to take two steps down before I reached the ground. I had practiced going up and down these hard concrete steps in my three-inch lacy heels and now I told myself to be careful. But first I took one more quick moment to look around the garden, to stare out at the view, and to study the faces of my friends and family. I wanted to memorize this moment so I would never forget it. I saw my father standing and beaming at me from thirty feet away, ready to walk me down the aisle. Everyone in the crowd continued to smile as I prepared to move their way.

Then, as if in slow motion, their expressions turned to horror. A woman screamed. My father shouted, "No!"

What in the world? Had I suffered a wardrobe malfunction? Was my dress slipping off? Was my veil caught on something?

All of a sudden someone grabbed me from behind. He wrapped one arm around my neck and shouted, "Anyone comes close and I'll cut her."

That's when I felt the blade of a sharp knife pressing into my throat. I could smell the vague stench of fear and panic wafting up from my attacker. All I could see was the anguished face of my father. And then I knew.

"Rod," I said, and swore out loud. "Doesn't it figure you'd show up where you're not invited?"

Dad took a step and Rod yelled, "Stay back!"

Dad froze. His face had turned completely ashen and I knew he felt powerless to do anything. It broke my heart and in that moment I despised Rod Martin more than I'd ever hated anyone in my life.

"I'm okay," I said as loudly as I could manage, and gave my father a weak wave of my hand. "Don't worry, Dad."

Derek walked cautiously but purposefully up the aisle followed by his four brothers and my two. Inspector Lee marched right behind Austin and Jackson, her hand on the butt of her gun, still holstered. Gabriel and Alex followed closely behind her. My stalwart bridesmaids came, too, and my mother, Meg, and John. The rest of the crowd stayed where they were but remained watchful.

They all moved to get within twenty feet of us and together they formed the most impressive show of force I'd ever seen. I couldn't have been prouder to have them defending me. Unfortunately, I still had a knife shoved up against my throat, so it was a little early to be lauding my liberators.

"Don't come any closer," Rod said, clutching the knife more tightly.

From the corner of my eye I saw another man creeping toward us, and it threw me for a loop. It was the ex-FBI guy. What in the world was he doing here? Derek saw him, too, and flashed him a series of rapid hand signals. The guy responded in kind and remained partially hidden along the side of the building, out of the range of Rod's vision. If Rod caught sight of the guy, he might lose control of the knife. And I might die on my wedding day—before I could even get married!

That was when I snapped.

"Listen, you creep," I snarled. "You get one drop of blood on this dress and you're a dead man."

I was pleased that my voice sounded clear and deceptively calm despite the terror I was feeling inside. I knew my family shared that terror. Somehow I had to find a way to escape Rod's grip on me.

His laugh was hollow. "Shut up. You're in no position to make threats."

"You wanna bet?" I countered, letting my gaze skim across

the faces of everyone I loved. "Have you taken a good look around? You're seriously outnumbered."

"Yeah, but I've got you, don't I?"

"You really think so?"

It struck me that he finally sounded like the blowhard I had always suspected he was. It was almost refreshing to see that he had dropped the nice-guy act. It had never suited him.

"Who's the one holding the knife?"

"You're right, Rod. You're holding all the cards," I said carefully. My throat was growing drier by the minute, but I kept my gaze on Derek and found the strength to keep going. "But here's a word of warning. You cut me, you injure me in any way, and I guarantee you will not leave this place alive. My fiancé will kill you with his bare hands and then he'll pass your mangled, bloody carcass over to his brothers and mine. And then Inspector Lee will shoot you in the head. And then—"

"All right, all right," he said, and now his voice sounded a little unsure. As if everything I'd just said had gotten through to him. I hoped so, because the scenario I'd spelled out for him was just the beginning of what would happen to him if he hurt me in any way.

"I just want the damn book," he ground out. "Hand it over nice and easy and I'll be on my way."

"You know, you're not the first person to come here today wanting that book. Lenny and Squiggy showed up, too. Are those two knuckleheads friends of yours? Because I've got to say, they were kind of lame." I forced a laugh. "My mom and my mother-in-law beat the pants off of them."

"I don't know who you're talking about."

"Sure you do. The two guys who kept freaking you out at the conference?" I felt his hand at my throat tremble a little at the memory of those two men. "The tall hairy guy and the short bald one? Remember how you threw yourself at me and cried like a baby? They were threatening you, right? They wanted the book, too, probably because you'd promised to sell it to them."

Then I remembered something Thuggy had said. I glanced up and met his panicky gaze. "Oh, wait. You already had their money, didn't you? That's why they were so demanding and that's why you looked so nervous all the time. Did they threaten to kill you if you didn't give them the book? Because that tall guy is pretty scary-looking. No wonder you were so freaked out."

He didn't say anything, but then, he didn't have to.

"Funny story," I continued, despite my throat getting drier. "The tall scary dude shot himself in the foot while trying to fight off my mother. Isn't that crazy? We laughed anyway."

"Shut up."

"Oh, and my new mother-in-law nearly blinded the bald guy with hairspray. It was a great fight. I'm really sorry you missed it." I looked up at him again. "Because my family could have kicked your butt earlier, and right now, I'd be married and dancing with my husband."

Rod bared his teeth at me. "You know, you're just not that funny."

"And you're not that charming." I managed to smile. "You never were. And by the way, I think I'm a laugh riot, but never mind. You'll think about it later and laugh. All the way to jail, because that's where you're going. You killed Sara and now you're threatening to kill me. In front of about a million witnesses. And a San Francisco Police Department inspector. That's just not smart."

"Smart," he hissed, and I watched his jaw tighten. "You always thought you were so much smarter than me. Guess this proves you're not."

I laughed again as he lowered the knife a fraction of an inch. "Haven't you been listening? Actually, this just proves how stupid you really are."

"Brooklyn, love . . ." Derek muttered, sliding a bit closer to me and Rod.

"If that man touches my girl, I want three minutes with him. Alone," my dad announced.

Rod glanced at him and visibly winced when Inspector Lee assured my father, "You'll have them."

I heard the side foyer door open and someone in the crowd gasped.

"Let me go," a woman cried out from behind us. "I didn't do anything!"

"Heather?" I whispered.

"Look who I found lurking behind the door." It was Mitch, Derek's associate, and he was pulling a woman across the steps and down to the garden.

"Tell them, Rod," she insisted. "Tell them I'm not involved in any of this."

"Oh, shut up, Cornelia," he said derisively.

Cornelia? Not Heather? So this was the woman Thuggy and Leon were talking about. I guess I owed Heather an apology.

"Don't tell me to shut up," she snapped. "I just followed him here to make sure he got the book back. It belongs to the college."

"So you and Cornelia, huh?" I whispered to Rod. "Sara must've loved you hanging out with her boss."

"Damn it, Cornelia." Rod was fuming and I was taking a big chance by provoking him. But I refused to give in to the fear. I was surrounded by people who loved me. Even with a knife at my throat, I felt somehow *safe.* And damn it, this was my wedding day.

Thankfully Rod managed to hold his temper, barely. I knew he didn't want to kill me—or maybe he did but knew he would be in a whole lot more trouble if I died. With clenched teeth, he said, "Just tell me where the book is and I'll leave you to your stupid wedding."

"I'll be glad to tell you, but I'm not sure you heard me a minute ago." I tried to swallow despite the pressure against my throat. "I know that you killed your wife."

His laugh was stilted. "Why would I do that?"

"Good question. That's what I wanted to know. Maybe you were growing tired of her. Or maybe you found someone new. Cornelia, for instance."

I heard the woman snort at those words.

"None of the above," Cornelia snarled. So it seemed that she and Rod weren't lovers after all.

"Yeah," Rod said. "Sara was defacing school property, which meant she was a criminal. I couldn't live with a person who would do that to a book."

"Oh, you're so honorable," I scoffed quietly.

"But you don't mind threatening my daughter?" My mother's shout came loud and clear.

"Just let me at him," Meg called out. "I'll show him how the British handle problems like this."

I smiled. God, I loved these women. But I had to keep Rod talking while Derek and our brothers all crept closer.

"This was never about the book, was it, Rod?" I said. "We both know it. This was about you getting tired of Sara and killing her, then blaming it all on her." But when I stared up at his face, I suddenly saw the truth in his eyes. "Oh, wait. I was wrong. *She* was tired of *you*. Did she want a divorce? Is that why you killed her?"

"Shut up."

"How about that? A woman wanted to dump you. I imagine she was making you a nice little bundle of cash by forging all those books. How much money did she make over the years? You were getting used to living the good life and couldn't afford to lose her, could you?"

"I said shut up." His gaze flashed from me to Derek and the others and I could tell he was wondering if they were closer or if he was imagining things. He wasn't.

"But once you knew she was tired of that life, you couldn't afford to keep her around, could you?" I kept him focused on me deliberately. "Was she sick of lying for you? Was she threatening to confess to the school what she was doing? Or maybe she just wanted to get away from you. Can't blame her for that. That must've been a blow to your fragile ego."

"You're wrong about everything." Rod held me tighter. "I told you to shut up."

"And I heard you the first twenty times you said it."

I heard Robin snicker and gave myself a point for that one before continuing. "So did you offer to help Sara move the books the other night? Is that when you saw your chance to get rid of her? Or were you already lying in wait for her? Did Cornelia help you? Did she lure Sara into that cold basement while you huddled near the forklift, waiting for the exact moment to bury her under a ton of books and crates? You must have really grown to hate her, because that's a brutally awful way to kill someone."

"I didn't do anything," Cornelia wailed.

Rod bared his teeth at me. "You don't know what you're talking about."

"I'm talking about murder," I said. "You're a cold-blooded killer and you're going to rot in jail."

"I said shut up," he shouted.

I made eye contact with Inspector Lee, whose teeth were clenched and whose fingers were white from the pressure of holding her gun so tightly. She looked ready to kill Rod at a moment's notice and somehow that comforted me.

"Okeydokey, Rod." My throat was so dry I could barely speak anymore, but I stared up at him and managed to keep talking. "My husband has the book. If you take the knife away from my throat, he'll bring it to you and then you and your delightful friend Cornelia can go." I stared at Derek. "Tell him you'll give him the book."

Derek moved a few feet closer. "I don't think he cares about the book, darling."

I stared at him. "What do you mean?"

"Just bring him the damn book," Cornelia shouted.

I glanced up at Rod and saw his eyes widening in fear. What was Derek talking about? But I played along. "Is it the book you want, Rod? Or something else?"

He swallowed nervously. "I need the book."

Derek pulled a slip of paper from his pocket and waved it. "Or is it this list?"

"Derek?"

"Give that to me," Rod demanded.

"What is it?" I asked.

Derek glanced at the list and then looked at me. "It's a long list of books that Sara worked on, with names and dates and sales information."

I gazed up at Rod. "Was she going to blackmail you?"

But he was glaring at Derek. "Bring me that list."

"Or what?"

He gripped the knife even tighter. "Or I'll end it all right here."

"And you won't make it out of here alive." Derek's voice was coldly dangerous and Rod was too self-involved to realize who he was dealing with.

"Get the list, Rod," Cornelia shouted.

It sounded as though she had given up playing the helpless sidekick.

Rod seemed to make up his mind in that moment and jerked his arm tighter. "You're coming with me."

"Are you crazy? In case you didn't notice, I've got a wedding to go to."

He scowled. "There you go again, thinking you're funny. But I'll have the last laugh."

Why did he sound like Snidely Whiplash all of a sudden? *I'll have the last laugh, my pretty.*

Rod pulled the knife away and wrapped his arm across my shoulders, then jerked me around to face the door leading into the foyer. Glancing back at the crowd, he shouted, "Don't even think about following us, or she gets it."

"You've been watching too many B movies." Seriously, could he drag out more clichés? I wondered. I tried to concentrate on the moment. The knife was no longer a threat, for the moment anyway, so I could take my best shot to hurt him. I just had to remember my self-defense moves that Alex had been drumming into me for the past year.

Rod dragged me another step toward the door.

I had run out of time and needed to make my move now. I took another step and faltered. "Sorry, I tripped on my dress."

"Be careful," he snapped.

"Yeah." I slipped again and his grip loosened. I elbowed him in the solar plexus and heard him gasp. He dropped the knife. Then I stomped on his instep with my three-inch heels and his wail of pain sounded like choir music.

I heard Alex shout, "Yes!"

I pivoted and used my elbow again, this time aiming for his face. He screamed and I scurried backward, praying there was no blood about to spurt out and hit my dress.

In the confusion Cornelia broke away from Mitch and scrambled for the knife, but I beat her to it. Grabbing it, I pointed it right at her with one hand, holding the hem of my dress with the other to keep it from getting dirty. "Not so fast, you cow."

Inspector Lee was already there, grabbing Cornelia's wrist and wrenching it behind her back. "Good girl," she said.

Derek grabbed on to me and lifted me into his arms.

I vaguely heard the crowd screaming and clapping as Derek took one long stride off the steps, landing on the ground with me still in his arms. I held on to him for dear life until we were a safe distance away.

Our brothers surrounded Rod and shouted threats. There were so many of them that I could no longer see the weasel who'd tried to kill me. I was okay with that.

Inspector Lee, still clutching Cornelia's wrist, signaled to one of her officers standing a few feet away. "Take her out of here."

"I didn't do anything," she whined. "Rod and Sara were in on the whole thing together. I was only here to save the books."

"Yeah, you're a real patriot," Inspector Lee drawled.

Cornelia was shuffled off to a patrol car while Inspector Lee watched and waited for the men to finish with Rod. I could hear his screams, but I seriously doubted that the brothers were hurting him too badly.

"My hand," Rod shrieked. "You're standing on my hand!"

"That must hurt," Austin mused. "Dalton, maybe you should step back."

I smiled into Derek's chest. My heroes. My family. My miracles.

"Okay, break it up, guys," Inspector Lee said, her voice almost cheerful as she nudged her way through the crowd of good-looking men. They moved aside for her and I could see Rod writhing on the ground, whimpering. He didn't look as though he'd been harmed much, at least not by any of the men. He just looked pathetic.

I had managed to give him a bloody nose, so that gave me a little thrill. Especially since I was a safe enough distance away from the possibility of staining the dress. I considered it a real miracle that my dress remained unsoiled through all of the insanity.

Derek finally set me down, but we kept our arms around each other's waists, unwilling to let go. We both knew how easily Rod's self-control could have shattered. I could've died. The thought of leaving Derek alone without me was almost unbearable. So I clung to him as the aftermath of the danger carried on around us.

"How did you find that list?" I asked. "I examined the book and never saw it."

"Did you look all the way through the book?"

I thought about it. "No, darn it. I stopped at the title page because the paper felt different from the previous pages."

"When I handed the book to Ian, he glanced through it and the list fell out. I looked at all the books and information and made an educated guess. I put it in my pocket, thinking I would show it to you later."

"You saved the day," I marveled.

"No, darling. You did that all on your own."

And now I had to wonder if Sara had wanted me to find the

list. Had she been trying to redeem herself? I guess I would never know for sure.

As soon as Inspector Lee slapped the handcuffs onto Rod's wrists, two uniformed officers came over to guard him until they were ready to escort him off to jail. Then she walked over to me.

"You are a complete pain in the ass," she said. "What were you thinking, taunting him like that?"

"That wasn't taunting," Robin put in. "That was just Brooklyn."

I smiled at Inspector Lee. "I wanted him to confess to Sara's murder."

"He had a knife to your throat, for God's sake." She shook her head in despair. "You scared me half to death. What am I going to do with you?"

"I'm sorry," I said, and I meant it. "This wasn't actually part of our wedding plans. We all should've been drinking champagne by now. I'm not even married yet." I was feeling close to tears now that the adrenaline rush had left me.

Derek wrapped a protective arm around me. "Let's take care of that right now, shall we?"

"Yes, let's do it."

"Come here." Inspector Lee reached out and gave me a tight hug. She whispered, "You did good, kid." And then she let me go.

I was left dumbfounded while she carried on as usual, giving orders to the guys in uniform. Glancing up at Derek, she said, "Just give me a minute to make sure all of your uninvited guests are taken care of. Then you can start the ball rolling again."

"Thank you, Inspector," he murmured, and she winked at me.

She walked away and I saw her stop to talk to the ex-FBI agent, who didn't seem inclined to leave anytime soon. I would have to ask later if this was the guy hired by Glen Cove College to hunt down the stolen books. If so, I was fairly certain he had found his suspects.

Inspector Lee suggested to the uniformed officers that they put Rod in a cell with Thuggy and Leon until she was ready to come in and do the paperwork.

"That could take days," she admitted, and I laughed for the first time since I walked out that side door and got ambushed by a stone-cold killer.

Everyone was back in their seat. Ten minutes later, after Laura the makeup-and-hair wizard had given me a quick do-over, the music began anew. My bridesmaids were less restrained this time as each of them counted to ten before heading out of the foyer to do a little boogey down the aisle.

"Restraint be damned," I muttered, and this time I walked out the door with my arms raised in victory. The crowd went wild and I laughed out loud. With family and friends cheering, my father took my arm and we walked together down the aisle toward my new life as Derek Stone's blissfully happy wife.

And as I got closer, I could see that Derek looked pretty darned blissful himself. Rather than wait patiently, he walked toward me, shook my father's hand, and kissed me. Then he lifted me into his arms and carried me the rest of the way.

"This isn't necessary," I whispered in his ear.

He kissed my neck where the faint impression of a knife blade still showed. "I almost lost you. I don't want to take a chance on losing you again."

I pressed my hand against his cheek. "You could never lose me, love. I'm yours forever."

"And I'm yours."

After a long moment of soulful gazing, we glanced at Robson, who smiled beatifically. "Let's do this, shall we?"

I laughed. "Yes. Absolutely yes."

All the way through the ceremony, the bursts of applause almost drowned out Robson's words. But nobody cared. Not until the very end, when he finally, finally said, "I now pronounce you husband and wife."

And the crowd went wild all over again as Derek Stone kissed his blissful bride.

Epilogue

"But how did you figure out that he killed his wife?" Meg asked, as she nibbled on pâté and crackers. John, sitting next to her on the couch, was partial to the miniature blinis stuffed with caviar, chives, and crème fraîche.

It was the day after the wedding and we had invited the entire family over to our place for leftovers. Most of Derek's family had spent the week up in Dharma getting to know my family, but Derek and I had hardly spent any time with them at all. We wouldn't be leaving for Paris until tomorrow night, and since we were already packed and ready to go, we wanted to hang out with our loved ones for the day.

I glanced at Derek, who happily deferred to me.

"We suspected Rod all along," I said, stroking Charlie's soft fur. The cat was happy to play the role of security blanket for the moment. "Not only because the husband is usually the most likely suspect when the wife is killed, but also because Rod was such a jerk. And who else would've done it? Of course, it turned out that Sara's boss, Cornelia, was also involved. But we also considered Heather for a while, and even Thuggy and Leon."

Daphne chuckled. "Did you ever learn their real names?"

"Not yet. Frankly," I continued, "I don't care what their names are. They're horrible people and I hope they wind up spending lots of quality time in a rat-infested prison somewhere."

"Here, here," Mom said.

It turned out that my scenario was as close to the truth as anyone had guessed. Sara had announced that all the books had been brought to the booth in the conference center, but Cornelia didn't believe her. She had insisted on going back into the basement with Sara, and that was when Rod suddenly fired up the forklift and dropped several crates filled with books on top of her.

The nature of the crime made me think that Cornelia had to have been the mastermind. Rod wouldn't have had a clue about book storage at a conference, but Cornelia would've known and she would've told Rod exactly what to do. So even though Rod had been the one who actually killed his wife, Inspector Lee was determined to hold Cornelia equally responsible for Sara's murder. And I couldn't have been happier to hear it.

"Heather seemed like such a nice girl when we met her at the restaurant the other night," Meg said.

"She is very nice," I said, and thought of the phone call I'd made earlier that morning. Heather was already back home in Valley Heart, Wisconsin, and getting ready to go back to her job at the local library.

I'd told her everything that happened at the wedding and we

commiserated for a few minutes about Rod and Sara. I begged her to stay in touch and she promised she would.

"I want to hear what happens with Gus," I said.

She laughed. "I'll keep you posted."

"Look, Heather," I said hesitantly. "I wanted you to know that while Inspector Lee was investigating Sara's death, she called to talk to your boss about a few things."

"I don't like the sound of that. But go ahead, tell me everything."

"It sounded pretty ominous," I admitted. "But I'm sure it's all easily explained." At least, I hoped so. "Your boss mentioned an anonymous donor that had raised suspicions over the past year."

"Anonymous . . . Oh, Mrs. Freeling," Heather said. "She's a sweetie."

"What did you do for her?"

"Well, let's see. She's a junkie for true crime so I hold all the gritty bestsellers for her. And she loves romance, too."

"She sounds like a good customer," I said lightly.

"She's the best. She's eighty-nine years old and sometimes forgets her coat, so I always have a shawl for her to wear. Sometimes I'll drive her home when I find out she walked to the library. It's almost a mile away from her house, so I worry that she'll fall or hurt herself."

"You're a nice person."

"Well, I like her." She chuckled. "And her family bugs the heck out of her. They keep waiting for her to die so they'll be able to split her fortune among themselves."

"That's creepy."

"I know," Heather said. "So she started giving her money to the library. I mean, a lot of money. But she doesn't want her relatives to know, so she insists on anonymity. She's worried that if they find out, they'll have her declared incompetent."

"I can't believe what some families do to each other."

"That's the real crime," she said staunchly.

"Well, Mrs. Freeling sounds like a crackerjack."

"Oh, she's a doll. Feisty with a heart of gold. I don't look forward to losing her anytime soon."

"I don't blame you."

We talked for a few more minutes and then I hung up. I really hoped that Gus would make her happy. She deserved it after all those years of suffering at the hands of Sara and Rod Martin.

Sitting back on the couch, I watched Robin pick up the platter of leftover slices of Beef Wellington—which Derek had insisted on serving at our wedding dinner. I had gleefully agreed. We served it with a yummy Swiss cheese sauce but Robin had also found a spicy mustard in our refrigerator and spooned some of it into a small bowl. She strolled around the room offering it to our guests. We also had some of our vegetarian selection left over—cauliflower steak with a savory sesame-ginger dip—so Savannah and Daphne and her children were happy. We had six more huge platters of leftover wedding hors d'oeuvres and side dishes, so I was anxious to get rid of everything before we left for Paris. And I knew I could count on my family to do the job.

"You were very brave, Brooklyn," Daphne said, swirling her wineglass. "If you ever want a job hunting down cyber spies, please call me."

My eyes widened and I shot a glance at Derek, who just chuckled at the idea.

"Is that what you do?" I asked, dying of curiosity about the woman.

"Among other things," Daphne said with a light shrug. "Mostly I'm a mom."

I had to laugh. Not that being a mom wasn't awesome, but Daphne had said that very thing when I first met her. Now I was pretty sure it was a vast understatement of what her life truly entailed.

She gave me a wink, then set her wineglass down on the coffee table and reached for Charlie to snuggle for a moment. "I need this kitty."

"She's a sweetheart," I said.

"Indeed she is." Charlie seemed happy to oblige her and purred contentedly.

"Hunting down cyber spies sounds super exciting," I said. "But I suppose I'm a bookbinder down to my soul. Thanks, though."

"The world should be grateful for that," Douglas said. "You have a real gift, Brooklyn."

"Oh, thank you, Douglas. But how . . ."

"Ian gave us a tour of your work on exhibit yesterday," Daphne said. "You are a true artist."

"Wow, I didn't know that Ian was doing that."

She smiled. "I believe he'd had several glasses of champagne before we were able to coax him into it."

I laughed. "He probably would've done it stone-cold sober

because he's very proud of the Covington collection. You couldn't have asked for a more expert guide."

"I'm craving a Twisted Honey right about now," London admitted. "God, those were good."

"I'll be happy to make a pitcher," Derek said jovially.

I stood and rounded the room to make sure everyone was eating and drinking enough. I stopped at the kitchen island, where Dad was doing an impromptu wine tasting with Derek's father and two of his brothers, plus Douglas's wife, Delia, and my sister China. Robin joined us, still carrying the platter of Beef Wellington slices, and the wine-tasting group jumped on it.

I smiled as Dad took the opportunity to turn the moment into a wine pairing mini-lecture.

"What about that FBI guy?" Robin asked. "What was he doing there?"

Derek took that one. "Inspector Lee talked to him and got the whole story. He admitted that he'd been hired by Sara's college to investigate all of the stolen books. It turns out that they had lost over five hundred thousand dollars' worth of rare books in the last three years."

"Wow."

"Yeah," I added. "And Rod was perfectly willing to blame all of it on Sara."

"Well, she did the work," Robin said.

"I know. But he was such a skeevy jerk, I wouldn't be surprised to find out that he had somehow forced her into it." I thought about that for a long moment and finally had to face facts. Yes, Sara had given me *The Three Musketeers* in the first place in order to one-up Heather. But it was becoming more and more apparent that she had also wanted to stick it to Rod. I hoped that was true, anyway, because I wanted my memories of Sara to include at least a few redeeming qualities. Now I had to wonder if maybe Sara had been a bit of a grifter herself.

"Skeevy," Robin repeated. "Is that really a word?"

"It should be, don't you think?" I took a sip of champagne and leaned into Derek. My *husband.*

She nodded. "I like it."

Derek stood and raised his glass. "I would like to propose a toast."

"This makes number three hundred and twelve," Dylan said, chuckling.

"We did have quite a few toasts last night," Derek admitted, grinning. "So here's one more." He gazed at me. "To the love of my life. May we always have interesting times together."

"Is that a toast or a curse?" Douglas wondered out loud.

I laughed. "I was thinking the same thing. But I'll certainly toast to that."

"My life since I met you," Derek said, gazing into my eyes, "has been an adventure that I wouldn't have missed for anything. I look forward to another fifty years of it."

My eyes filled with tears and this time I let them fall. "Our adventure is just beginning, Derek." I raised my glass and looked up at him. "I love you forever."

"And I love you more." He took a sip, then added with a wink, "But, darling, let's try to avoid running into any dead bodies while we're in Paris, shall we?"

Recipes

These recipes are just a few of the delectible items served at Brooklyn and Derek's wedding! Now it's a well-known fact that Brooklyn can barely cook an egg, so she requested that we make these recipes easy to follow with ingredients that can be found at the local supermarket. Brooklyn shyly admits that she dreams of someday preparing these recipes herself. Her sister Savannah, the professional chef in the family, finds this idea hysterically funny (and frankly, so do we). But since it's all about Brooklyn, we will comply with her wishes. We hope you'll find them easy to prepare. And Brooklyn hopes you'll enjoy them!

TWISTED HONEY

BROOKLYN AND DEREK'S SIGNATURE COCKTAIL

1 oz. VSOP cognac
(Derek uses Camus, but any good cognac or brandy will do)
½ oz. fresh-squeezed lemon juice
½ oz. honey syrup (combine equal parts honey and water, both at room temperature)
½ oz. Cointreau (or other fine orange liqueur)
Lemon twist for garnish

Combine first four ingredients in a shaker filled with ice. Dip rim of martini glass lightly in lemon juice and then fine white sugar. Garnish with a generous lemon twist.

STUFFED MUSHROOM CAPS

APPETIZER

8 oz. mushrooms, stems removed
5 oz. Boursin garlic & fine herbs cheese
¼ cup bread crumbs
1 Tbsp. butter, melted

Preheat the oven to 400 degrees. Discard the mushroom stems. Stuff each mushroom cap with cheese. Mix together bread crumbs and melted butter, then sprinkle over the mushroom caps. Roast until brown, 20-25 minutes.

BEEF WELLINGTON WITH SWISS CHEESE SAUCE

Main Dish for the Meat Eaters

1 3-lb. beef tenderloin
Garlic salt and black pepper
8 oz. mushrooms, diced
2 medium shallots, diced
2 Tbsp. olive oil
3 cloves garlic, minced
2 Tbsp. steak sauce, such as A1
1 sheet puff pastry, thawed but still cold
4 thin slices Swiss cheese
1 egg, whisked with 1 Tbsp. water

Liberally sprinkle the tenderloin with garlic salt and black pepper. Broil 5-7 minutes (until well browned), then turn and broil the other side for 5-7 minutes until browned. Chill in the refrigerator until cool to the touch.

Sauté the mushrooms and shallots in olive oil over medium heat for 5 minutes, stirring frequently. Add garlic and sauté until fragrant, about 30 seconds longer. Remove from heat and stir in steak sauce.

Preheat the oven to 400 degrees. Unfold the sheet of puff pastry on a lightly floured surface. Roll just enough so that it will completely wrap around the tenderloin. Put mushroom mixture along the center of the puff pastry in a rectangle the length and width of the tenderloin. Cover the mushroom mixture with thin slices of Swiss cheese, then put the beef on top. Wrap the puff pastry around everything, pinching to close. If you have extra puff pastry after wrapping the tenderloin, you can cut out leaves or other decorations. Affix the decorations to the puff pastry with egg wash, then brush the egg wash over the whole thing.

Place seam side down in a roasting pan. Roast 45 minutes to an hour. Check halfway through, and if the puff pastry is looking too brown, tent loosely with aluminum foil. When the meat in the center reaches 135 degrees, remove from oven and allow to sit while you make the Swiss cheese sauce.

SWISS CHEESE SAUCE

2 Tbsp. butter
2 Tbsp. flour
2 cups milk
8 oz. Swiss cheese (or whatever's left after the 4 thin slices are cut), shredded

Melt butter in a small saucepan. Add flour a little at a time and stir thoroughly. Then add the milk just a little at a time, stirring until incorporated each time. Once all of the milk has been added, heat to a simmer, stirring frequently, and simmer until thickened. Stir in the shredded cheese a little at a time.

CAULIFLOWER STEAK WITH SESAME-GINGER DIP

Main Dish for the Vegetarians

1 head cauliflower, cut into 1-inch thick slices
½ cup olive oil
2 cloves garlic, minced
1 tsp. red pepper flakes
½ tsp. salt
1 tsp. lemon juice

Preheat the oven to 400 degrees. Slice the cauliflower. If florets fall off, it's fine. Just try to keep the chunks 1-inch thick as much as possible. Mix together the olive oil and lemon juice and brush all over both sides of the cauliflower. Roast 15 minutes, flip, and roast another 15 minutes. The outside will get nice and crispy, and the inside soft.

SESAME-GINGER DIP

¼ cup olive oil
2 Tbsp. rice vinegar
1 Tbsp. soy sauce

1 Tbsp. toasted sesame oil
1 Tbsp. fresh ginger, minced
1 Tbsp. brown sugar
1 tsp. Dijon mustard
½ tsp. red pepper flakes

Put all ingredients in a food processor and combine. Serve in small bowls alongside the cauliflower.